Incredible Tales That Take
You Off the Main Road

D0846951

Incredible Tales That Take
You Off the Main Road

RICK PASCAL

Printed in the USA.
ISBN: 978-1-943190-22-5

Cover and book design by Bobbi Benson
wildgingerpress.com

For Maxine

CONTENTS

INTRODUCTION

FOR AS LONG AS I CAN REMEMBER, I've been a fan of the macabre: eerie fantasy, sci-fi and spooky tales of horror. When I was a young boy, my comic book collection included *Tales from the Crypt, Vault of Horror* and *The Haunt of Fear.* I enjoyed the "normal" comic books of the period that the boys of my generation enjoyed, such as *Superman, Batman, Blackhawks* and *Captain Marvel* just as much. I'd like to think that if my mother hadn't tossed them away, I'd be wealthy by now. Radio and television also offered scary programs such as *Lights Out,* narrated by Frank Gallup, whose creepy voice often gave me the chills. When I was a teenager, I was enthralled by Rod Serling's *The Twilight Zone,* followed by *The Outer Limits.* The science fiction genre of the 1950's continued to capture my fascination with films like *Invaders from Mars, When Worlds Collide* and *The War of the Worlds,* to name just a few. My interest in this genre gave rise to my enjoyment of short stories by O. Henry, Edger Allen Poe and, one of favorite authors, Stephen King. It should be no surprise, therefore, that my first book of short stories follows this path.

The first short story I wrote, *They Answer Our Prayers,* incubated in my psyche for about twenty years before I began to write it, first as a one-act play. I even thought that it might make a good *Twilight*

Zone episode. By the time I wrote it, however, *The Twilight Zone* was no longer airing. The local Community Theater group to which I belonged passed on producing it, feeling that the staging was cumbersome. I decided to expand it into a short story, developing the plots and characters' backgrounds to a greater extent. One thing led to another and I wrote another one-act play and short story inspired by *The Twilight Zone,* called *Stay With Me.*

Having completed two short stories, I was on a roll. Online research gave me much more information about writing short stories, plot ideas and style. Writing this book has been an exciting challenge as well as a joy. I hope that you enjoy reading these stories as much as I have enjoyed writing them. Oh, one more thing. My father loved to write poetry, most of which were love poems to my mother. One of his poems, however, was written for my children. I'm glad to include *The Double Dee Dee* in this collection as a tribute to him.

Eduardo's Death is a work of fiction, inspired by true events. All the other stories in this compilation are complete fiction. Any similarity to anyone, living or dead, is purely coincidental.

Money Hungry

CHARLIE FLUNK was a victim of his name. As a child, his grades in school were barely mediocre. During recess he was the last boy chosen for every team sport, if he were chosen at all. He was bullied at school so much that he feigned sickness in order to stay home. As a teenager he had a horrible acne condition and his overall appearance was sloppy and unkempt. He had no friends. He was never invited to parties. Girls avoided him. Boys teased him. He didn't attend his high school prom. Everyone considered Charlie the town loser.

In his loneliness, Charlie became depressed. To alleviate his depression, he found comfort in food. He ate whenever he felt low, binged on candy and became seriously overweight. His attempts to fight obesity were thwarted by his lack of will power. He took diet pills, but his appetite for food was too strong. He contemplated suicide, but did not even have the courage to make a serious attempt at it.

As a result of his obesity and poor grades, Charlie Flunk was unable to find any job that afforded him a sense of accomplishment or chance for advancement. He drifted from menial job to menial job in a downward spiral of disappointment, earning scarcely enough to rent the one small room in the town's only boarding house.

As Charlie returned home one Friday evening from his part-time job stacking boxes at a local warehouse, he was greeted by his landlady, Mrs. Ilse Radford, who was waiting to confront him the moment he opened the front door. She didn't even give him the opportunity to remove his jacket before pouncing on him.

"You gonna have rent on time this month, Charlie?" she demanded.

Mrs. Radford wasn't a bad person, but business was business. She had bills to pay. Her husband had left her some years back, and her only means of income was from the boarding house where Charlie had been living for the past six months. "Give me just a few more days and I'll have it for you, Mrs. Radford, I'm a little short this week, but I promise I'll pay you," he responded.

"Tell you what, Charlie old boy. I'll let you have until next week," she said. "Otherwise, you'll have to find someplace else to live, got it?"

"Yes, ma'am," Charlie answered, sheepishly.

Dismayed and dejected, Charlie plodded up the stairs to his room, hung up his jacket, and lay on his bed staring at the ceiling. After ten minutes of emptiness in his heart, he went to his dresser drawer and took out the cigar box that contained his valuables: a pair of pearl cuff links left to him by his father, a gold tie clip, silver key chain, tape measure, a few postage stamps, $37.83 in cash and his bank book with a total of $280. He took out his wallet that held $60. In his pocket and found another $2.45 – not enough money to pay his rent. He wouldn't receive his meager paycheck for another two weeks, so how would he be able to come up with the $500 he needed to pay Mrs. Radford in one week?

Well, I'll just have a week to figure it out, he thought, and decided to treat himself to dinner at The Empress Diner, a short walk from the boarding house. As Charlie strolled over to the diner, he couldn't help notice people staring at "the town fat man." He continued on his way with his head down, staring at the sidewalk, in shame.

Charlie opened the glass entrance doors of The Empress and walked immediately to the far end of the counter to avoid being noticed. He ordered a grilled cheese sandwich, a cup of coffee, and a slice of peach pie for dessert. The check came to $9.95 and he left a tip of $1.00. Even though he was broke, he couldn't deny himself a meal. As Charlie rose from the red plastic covered counter stool, he heard a dreadful sound coming from behind. It was the sound of fabric tearing, r-i-i-i-p-p-p. *Oh no,* he thought, *my pants tore.* Sure enough, the seam on the back of Charlie's pants was completely slit, tearing some of the fabric along with it. He immediately became aware of several chuckles coming from some of the other patrons and, his face turning crimson with embarrassment, wrapped his jacket around his waist to cover his exposed boxer shorts. He shuffled out of the diner and walked the two blocks back to the solitary room in the boarding house as quickly as possible to avoid any further scene.

The following morning, Charlie put on his one pair of old jeans and walked five blocks to the Goodwill store. "I need a pair of pants," he said to the clerk.

"I remember you," said the clerk. "I'm Cindy Cheek. We were in grammar school together. The Big and Tall section is in Aisle Ten, over there, Charlie," she continued, pointing toward the back of the store. "Thanks," Charlie muttered, as he followed Cindy's directions, while she turned her back and snickered with her hand covering her mouth. Charlie remembered her, too. Cindy Cheek was just as nasty as she had been when they were school kids. *"Wait till I tell everyone who I saw buying fat pants at the Goodwill,"* Cindy cackled under her breath, as she continued to fold clothes into neat piles...for minimum wage.

Charlie searched earnestly to find a pair of pants his size but found only two. One had a broken zipper. The other was a dull brown with a yellow stripe, the pants from a two-piece suit from which the jacket went missing. They were marked $4. With not much choice, he tried them on. The pants were only slightly larger than his 50-inch waist, which was fine with him; he could cinch them with a belt. The length was perfect; there was no need to spend any money on tailoring. As he adjusted the pants on his hips, he inadvertently put his hand into the right pocket and pulled out a piece of paper. It was a brand new ten-dollar bill. *My goodness*, Charlie thought, *the person who donated these pants must have left this money in the pocket. Well, it's mine now*, he mused. *It'll pay for the pants and I'll have an extra six bucks in the bargain.* The Goodwill store cashier placed Charlie's new pants in a generic plastic bag and handed him the $6 change. Charlie whistled a happy tune all the way home.

Back in his room, Charlie wondered if the previous owner had left more money in another pants pocket. He removed the pants from the bag and stuck his hand in each of four pockets. Alas, he found no more money. *Oh, well*, he thought, *I didn't really expect to find any more money*, although he hoped that he would. He took off his old jeans and put on his new pants, this time with a belt to see how much cinch he needed. Once again, he casually put his hand in the pocket to strike a pose in front of the mirror. Lo and behold, he felt

4

a piece of paper in the pocket again. It was another ten-dollar bill. Amazed and baffled, he lay the $10 on his bed and put his hand in the pocket once more and came out with another $10 bill. Over and over, he retrieved $10 bills until he had placed more than $1,500 on his bed. *Holy Moley*, he thought, as he stared at 150 ten-dollar bills spread out on his bed. He put his hand in his pocket once more, pulled out another $10 bill and threw it on the bed. Then once again with the same result.

There seemed to be no end to the cornucopia's bounty. Charlie removed the pants and decided to put them away for now, fearing that he might tear the pocket if he continued for too long. Standing in his boxer shorts holding the pants, Charlie attempted to retrieve some money once again. He put his hand in the pocket and, to his chagrin, found that the pocket was empty. *Oh, no*, he thought, *I've ruined it*. Again and again he tried to find the magical $10 gifts, but to no avail. *Let me put them back on*, he thought. Once he was wearing the pants, he reached into the pocket and smiled. He pulled out a new ten-dollar bill! *Aha*, he concluded. *I can only get the money when I'm wearing the pants*. Charlie folded his new pants neatly and stowed them in his bottom dresser drawer. He put his old jeans back on, counted out $500 from the stack of $10 bills that lay on his bed and went downstairs to Mrs. Radford's room. "What's all this?" Mrs. Radford asked.

"Here's my room rent for the next month," Charlie said, with a Cheshire cat-like grin. "I, uh, just came into some money," he added.

"Oh, how so?" Mrs. Radford asked.

"Well, it was a sort of inheritance," Charlie replied. "Gotta go now," he added, as he turned and hustled, as best he could, given his size, up the stairs and back into his room. An astounded and suspicious Mrs. Radford watched Charlie run upstairs. She immediately closed her door and telephoned her friend, Ida Prattler. Ida was a teller at the local bank and took specific interest in each of the townspeople's deposits and withdrawals. She enjoyed sharing that information with her close friends, Ilse Radford being one of them.

"Ida," Mrs. Radford said, "I'm not a gossip, but you know that Charlie Flunk who rents a room in my boarding house?"

"You mean the fat one?" Ida responded.

"Yes, him," Ilse said. "He claims to have come into an inheritance. Have you heard anything about that?"

"Well, no, I haven't," Ida said with consternation. "How come I don't know that, working at the bank and all?" she added.

"Yesterday he didn't have enough for his room rent, and today he handed me $500 in cash, all ten-dollar bills. He hasn't robbed the bank, has he?" Ilse asked.

"Not that I know of," Ida said. "But I'll ask around and keep my eyes open. I'll let you know if I hear anything."

Charlie opened his bottom dresser drawer, took out his new pants and put them back on. He barely noticed that the waist was not as loose as it had been when he first tried them on. For the next hour Charlie continued retrieving ten-dollar bills from his pocket. The skin on his hand was sore and beginning to chafe when he ceased reaching for money. He had amassed a total of $15,000 which now lay strewn all over his bed. As he played with the bills, laughing and tossing them around, he noticed that the waist on his pants felt uncomfortably tight and realized, for some strange reason, that they must have shrunk. He even had a bit of difficulty undoing the top button while trying to take them off. Then it dawned on him. Each time he removed money from the pocket, the waist got smaller. No problem, Charlie reasoned. He'd take them to the tailor right away and have them let out.

He stashed his money in a shoe box and hid it in the back of his closet, planning to deposit most of it in the bank on Monday, except for a couple of hundred for pocket money.

"Sorry, Charlie," said Moe, the tailor. "There's no extra material to let out these pants." After measuring the waist, Moe said, "The waist on these pants is 44 inches. You should lose some weight if you want to wear them again," he added advisedly.

Dejected, Charlie took the pants and returned home. Try as he might, he could not fit back into the pants. There was no way Charlie could retrieve any money from the pockets of his pants unless he wore them with the zipper zipped and the waist buttoned at the top. His waist was still 50 inches so he had to lose both weight and inches from his waist in order to wear them again and profit from his newly found good fortune.

Charlie had never dieted. He wasn't even sure how much he weighed. He went to the local CVS and purchased a scale and a package of diet pills. Back in his room he stepped on the scale. Charlie flinched when he saw the needle strain to go beyond the 320-pound limit. The tape measure from his cigar box indicated that he had a 50-inch waist. Moe told him that the waistline on his pants was 44 inches, so he'd have to shrink his own waistline by 6 inches. *Time to*

get this diet started, Charlie said to himself, as he downed two diet pills. *I'm gonna be hungry, but the money will be worth it.*

On Monday morning, Charlie took $14,000 out of his shoe box to deposit in his bank account before heading to work. "Hi Charlie," Ida Prattler said. "Come into an inheritance, did ya, Charlie?" she added sarcastically, while she stamped his passbook.

"Who told you that?" Charlie asked with concern.

"Oh, no one. Just figured," Ida said.

"As a matter of fact, yes, I did inherit some money." Charlie said with a new air of confidence. "Bye now," he added with the same Cheshire cat smile he had offered to Mrs. Radford. His next stop was at Kilroy's, the town's only supermarket, where he purchased two apples for lunch and a bunch of carrots that he'd have for supper. He finally found the will power to lose weight. His hunger for money eclipsed his hunger for food.

For the next six weeks Charlie's diet consisted solely of fruits, vegetables and an occasional hard-boiled egg. His weight dropped from 320 pounds to 295. His waist decreased by five inches, only one inch more than the pants that were still in his bottom dresser drawer.

Charlie attempted to put the pants back on after having suffered the pangs of hunger for the past month and a half. Even though he felt himself growing weaker each day, he was too happy about his weight loss to care. To his delight, even in spite of the one-inch difference between his waist size and the pants, he was able to zip them up and close the top button with only a minimum amount of difficulty.

While standing in front of the mirror, proud that he looked slimmer than he had been in years, Charlie reached into his pocket and was thrilled to find another brand new ten-dollar bill in his hand. A feeling of euphoria swept over him as he continued removing $10 bills as quickly as he could for the next hour, accumulating $16,000. But at the same time, he began experiencing the discomfort of his pants shrinking during the process. He tightened his stomach and held it in for as long as he could, but lasted only ten more minutes. He amassed another $2,500 before the top button popped off the pants and onto the floor, bouncing underneath his bed.

I've just got to lose a lot more weight this time, Charlie thought, *but I have to find that button first.* Frustrated that he couldn't locate the button, even with a flashlight, Charlie began to panic. *If I can't get that button back on my pants,* he thought, *I might never be able to use its magic again.* Finally, he thought to look inside one of his bedroom slippers, where it lay in the toe area. Heaving a sigh of relief, he sewed the button back on his pants. He took out his tape measure again and checked his waist...still 45 inches. However, as a result of Charlie's recent frenzy, the waistline on his pants now decreased to 38 inches. *Jeez,* he thought, *I really have to lose more weight.* He folded the pants neatly and stowed them away again in his bottom dresser drawer, determined to lose more weight as quickly as possible.

Word soon spread around town that Charlie Flunk had come into money. People he hadn't seen or spoken to for years began to greet him in the street, often commenting on how good he looked. Cindy Cheek passed by him in the street one day. "Hi Charlie," she said, coyly. "Remember me? Cindy from the Goodwill. Gee, you look great."

Charlie just continued on his way, nodding but not engaging in conversation. Meanwhile, Charlie's bank account had now risen to more than $30,000. He was unrelenting in his quest to lose weight and become thinner and richer. He would eat no more than 500 calories a day for as long as it took to reduce his waist by another seven inches.

For the next several weeks, Charlie ate only two apples, one hard-boiled egg and three carrots a day, virtually starving himself. He continued to fight off the hunger as he lost weight while at the same time growing weaker and more tired each day. After three more weeks, not yet reaching his ultimate goal, Charlie felt faint and collapsed in the street on his way to work. By the time anyone noticed him lying on the ground and called the EMTs, Charlie's heart had failed. By the time they arrived at the emergency room, Charlie was already dead.

Mrs. Radford entered Charlie's room in order to clean out his belongings and see what she could salvage for herself. She pocketed the $1,500 that she found in the shoe box in Charlie's closet and the small amount of cash from the cigar box in his dresser. She discarded everything else except some of his clothes that she felt inclined to donate to the Goodwill store. Unfortunately for Ilse Radford, the money she noticed in his bank account would be turned over to the state. Sorting through his clothing, she noticed a pair of brown pants with a yellow stripe.

"Wow," she remarked, "These must have been Charlie's fat pants. The waist on them is huge. They must be at least fifty inches." Ilse

Radford bagged the rest of Charlie's clothes and brought them to the Goodwill store. She asked for a receipt for tax purposes. Mrs. Radford returned home and put a "Room For Rent" sign on her front door, after which she telephoned her friend, Ida Prattler. "Hi Ida," she said. "Did you hear what happened to Charlie Flunk?"

Tomorrow, Today

I do not believe in a fate that falls on men however they act;
but I do believe in a fate that falls on them unless they act.
– Buddha

BRUCE COZENER loved to gamble. He gambled on horses, sporting events, penny-ante stocks, slot machines, and other casino games. Occasionally he'd win, sometimes big. He often bragged about his big winnings to his best friend, Phil Cooper. On balance, however, Bruce lost more than he won. He rarely thought about his losses. He had been born into wealth, and inherited $3 million from his father.

Bruce was an executive at a major insurance firm in New York City. He lived alone on the Upper West Side in an apartment that was too large for him after his wife, Corey, divorced him. Corey had become frustrated with Bruce's gambling and his lack of emotional attention to her. After the divorce she moved back to Texas, along with the children and the dog, to be closer to her family – and far away from Bruce. Bruce kept the apartment because it was convenient to his office and The New York Athletic Club on Central Park South, where he played racquet ball with Phil at 8 am every Tuesday.

Sunday, July 5

Bruce sat at his kitchen table, sipping his coffee. He had no plans for the day. The clock over the doorway read 10 am. He picked up the phone and called Phil.

"Hi Phil, whatcha doin' today?" he asked a sleepy Phil who had just awakened after a late Saturday night out with his wife, Susan, who was still asleep.

"Bruce, what time is it?" Phil inquired, rubbing the sleep from his eyes.

"It's already ten o'clock, Phil," Bruce taunted. "Time to get moving. Do you want to make it out to Belmont today?"

"I guess so, why not," Phil replied. "What time do you want to leave?"

"I'll pick you up in front of your building at 11:30," Bruce instructed. "That should give you enough time to eat breakfast and get ready. I want to be there in time for the Daily Double."

Phil nudged Susan and told her that he'd be spending the afternoon with Bruce at the track. In spite of Bruce's gambling problem, Susan was completely understanding of her husband's friendship with Bruce. She knew that they had been childhood friends and didn't want to come between them. She was also aware that Phil would never forgive her if she did. She didn't really mind the fact that once in a while Phil went to the track with Bruce. This Sunday was one of those days. "Go on," Susan told Phil. "Have some fun, and for heaven's sake, don't lose too much," she said. That was Susan's catch phrase every time Phil went to the track.

Bruce telephoned the doorman to have his car ready for him at 11:15. He nuked a bagel from his freezer, poured himself another cup of coffee and perused the list of horses and jockeys in the *Daily News* that would be running today. He slipped into his denim shorts, blue tee shirt and tennis shoes and took the elevator down to the front lobby, where he was greeted by Irv, the doorman.

"Good morning, Mr. Cozener," Irv said. "I have your car right out in front for you, as you asked," as he opened the front door.

"Thanks, Irv," said Phil, slipping a five-dollar bill into the outside breast pocket of Irv's uniform.

"Thank you, too, Mr. Cozener," said Irv. Bruce slid into his black BMW convertible and drove away.

Bruce and Phil pooled their money, $100 each. They lost the daily double, and after the first five races decided to return home, minus $100 each.

Phil Cooper and Bruce Cozener had been close friends since childhood. After high school, Phil enrolled in Pratt Institute where he studied architecture. Bruce opted to forego college and joined Northeast Insurance as a sales trainee. Before long, his drive and initiative led to him becoming one of the firm's top executives.

Phil joined the Alpha Kappa Psi fraternity where, as social chairman, he organized several parties to which he often invited Bruce. Phil's fraternity brothers were fond of Bruce because of his vibrant personality, his sense of humor, and the fact that he often brought a case of beer to their parties.

Phil met Susan Matthews at a frat party during his sophomore year. Susan was the sister of one of Phil's fraternity brothers, and was attracted to Phil instantly. She had been a student at FIT in New York City, where she studied fashion design. She invited Corey Davis, her roommate at FIT, to an AKP party where she met, and eventually fell in love with Bruce. Corey was raised in West Texas. Her dream had been realized when she earned a scholarship to FIT to study art.

After graduation, Phil joined the architectural firm of Held & Associates in midtown Manhattan. The following year he married Susan. Six months later, Bruce and Corey were wed. Both served as Best Man at each other's weddings. The two couples remained close for several years, until Corey divorced Bruce and moved back to Texas to teach art in high school.

Bruce was always obsessed with winning. He and Phil were regulars at Belmont Park and Yonkers Raceway. From time to time, they went to the casinos in Atlantic City, New Jersey. Bruce tried to persuade Phil to go to the track or the casinos more frequently, but Phil, being more grounded than Bruce – and still married – often begged off.

"Bruce, I've got work to do," he'd say. "Bruce, I want to spend some time with Susan." But to no avail. Bruce became adamant about going to the track. When Phil declined Bruce's persistent requests, Bruce went alone, but their friendship always remained intact.

Tuesday, July 7

Every Tuesday morning Phil and Bruce had a standing reservation at the New York Athletic Club for an hour of racquet ball. They were pretty evenly matched and, as usual, would bet $10 on the outcome. Bruce always wanted to raise the stakes, but Phil insisted on keeping it at ten.

"Ready for a whuppin?" Bruce said to Phil as they entered the court.

"In your dreams," Phil replied with a grin. "Rough or smooth?" he continued as he twirled his squash racquet and covered the label. One side of the label was shiny, the other side was dull.

"Smooth," said Bruce.

"Hah," said Phil. "My serve."

After the match, both men showered and dressed. Bruce took a ten-dollar bill out of his wallet and said, "Here's your lousy sawbuck."

"Thanks for the tenner," Phil responded as he pocketed his winnings. "Better luck next time."

"Talk to you later," Bruce said. "See you next week."

"Right, buddy," said Phil, as they gave each other a man hug.

They emptied their lockers, left the Athletic Club and headed toward the Columbus Circle Metro Station at 59th Street to begin their work day.

Saturday, July 11

It was a beautiful sunny morning with low humidity and the temperature hovering at about 70 degrees. Bruce wore his new Armani sunglasses which, he thought, made him look "cool". He often wore his Armani sunglasses even when the sun wasn't shining as part of his persona. He walked to Nick's Olympic Diner on 80th Street to take advantage of their Saturday morning breakfast special of eggs, sausage, juice, toast and coffee for only $9.95, a good deal if you ordered before 10:30 am. He'd have a leisurely breakfast and read the morning edition of *The Daily News* while drinking a second cup of coffee.

After receiving a cordial "Good morning Mr. Cozener," from Nick himself, Bruce went to his favorite booth that had been cleaned and re-set with a paper placemat (replete with sketches of a map of the Greek isles, the Parthenon, Acropolis and statues of Greek gods). As Bruce took his seat, a gentleman leaving the diner stopped at Bruce's booth and offered him his copy of *The Daily News*. Bruce noticed with curiosity that the man was wearing a raincoat and a plaid cap.

"Here, you go, I'm finished with the paper," he said, cordially. "Enjoy your day."

"Thanks," Bruce said, surprised at the stranger's generosity.

After paying his bill, the man turned toward Bruce, tipped his cap and waved. Bruce waved back.

"Hi, Mr. C," said Gloria, the waitress. "What'll it be this morning?"

Gloria Gomez was a stunning Latina who had emigrated from Mexico with her family when she was ten years old. She had long, dark hair and deep brown eyes with a figure that most men desired. And she enjoyed the lustful looks men gave her. One of Corey's big complaints was that Bruce couldn't take his eyes off Gloria whenever they went to Nick's.

"You sure you're not having an affair with her?" Corey would ask, suspiciously.

"Don't be ridiculous," Bruce would counter.

"Hi Gloria," Bruce responded. "Let me have the Number 3, two eggs over easy, sausage, hash browns well-done, whole wheat toast, cranberry juice and coffee."

"You got it," said Gloria as she jotted down the order and headed toward the kitchen. Bruce stared at Gloria from behind, as she walked away with a sexy wiggle of her derriere. He picked up the stranger's newspaper and read the back sports page.

Yankees Top Baltimore, 8-6 in 12th
Judge Hits 2-Run Walk-Off Homer #20

A picture of Aaron Judge being greeted by his teammates with high-fives filled up the rest of the page. That's odd, Bruce muttered to himself. Baltimore beat the Yanks last night, 3-2, if I remember correctly. Chapman lost it in the bottom of the ninth.

Gloria placed a glass of cranberry juice and a cup of coffee in front of Bruce, careful not to spill anything on his newspaper. "Your eggs will be up in a jiff," she said, and returned to the kitchen. Bruce put his usual three teaspoons of sugar in the coffee, added milk and sipped it slowly. Then he returned to the sports page of *The Daily News* and re-read the headline.

Yankees Top Baltimore, 8-6 in 12th

The same picture of Aaron Judge and his Yankees teammates celebrating was still there.

Am I dreaming or what? Bruce was perplexed. Then, turning to the front page he noticed the date at the top of the page: Sunday, July 12. *This can't be*, he muttered under his breath.

"Enjoy," Gloria said, as she lay his breakfast plate in front of him.

"Hold on a minute Gloria," Bruce said. "What day is today?"

"What do you mean?" asked Gloria, pondering such an odd question.

"I mean, is today Saturday or Sunday?" Bruce asked.

"C'mon, Mr. C., is this a joke? It's Saturday, July 11," said Gloria. "And in case you're wondering," she continued, glancing at her wristwatch, "it's also 10:25 am, if you want to know what time it is. Now eat your breakfast," she added with a wink, and sauntered off wiggling her hips to tend to another customer, knowing that Bruce was watching her every step.

Bruce rose from his seat at the booth and walked to the front counter, where Nick was at the cash register. "Nick, do you have today's *Daily News?*" Bruce asked.

"Sure, Mr. C., right over there," pointing to the rack of newspapers.

Bruce picked up a copy of *The Daily News* and looked at the front page. The date was indeed Saturday, July 11. The lead story on the sports page was:

B'more Defeats Yanks 3-2, Chapman Blows Save

He handed $1 to Nick for the newspaper and returned to his booth, staring silently at his unfinished breakfast which, by now, had turned cold.

Bruce was stupefied. How could this be? And who was the man in the raincoat who gave him this newspaper? *Tomorrow's* newspaper!

He then turned to the horseracing section to see the results listed at Yonkers Raceway. The winners and payouts for each of Saturday night's races were shown as:

1st Race: #2-Love Story: $5.40

2nd Race: #2-Mr. Hyde: $18.20

3rd Race: #5-Blue Chip: $7.40

4th Race: #4-Photo Shoot: $3.10

5th Race: #7-Hangover: $18.60

6th Race: #6-Gloria's Own: $10.40

7th Race: #3-Crown Gold: $8.40

8th Race: #1-Royal Blue: $3.20

Daily Double: #2 & #2: $146

Bruce laid the racing section of Sunday's *Daily News* on the table adjacent to the racing pages in Saturday's *Daily News*. He compared the winners shown in Sunday's paper to the entries shown in Saturday's paper. Sure enough, the names of the winning horses matched the entries shown in Saturday's paper. By now his head was reeling. *What momentous spin of the wheel of fate had landed on his number? And why me?* he marveled.

"More coffee?" Gloria said, interrupting Bruce's seemingly vacant stare.

"What? Oh, yeah, please."

As if waking from a dream, Bruce made the decision to go to Yonkers Raceway that evening and bet on each of the reported winners. If the listings in the newspaper were true, he could make some big money, lots of money. He considered asking Phil to go with him, but if this newspaper were some kind of joke, he'd look like a fool. Better to go alone. Maybe this information was not meant to be shared. But if it were true, why not share the wealth with his best friend? He wouldn't have to tell Phil how he got the information, or even that he had any information at all. Bruce finally called Phil.

"I'm feeling really lucky, let's go to Yonkers tonight," he said.

"Great, it's Susan's Mah Jong night and I'd love to go to Yonkers, Bruce. What time do you want to leave?"

"I'll pick you up at six so we can get there in time for the Daily Double. Wait in front of the building for me as usual."

"You got it," Phil replied. "See you later."

Bruce picked up his special copy of Sunday's *Daily News*, clutching it tightly to his chest as if it were a valuable family heirloom and returned to his apartment. He stopped first at his bank and entered the ATM lobby, hoping no one else would be there. He would have preferred to go to a teller's window to withdraw a large amount of cash, but on Saturday the counters were closed. Looking over his shoulder to make certain that no one was watching, Bruce inserted his ATM card, entered his PIN and withdrew $2,000 from his passbook account. Carefully and quickly removing the stack of one hundred $20 bills from the machine, he stuffed them into his pockets just as another customer was entering the lobby. Bruce brushed past him and hurried to his apartment.

"Hi Irv," Bruce said to the doorman. "Please have my car ready at a quarter to six this evening."

"Roger, wilco, 5:45 pm it shall be," said Irv. "See you later, Mr. Cozener." Irv was always eager to please Bruce, who was a good tipper.

Bruce took the elevator up to his apartment, sat down in the kitchen and placed one hundred $20 bills onto the kitchen table into ten piles. After staring at them for a few moments, he went into his bedroom and retrieved a black leather pouch (Phil called it Bruce's 'man-bag') that Corey had given him for his thirtieth birthday and put the money neatly into it. He didn't want to take the Sunday newspaper with him to the track fearing someone might see it. He copied the names of each of the winning horses, their post positions and the payoffs on a small piece of paper and slid it carefully into his wallet. He made another copy and placed it in his shoe.

Bruce's body flowed with electricity. He could hardly contain his excitement at the prospect of the evening's rewards. Yet in a remote corner of his mind, an iota of uncertainty lingered. How to stem that uncertainty was his dilemma. He noticed it was 12:55 pm. The Yankee/Baltimore game would begin in ten minutes. He turned the television on to the YES Network and caught the end of the Bob Lorenz pre-game show and waited for the game to begin.

"Yankees 8, Baltimore 6, in 12 innings," he said to the TV. "Now, Mr. Tomorrow's *Daily News*, let's see if my boy, Aaron Judge will hit a two-run, walk-off home run." He opened a bottle of his favorite beer, Blue Moon, plopped himself down in his La-Z-Boy, pulled back on the reclining lever, and relaxed to watch the game and wait for the evening.

By the middle of the fourth inning, Baltimore was leading by a score of 5 to 1. A tinge of skepticism began to creep, ever so slightly, into Bruce's mind. *But then, they're the Yankees,* Bruce thought, *and the special newspaper said they'd win in twelve.*

Gio Urshela walked to lead off the bottom of the fourth inning. Gleyber Torres followed with a fly ball to center field, which was caught for the first out. On the first pitch, Brett Gardner hit a blast to right field into the second deck. Ford and Frazier made the next two outs. The Yankees were moving now, down only two runs. They scored one run again in the bottom of the fifth and another in the bottom of the seventh, tying the score at 5 to 5. The Yankees took the lead in the bottom of the eighth inning with a home run by Didi Gregorius. But in the top of the ninth, Baltimore tied the score again at six runs apiece. The Yankees failed to score in the bottom half of the ninth inning forcing extra innings. Bruce's head was in a whirl. *They're going to do it*, thought. *They're gonna win in twelve!*

It was 4:00 pm. Bruce was getting hungry, but he was too excited to eat, let alone walk away from the television. Certain that neither team would score a run in either of the next two innings, he decided that he had enough time to go into the kitchen, make a sandwich, open another bottle of Blue Moon and return to the living room to watch the end of the game.

Clint Frazier led off the bottom of the twelfth inning with a single. After DJ LeMahieu struck out, Aaron Judge took two strikes before hitting a rocket over the center field fence into Monument Park in center field. The Yankees won in the bottom of the twelfth inning by a score of 8 to 6 exactly as described in Bruce's copy of Sunday's *Daily News*. Bruce sat back in his La-Z-Boy, clutching his beer bottle, his eyes wide and his mouth agape.

Oh my god, he whispered. He then stood up, his arms over his head and shouted, "I'm gonna be rich!"

Bruce was now completely convinced that he had been the recipient of something special, out of the ordinary, eerie even. *Am I dreaming? Am I being rewarded for good deeds in a past life?* Whatever the reason, Bruce was going to enjoy his good fortune. He glanced at his wristwatch, noticing it was nearly 5 pm. He took a quick shower, put on some fresh clothes. At 5:40 Bruce exited the elevator to greet a smiling Irv, who said, "Your car's ready, just as you asked." Bruce handed Irv a $10 bill instead of his usual fiver, saying, "I'm feeling lucky tonight, Irv."

"Hey, thanks a lot, Mr. Cozener. I sure hope you're right. You have a wonderful evening," Irv responded, his smile stretching from ear to ear as he shoved the $10 bill into his pocket and rushed ahead to open the front for Bruce.

Bruce pressed the Voice Command button on the dashboard and stated, "Call Phil." Phil picked up the phone on the second ring. "I'll be there in ten minutes," Bruce said.

"See you then," Phil responded.

As promised, Phil was ready when Bruce drove up to the front of his building. The BMW's top was down and they felt the warm breeze enveloping them as the car sped uptown towards Yonkers.

"So, how come you feel so lucky today?" Phil asked.

"Sometimes, you just get that feeling," Bruce responded.

"What's in your man-bag?" Phil asked.

"Just some extra cash to bet with tonight," Bruce replied. Phil stared at him quizzically. He was dying to tell Phil about his experience with the *Daily News* from this morning, but he held back, feeling that Phil would think he was crazy. Bruce decided that it would be better to just let it unfold.

Traffic was light. He pulled into the Yonkers Raceway parking lot at 6:45, giving them just enough time to get to the betting window in time to bet on the Daily Double before the 7:10 post time.

"Five hundred dollars on #2 and #2," Bruce said to the ticket agent.

"Wow," Phil remarked. "That's an awfully big bet. Do you really feel that lucky?"

"Don't worry, I got it covered," Bruce replied. "Give me another $500 on #2 to win in the first," he said to the clerk.

Staring wide-eyed as a result of watching his friend bet what he thought was a fortune, Phil stepped to the window and said, "$10 on #2 to win." Then, turning to Bruce, he added, "I'm just going to bet on the first race by itself. I hope your hunch is right."

When Love Story, the #2 horse paid $5.40 to win, Bruce's collected $1350. Phil won $27. Even more certain that his newspaper was prophetic, Bruce proceeded to bet $500 on Mr. Hyde to win the second race.

"Come on, Phil, bet with me on this race," Bruce implored. "Bet $50 to win on #2."

"Are you crazy, Bruce? That's too big a bet for me."

"Tell you what, Phil," Bruce suggested, "if you lose, I'll cover your $50."

"Now I know you're crazy, but okay," Phil laughed. He dug into his wallet and placed a $50 bet on #2 to win.

When Mr. Hyde barely nosed out the favorite, Bruce and Phil hugged each other with delight.

"What's your secret, Bruce? How did you know he'd win? Was the race fixed?" Phil whispered, not wanting anyone to hear him.

"I told you I was feeling lucky," Bruce said as he slapped Phil on the shoulder. "Now let's go collect our money."

After two races, Phil's nearly $500 winnings were dwarfed by

Bruce's net of $30,000 after the IRS took their cut. Bruce placed his cash in the black bag and clutched it tightly.

"I can't believe what just happened," Phil said. Let's take the money and run."

"I'm just getting started, Bruce smirked.

"Five hundred to win on #5, Blue Chip in the third," Bruce said to the ticket agent.

"Oh, screw it," Phil shrugged, and placed a $100 bet on Blue Chip to win.

After Blue Chip won by two lengths, they won $1,850 and $370 respectively.

Bruce knew that Photo Shoot would win the fourth race, but would pay only $3.10, so he decided that they should sit this one out and have dinner. "Let's take a break," Bruce said. "Dinner's on me."

Steak dinners at *The Pub* were a little pricey – the tab came to $250. But with Bruce's winnings, it was a drop in the bucket. During dinner, Phil asked Bruce not only how he was able to pick the winners in the first three races, but how was he so certain as to wager so much money on the outcomes. He knew that Bruce was a gambler, but he never thought that Bruce was reckless.

"I have a new system," Bruce admitted, "Foolproof, I think," he added. "Give me a few days and I'll let you in on it. Meanwhile, just trust me."

"So long as we keep winning," Phil said excitedly.

"Don't you worry, Phil," Bruce said, "I told you it's foolproof. Two more races and then we'll leave, okay?"

By the end of the 6th race, Bruce's overall winnings were $45,000 while Phil walked away with $4600.

Phil noticed that Bruce's black leather pouch was bulging. "That's a lot of cash to carry around, Bruce," he said.

"You're right. Wait here." I'll be right back." Bruce walked to the pari-mutuel window and whispered something to the clerk. Soon, a uniformed armed guard approached Bruce. He beckoned to Phil, who crossed over to him. "Okay, we're all set to go to the parking lot," Bruce said. "We have an escort."

For the short walk from the cashier's office to the car, Bruce tipped the guard $100, a small sum, he believed, to ensure his safety. Phil and Bruce sat quietly in the car for several minutes. Then, safely on the road back to Manhattan, Phil broke the silence.

"I can't believe what happened tonight. 'Feeling lucky' hardly described what you did. Did you make some pact with the devil or something like that? And how do I tell Susan I won over $4,000?"

"Don't," Bruce replied. "Just stash it away someplace safe for the next time we go to the track. I'll let you in on my secret soon."

Phil was too excited to engage in any more conversation. He turned on the radio and, ironically, sang out loud to accompany Rod Stewart singing, "Some Guys Have All the Luck."

The BMW stopped in front of Phil's building. "Thanks for a great evening. Let's do it again soon," he added.

"We will, my friend," Bruce responded. He put up the BMW's top and drove directly home and into his parking garage. The elevator took him from the garage to his floor. Cautiously eyeing his surroundings, he quickly entered his apartment. He never loosened his grip on the black leather case bulging with over $45,000 in cash. Bruce bolted the door behind him and sank onto the sofa. He couldn't tell whether he felt relief or disbelief.

Phil hid his winnings in one of his dresser drawers where he was sure that Susan wouldn't find it.

"How was your evening?" Susan asked when she came home from Mah Jong. "Lose much?"

"It was great," Phil said. "I actually won a couple of bucks. How was Mah Jong?"

"Oh, the usual," Susan replied. "The other husbands asked for you, but I told them that you had made plans with Bruce, and they dropped it."

Phil was so elated from the experience of his evening that he had a hard time falling asleep. "I'm going to take a shower," he said to Susan. "How about you?"

Susan recognized, Phil's 'How about you?' as a hint that he wanted to make love to her.

"You go in and I'll be right in there with you," Susan said as she slipped out of her clothes slowly and invitingly. After showering together and sharing their love in bed, Phil had no problem falling asleep.

Bruce, on the other hand, was unable to find sleep. His mind remained stimulated with the excitement of having won so much money. His head whirled with ideas about taking advantage of his new-found method of winning. But he was plagued with doubts, too. *What if tomorrow's newspaper were just that, Sunday's paper? What if yesterday's windfall was an aberration, an extraordinary, one-of-a kind event?* Bruce continued to stare at the ceiling. At 3 am he got out of bed, poured a glass of milk and warmed it in the microwave for a minute, set his alarm clock for 10, and returned to bed. After fifteen minutes, he drifted off to sleep.

Sunday, July 12 - 11 am

Bruce went to Nick's diner in the morning to see if the mysterious stranger who gave him the newspaper would reappear. "You look like hell," Gloria said, as Bruce walked in. "Go find a seat and I'll bring you some coffee."

"Make it black," Bruce answered as he headed to his favorite booth. He sat down and opened the large menu to the page with the heading *Breakfast Anytime*. Still a bit foggy from lack of sleep, Bruce failed to notice the man wearing a raincoat enter Nick's right after him. He walked past Bruce and sat at the rear of the diner.

"You look like you were up all night," Gloria said.

"I'll be all right after I have something to eat," Bruce responded. He thought about the $45,000, still in the black leather pouch on the top of his dresser and added, "In fact, I'm beginning to feel better right now."

"That's good," Gloria said. "What'll it be?"

"Let me have the eggs benedict, hold the potatoes," Bruce said. "And some more coffee, please."

Bruce was so eager to enjoy his breakfast that he didn't notice the stranger in the raincoat sit down across from him in the booth. Bruce looked up, startled. The man seemed to appear out of nowhere. Bruce immediately flinched, spilling some of his coffee onto the table top.

"Sorry to surprise you," the man said. He placed a copy of *The Daily News* on the table. "Mind if I join you?"

Bruce stared at the man, then at the newspaper, then back the man without uttering a word. He thought how peculiar it was that the man was wearing a raincoat on a warm day in July.

"I trust you had a successful day yesterday," the man said.

Bruce's eyes were fixated on the man. He remained speechless. Finally, Bruce asked, "Aren't you the man who gave me the newspaper yesterday?"

"My name is Michael," said the stranger. He nudged *The Daily News* towards Bruce and continued, "This is for you. Use it wisely."

He rose suddenly from the table and added, "You'll want to wipe up that spilled coffee before it runs into your lap. Have a nice day. Perhaps I'll see you tomorrow." Michael rose and walked out of Nick's as suddenly as he had appeared. Bruce watched him walk out the door. He ran to the front door in an attempt to follow Michael, who had vanished into the Sunday morning crowd. Dazed, he returned to the diner and, turning to Gloria, said, "Did you notice which way that man went?"

"What man?" she responded.

"The man, Michael, who was sitting at my booth. The guy that gave me the newspaper. The man in the raincoat," Bruce replied.

"I didn't see any man," Gloria said, as she continued to clean one of the tables.

"You must have," Bruce insisted. "He rushed right by you a minute ago."

"I don't know what you're talking about," Gloria said, casually. "Are you okay, Mr. C?"

Bruce was flummoxed. He stared at Gloria for a moment and then said, "Yeah, I'm fine." He returned to his booth, sat down and examined the newspaper.

"More coffee?" asked Gloria, as she refilled Bruce's cup without waiting for a response. By the time Bruce said, "Yes," she had already walked to the other end of the diner to attend to another customer.

Bruce perused the *Daily News* with the date, Monday, July 13 on the front page. Slowly regaining his composure, Bruce turned to the sports page.

Yanks Over B'More 8-2
Judge, Gardner Each Hit 2 Four-Baggers

This is truly astonishing, Bruce thought, as his mind once again swirled around the fact that he was being favored with advance knowledge of today's events. *Why me?* he thought again. *Who is this Michael guy and why was I selected to know the future?* He sipped his coffee and said to himself, *What the hell, enjoy it and get rich.* He flipped the page over to the horse racing results and jotted down the winners at Belmont Raceway for that afternoon. He thought of inviting Phil to join him but decided against it. No need to have to explain it. At least not yet.

Bruce's winnings at Belmont Raceway amounted to just over $200,000. When Bruce inquired about an armed escort, the pari-mutuel clerk suggested that he take a check for his winnings. It would be so much easier to carry and much safer than cash. Bruce agreed, thinking, *why didn't I come up with that idea myself?*

When he returned to his apartment, he poured a glass of Chivas, plopped down on the sofa, ordered in some Chinese food, and turned on the YES Network. He caught the post-game interview with Yankees Manager Aaron Boone, who was discussing the two home runs hit by both Aaron Judge and Bret Gardner in the Yankees 8-2 victory over the Baltimore Orioles.

Still dumbfounded about his good fortune, Bruce went for a walk to get fresh air. Without taking specific note of where he was walking, he found himself in front of Nick's Olympic Diner. *Might as well go in and get a cup of coffee*, he thought. *Who knows, maybe my new benefactor, Michael, might just be there.*

Bruce sat in his favorite booth, ordered coffee and a slice of Nick's famous strawberry rhubarb pie, and kept his gaze focused on the front door, thinking that Michael might appear. Tired of waiting, he finished his pie and coffee and went to the cash register to pay. He handed a $20 bill to Marina, Nick's wife. Handing him his change, Marina said, "Oh, Mr. Cozener, a man left this envelope for you. I don't know how he knew you'd be here this evening, though. Coincidence, I suppose."

Bruce quickly tore open the envelope and read the note. *"See you tomorrow morning."* It was signed, *Michael.* Bruce put the note in his pocket. *What the hell is going on?* He wondered.

"Did the man say anything when he left this note?" Bruce asked.

"Actually," Marina said, "He didn't really hand me the note. He left the envelope with your name on it on the counter. I only saw him from behind as he left. All I remember was that he was wearing a raincoat. Don't you think that's strange? I mean, why was he wearing a raincoat in July?"

"Thanks, Marina," Bruce replied. He walked home slowly, trying to make some sense of it all. Still puzzled, he poured another glass of Chivas, sat on the sofa, turned on the television to TCM, the classic movie channel. He thought how ironic it was that "Brewster's Millions" was playing. He took an Ambien at midnight and fell into a deep sleep.

Monday, July 13 - 7:30 am

Bruce's alarm beeped for almost 30 seconds before he awoke. Shaking the effects of the sleeping pill out of his head, he showered, dressed and walked quickly to Nick's for breakfast. The anticipation of meeting Michael that morning was foremost in his mind. What did Michael have in store for him today?

Bruce was greeted by Gloria with a cheerful, "Good morning, Mr. C," who escorted him to his favorite booth, placing the menu in front of him. "Coffee?" she asked.

"Black, and I'll have the usual. Has anyone asked for me?"

"Not that I'm aware of," Gloria responded.

Gloria returned with his coffee and food. With every bite of his breakfast, Bruce looked around the room but did not see Michael anywhere. As he was sopping up the last bit of egg yolk with his toast, he looked up and there was Michael, sitting across from him clad, as usual, in his raincoat.

"You were so engaged in your breakfast that you probably didn't see me come in," Michael said to a stunned Bruce.

"I guess not," Bruce replied. "I'm a bit tired this morning."

"Good day, yesterday, was it?" Michael asked, knowing the answer.

"Pretty good," Bruce said.

"Let's talk," said Michael. But before Bruce could respond, Michael continued. "You know, Bruce, the future is not always all what it seems to be. Or can be. Or is destined to be. Everyone has choices, choices that can affect their own future. Do you understand what I'm saying, Bruce?"

Bruce nodded, "I think I know what you're saying."

"I hope so," Michael continued. "The future may look bleak,

or it may look bright. But bleak doesn't have to turn out bleak and bright may not always be bright. It all depends on your choices, Bruce. What I'm saying now is that your future, and yours alone, is up to you. I hope you truly understand that."

"Who *are* you?" asked Bruce, attempting to figure out who this enigmatic man was.

Without saying another word, Michael stood up and was out the door in a flash, leaving behind a copy of *The Daily News* on the table showing the date Tuesday, July 14. Bruce caught a glimpse of Nick's front door as it closed, and the back of the mystery man in the raincoat as he disappeared into the crowded street. He continued staring at the door, then at the newspaper, tomorrow's newspaper, that Michael left on the table in front of him.

Finally, he picked up Tuesday's *Daily News* and thought, *Let's see what's going to be new in the world today.* Reveling again in his good fortune, Bruce turned straight to the horse racing results, taking note of the the winners of this evening's races at Yonkers. *I can always use another few hundred grand,* he mused.

Bruce paid his check and left a handsome tip for Gloria. He then hailed a cab to take him to his office, making sure he had tomorrow's *Daily News* with him. He kept it folded under his arm so no one would recognize Tuesday's date. Bruce's secretary, Judy, handed him a cup of coffee as he walked into his office. "Nice weekend?" she asked.

"Magnificent weekend," Bruce replied. "Hold my calls for a while," he added. "And close the door, would you please?"

"Sure thing, Bruce," Judy said as she returned to her own desk.

For the past two days, all Bruce had read in each of his advance copies of *The Daily News* were the sports pages. He had all but disregarded the front-page headlines or any other part of the newspaper. But now, in his office, he thought he'd take the time to read more of tomorrow's newspaper to find out what else would be happening, other than sports. The front page read:

SENATE PROCEEDING WITH TRUMP
IMPEACHMENT VOTE

A picture of a scowling Donald Trump covered the rest of the front page. Beneath the photograph, was the caption: **"They'll Never Get Me Out of Office"**

Yeah, right, Bruce thought. *We'll see about that.* Turning to Page 2, he noticed a headline:

$Mega$Millions$ Jackpot Now $130 Million
Next Drawing Tuesday Evening 9 pm

Bruce continued scanning the remainder of the newspaper without taking much notice of any other news that wasn't of any specific interest to him or his chance to make a significant windfall. He finished his coffee and dialed Phil's office number.

"Phil Cooper's office," said a friendly female voice.

"Hi, Janet," Bruce said to Phil's secretary. "Phil in yet?"

"Oh, hello Mr. Cozener," Janet replied, recognizing his voice. "Sure, I'll put him right on."

Phil's voice was bright and cheery, even for a Monday morning. "How're you doin' ol' buddy?" he asked.

"Great," Bruce replied. "How was the rest of your weekend?"

"Phenomenal," Phil said, "Especially Saturday night, if you know what I mean."

"So, Saturday night at the track didn't cause any harm?" Bruce said, sarcastically.

"I'll let you be the judge of that, my friend," Phil chuckled back.

Bruce almost told Phil about his day at Belmont yesterday, but then thought better of it. *I'm not really ready to let Phil in on my secret for winning yet,* he thought.

"How about Yonkers again tonight?" Bruce asked. "I'm feeling really lucky again."

"You're kidding," Phil replied. "I can't make it tonight. We're on for racquet ball tomorrow morning at 8, right?"

Bruce was a bit disappointed and, at the same time, relieved that Phil could not make it to the track that evening. He didn't want to mention his winning method yet. "You bet," Bruce replied. "See you on the court at 8. And make sure you bring another ten-spot."

Bruce jotted down the names of the winning horses for Monday night's races at Yonkers, folded the newspaper carefully and put it back in his attaché case. He called Judy on the intercom and said, "What's on the docket for today?" Judy brought in a small stack of manilla folders, placed them on Bruce's desk and said, "Have fun with these."

Bruce plugged away for the rest of the day without much enthusiasm, anticipating another jackpot later that evening. He brought a sandwich back from Prêt a Manger and ate lunch at his desk. He worked until 6:30 then called an Uber to take him directly to Yonkers Raceway in time to bet on the Daily Double. By 10:30, Bruce was ahead more than $250,000. At that point he was tired and decided to go home and get a good night's sleep in anticipation for his racquet ball game with Phil.

Tuesday, July 14

Bruce's alarm clock woke him from a deep sleep at 6 am. He was in the middle of an erotic dream in which he and Gloria were having sex in the back room of Nick's Olympic Diner. At 6:15 his doorbell rang. *Who'd be ringing my doorbell at this hour?* he wondered. Still in his pajamas, he opened the door but saw no one there. He peered up and down the hallway but it was completely vacant. Looking down at his doormat he noticed a package wrapped in brown paper. Inside was a copy of *The Daily News* dated Wednesday, July 15. A yellow Post-It note was affixed to the front page with a hand-written note that read: *Enjoy the day... M.*

Stunned, Bruce removed the Post-It note and immediately saw the lead article.

$Mega$Millions$Jackpot Pays $138 Million
Winning Numbers: 3, 17, 22, 36, 38, 47 - Power No. 12

Bruce glanced at the date on the newspaper once again. It was Wednesday, July 15. Today was Tuesday, July 14. He was gazing at tonight's winning lottery numbers. Staring at an amazing fortune of $138 million. All he had to do was purchase a lottery ticket with the winning numbers, and he would be wealthy beyond his wildest dreams. His heart pounded. *Oh, my god,* he thought. *Am I in the Twilight Zone?* It took several minutes to regain his composure. *Breathe,* he thought. He took a deep breath. Then another. Just go to the Athletic Club, play racquet ball with Phil, buy the ticket and wait for the evening's drawing. That's all he had to do today. Forget about work. Forget about anything else.

It was now 6:30. Still plenty of time to get dressed, have breakfast and catch a cab to the Athletic Club. Without thinking, Bruce flipped to the second page of the newspaper and was horrified at what he saw.

A photo of an ambulance, a taxi cab and a crowd of onlookers taken, obviously, with someone's cell phone camera. The headline read:

Man Killed by Taxi Exiting Central Park

The story began: *"Phil Cooper, 46, was struck and killed by a taxi cab as he crossed 7ᵗʰ Avenue after leaving the New York Athletic Club Tuesday morning."*

This can't be, Bruce thought. *My best friend is going to die this morning. I can't let that happen.* His mind spun like an unbalanced top. Then he suddenly remembered his last conversation with Michael.

"You know, Bruce, the future is not all that it seems to be. Or can be. Or is destined to be."

Bruce remembered that Michael might have been implying that the future could be changed. That he, Bruce, could change the future by his own actions. All he would have to do is prevent Phil from crossing 7ᵗʰ Avenue and his life would be saved. *Now that I know this*, Bruce thought, *I'll get Phil into a cab and he'll be fine. That won't be difficult.*

Bruce regained his composure, dressed, boiled a couple of eggs, had a cup of coffee, packed his gym bag and took a cab to the Athletic Club. All the while he kept thinking, *who is Michael and why did he choose me?*

Phil beat Bruce in straight sets. "You owe me another ten bucks," he bragged.

"Glad to pay up," Bruce said. "You played well."

"You seemed to be preoccupied, Bruce," Phil said.

"Nah, just some stuff at the office. No problem." Bruce replied.

They showered, dressed and got ready to go to work.

"Catch up with you later, Bruce," Phil said as they walked out of the Athletic Club.

"Hold on, Phil," Bruce said. "It's 9 o'clock already. Why don't you take a cab to your office? My treat."

"Seriously? There's no need for that," Phil said. "I'll just walk across to Columbus Circle and catch the train."

"No, my friend, I insist," Bruce stated emphatically. He raised his hand and waved for a cab, which appeared instantly, as if it had been waiting for Bruce's signal. As Phil entered the cab, he turned to Bruce and said, "Thanks, Bruce. You have a great day. Talk to you later."

Feeling like the weight of the world had been just been lifted from his shoulders, Bruce sighed in relief as he watched the cab disappear into the southbound traffic on 7th Avenue.

I did it, Bruce thought. *I just saved Phil's life!*

Bruce removed the piece of paper from his wallet on which he had written the winning lottery numbers. There they were: 3, 17, 22, 36, 38, 47, Power No. 12. The news kiosk was directly across the street. As he crossed 7th Avenue, excited to purchase the lottery ticket that would make him ultra-rich, he failed to notice the taxicab careening out of control from Central Park.

"Look out!" someone screamed.

Bruce turned but it was too late. All he managed to see was the cab driver's horrified face through the windshield. Then everything went black. Bruce barely felt the torrent of pain surge through his body. The impact was so swift and great that in less than one second, Bruce Cozener's life came to an end.

Two checks payable to Bruce Cozener from the New York State Racing Authority totaling more than $450,000 lay on the dresser in his apartment. The next day, the headline in *The Daily News* dated Wednesday, July 15 would read:

$Mega$Millions$ Jackpot Now $225 Million

The story on the second page described the accidental death of Bruce Cozener, 46, Insurance Executive, by an out-of-control taxicab on 7th Avenue.

Fate, it seems, is not always written in stone. Or in the newspapers. The future cannot be predicted. We control our own destiny by the choices we make. We do not, however, have control over their consequences.

Detour

STEVE LEONHARDT enjoyed driving. He took particular pleasure in planning road trips with his wife, Eileen. "Give me my Cross-Country Volvo station wagon, an open road, and I'm in heaven," was Steve's credo. During the past ten years, they drove from their home in northern New Jersey to Maine, Quebec, New Orleans, Nashville, Chicago, Miami, and as far away as California and Washington State.

Before Steve retired, he had been director of FedEx's distribution center in Bergen County. He knew the streets, roads, and virtually every point of interest in the county like the back of his hand. He was an expert in finding alternate routes that avoided traffic lights, stop signs and streets with speed bumps that would slow him down.

Eileen, unlike Steve, did not like to drive. She enjoyed the road trips but took the wheel to relieve Steve only when it was necessary, about one hour at a time for every six hours driven by Steve. However, Eileen was an excellent navigator. She knew Steve's route preferences, and they were an excellent driving team. In fact, with Steve at the wheel and Eileen as navigator, they won first prize in the Northern

New Jersey Volvo Club's annual Road Rally three times in their last five attempts. They displayed their 10-inch high trophies proudly in their den for all their friends to marvel at. Each trophy was adorned with the colorful scarf that Eileen wore during the race.

Both Steve and Eileen retired at the same time. Eileen taught high school mathematics. Her students adored her because of the caring and thoughtful manner with which she helped them learn geometry and trigonometry. Her dedication earned her the distinction of *Teacher of the Year.*

Eileen did the cooking and food shopping while they were actively employed. However, retirement gave them the opportunity to share these activities. Steve was an excellent cook who enjoyed shopping, and was particular about selecting his own special ingredients from the gourmet and ethnic food aisles in the local supermarket. After forty-five years of marriage, blessed with four children and six grandchildren, Steve and Eileen looked forward to a retirement filled with long vacation trips and visits with their grandchildren.

"We should replace our bedroom shades with those blackout shades," Eileen said one morning as the sun forced its way into the bedroom. "It's only seven o'clock and I could use another hour of sleep."

"Sure," Steve responded as he sat up on the edge of the bed, stretching his arms over his head. "If that's what you want, you got it. I'll measure the window and we can go to the shade store right after breakfast."

"You're a doll," Eileen said. She rolled over to Steve's side of the bed and kissed him on his shoulder. "Want coffee?"

"Do you want to make breakfast this morning?" Steve asked.

44

"No, silly," Eileen said, laughing. "That's your job. I'll just put up a pot of coffee."

Steve prepared his unparalleled pancakes, the ones that his grandchildren craved every time they were fortunate enough to spend a weekend with him and Eileen.

"What makes your pancakes so good, grandpa?" they'd ask.

"My special ingredient is love," Steve would always respond, as each child giggled with delight. Steve's special "love" was a few thimblefuls of Amaretto liqueur, in addition to the mashed banana and applesauce he added to the batter.

After breakfast, Steve and Eileen drove to the shade and curtain store in Paramus and ordered the blackout shade for their bedroom. Upon returning home, Steve remarked "You know, I forgot to take something out of the freezer for dinner tonight. I'm going to run to the supermarket to pick up a few things. Do you want me to get anything for you?"

"Buy some cold cuts and American cheese," Eileen said. "And remember to ask them to slice the cheese thin, the way I like it."

"It's two o'clock. I'll be back before three," Steve said, as he kissed Eileen on the forehead and drove away in his beloved Volvo station wagon.

On his way home from the supermarket, Steve encountered yellow rubber construction cones blocking the road at the corner of Prospect and Grove Streets. "DETOUR" was in the center of the arrow on the sign that pointed left, toward Grove Street. Beyond the sign, for one block on Prospect south of Grove Street, Steve noticed that the roadway contained patches of broken asphalt. Another sign, just beyond the detour sign read, "ROAD UNDER REPAIR." Steve stopped and looked at the road ahead. *That's awfully strange,* he thought. *I don't recall seeing any roadwork being done on my way to the store. How did they do this so quickly? And it seems odd that there are no workers here right now.*

Not wanting to drive his precious Volvo on the broken pavement, Steve followed the detour sign and made the left turn on to Grove Street. He proceeded for about one-quarter mile until he reached Spring Street, where another detour sign pointed to the right. *That's funny,* Steve considered, *I was sure I knew every street around here. I thought Spring Street dead-ended here at Grove. I don't recall being able to turn right here.* To his consternation, Steve followed the detour arrow for another block until he was again directed to turn right by another detour sign onto Green Street. He followed Green Street back to Prospect where he made the left turn that put him back on his original path home. As he glanced to his right, he could see the broken asphalt under repair. *I must be going nuts,* he thought. *I suppose it might be possible that I took a different route to the store, but I can't remember. Funny about those streets, though. Why didn't I know about that section of Spring Street? Well, no worries. I'm back on track now.*

Steve arrived home and parked in his usual spot on the right side of the double driveway. He pressed the automatic garage door opener on his window visor which, to his surprise, failed to open the door. Shrugging his shoulders, he exited the car and pressed the four-digit code on the garage door key pad which, like the switch in his car, failed to open the door. *Looks like the door opener is on the fritz. Another expense to deal with,* he thought. "I'm home hon," Steve called as he walked through the front door carrying two bags of groceries. He placed the bags on the kitchen table and said, "Hey, Eileen, did you know there's something wrong with the garage door?"

Instead of hearing a response, Steve heard the garage door open as Eileen drove her car into the garage. She walked up the steps into the kitchen with a sense of urgency. "Steve, where the hell have you been for the past four hours?" she shouted. "Jerry and I have been worried sick. We finally went out looking for you."

"What do you mean?" Steve said, perplexed. "I've only been gone for about 45 minutes. And why is Jerry here? I didn't see his car. where are Alice and the kids?"

"Steve, you're not having one of your fits again, are you?" Eileen asked, her voice trembling. She was still upset about Steve's mysterious absence.

"I told you before that I was just going to the store to buy some stuff for dinner. Don't you remember?" Steve replied. "What's going on here?" he continued, unable to understand what to make of the situation.

"Stuff for dinner?" Eileen said. "I told you before that I was making a lasagna tonight. When I turned around, you were gone. And your car was gone. You scared the living daylights out of us. And what's all this about someone named Alice? Who's Alice?"

"Jerry's wife, Alice. Who else do you think I mean?" Steve replied, becoming agitated in his state of confusion."

"Steve, sweetheart, come sit down in the living room," Eileen said as she coaxed Steve into his favorite rocker-recliner. Jerry, their youngest son, followed them into the living room and sat on the sofa, while Eileen pulled up a dining room chair and held Steve's hand. "Steve, you know we love you," she said as Steve began to break in, "Eileen..."

"No, Steve, please let me speak. For the past several weeks Jerry and I have noticed a change in your behavior. The way you recall things – or can't recall them – you seem to be undergoing some kind of change. I don't know where you came up with the name, Alice. Jerry's never been married. Our other children, of course, are married. But there's never been an Alice. I think we should call the doctor and get you a complete checkup. Don't you think?"

"Dad, mom's right," Jerry said. "I think a complete physical exam would be in order."

Steve thought that perhaps something wasn't right in his head. "I could use a drink," he said, and walked into the den only to find that the liquor cabinet was filled with dishtowels, linen napkins and serving dishes. There was no liquor anywhere to be found. His prized road rally trophies were nowhere in sight. "Where's all my liquor?" Steve said, completely puzzled. "And what happened to our road rally trophies? And the scarves you wore as my navigator?" Turning his gaze to the wall above the bookcase left to him by his mother, he noticed the portrait of his children and grandchildren given to him and Eileen for their fortieth anniversary. Three of his children were posed with their spouses and children – four grandchildren, not six. Jerry was there by himself. *I must be losing my mind*, he said to himself. His thoughts were interrupted by his wife's voice.

"What are you talking about, Steve?" Eileen said. "We haven't had a drop of liquor in the house for a long time. You've been on the wagon for three years now. You haven't been drinking outside, have you? And what trophies are you talking about? We don't do road rallies. You know that I get carsick if I try to read anything while you're driving, especially maps."

Eileen stared at her husband with her hands on her hips. "Steve, you don't look well. Come over here."

As he approached his wife, Eileen stood on her toes, put her lips to his forehead and said, "No, I don't think you have any fever. Why don't you go upstairs and lie down while I get dinner ready? I'm sure you'll feel better in a half hour or so. Go, get some rest. Meanwhile, I think it might be a good idea if Dr. Berkowitz examined you. It's been a while since your last visit."

Still confused, Steve looked at his wife and son. "Okay, I'll lie down for a bit. You're probably right about my seeing Dr. Berkowitz. Would you make the appointment for me?"

As Steve was getting into bed that night, Eileen said, "Do you feel any better?"

"I'm not quite sure," Steve responded.

"Honey," Eileen continued, "why are you on my side of the bed?"

"Oh, I must have forgotten," Steve replied.

"I think tomorrow you should stay in the house and rest while I call the doctor," Eileen insisted.

"Sure," Steve said as he lay down on the other side the bed, the side that felt awkward.

Steve spent most of the next day watching television, still trying to understand what had happened. Eileen made the appointment with Dr. Berkowitz for the following morning. That evening at dinner, Steve turned to Jerry and in bewilderment, asked "Are you sure you don't know anyone named Alice?"

"No, dad, I honestly don't know anyone named Alice," he replied.

Eileen stared at Steve momentarily, shaking her head as she continued with her dinner, trying to hold back her tears.

"How long have you had this feeling of confusion?" asked Dr. Berkowitz, as Steve sat on the examination table wearing the uncomfortable paper gown that the nurse handed him. He felt self-conscious about the slit being open in the back, continually reaching behind to keep it closed. *At least I haven't lost my sense of dignity,* he reflected.

"I really can't say," Steve replied. "I thought it started yesterday, when I returned home from the supermarket, but Eileen and Jerry told me that it's been going on for a few weeks."

"Let's take a look at you," said Dr. Berkowitz.

After giving Steve a thorough examination that included an electrocardiogram and chest X-Ray, Dr. Berkowitz said, "Well, Steve, all things considered, you appear to be in good physical health. But I want to ask you a few questions. Please bear with me."

Steve felt a bit awkward about being asked what he thought were simple personal questions. He answered most of them correctly with a few exceptions. He was wrong about Jerry's age (off by 3 years), the length of his marriage to Eileen (off by 4 years), how long they had been living in their present house (off by 3 years) and the number and ages of his grandchildren.

"I want you to see a colleague of mine, Dr. Phyllis Taylor. She's a psychiatrist who has a lot of experience dealing with memory loss. I think you'll like her. I'm sure she'll be able to sort things out for you. How about I help set up an appointment?" Dr. Berkowitz said.

"I guess that'll be all right," Steve said.

"Just sit here for a few moments," Dr. Berkowitz said. He picked up the wall phone and asked the nurse to call Dr. Taylor. After a few moments, Steve heard Dr. Berkowitz speaking with her. He then turned toward Steve and asked, "Will tomorrow afternoon at 4 be convenient for you to meet with Dr. Taylor?"

"I suppose so," Steve responded.

"Okay, Phyllis," Dr. Berkowitz said. "He'll be at your office tomorrow at 4. Thanks so much for seeing him so soon."

Steve removed the examination gown, got dressed and proceeded to the waiting room accompanied by Dr. Berkowitz, where Eileen sat reading People Magazine. "Well, what's the damage?" Eileen asked, looking up from the magazine.

That's peculiar, Steve thought, *Eileen never liked 'People' magazine.*

"Everything's going to be just fine, Eileen," said Dr. Berkowitz, offering the kind of reassurance that gave her some comfort. "I've arranged for Steve to visit a good friend and colleague of mine, Dr. Phyllis Taylor, tomorrow at 4 pm. She's one of the best psychiatrists in the area. I'm sure she'll help him sort things out."

"That's wonderful," Eileen said. "Steve, are you ready to go home now?"

"I guess so," Steve replied. Doubt and confusion still dominated Steve's mind as he attempted to grasp what was happening to him.

Steve awoke the next morning feeling relatively normal – if "normal" was the right word under these circumstances. But he still couldn't shake the confusion that occupied his brain. Eileen set the table, brewed the coffee, scrambled the eggs, made the toast, and poured the orange juice – all the things that Steve was used to doing. They ate breakfast quietly, after which Steve went into the living room and sat in his recliner while Eileen washed the dishes. He stood up and began pacing back and forth, thinking, *how did this happen to me? When did it start?* After a minute he called out to his wife, "Eileen, I'll be right back. I'm going to take a quick drive around the neighborhood and clear my mind. Don't worry about me, I won't be long."

"All right, Steve. Just be careful and don't get lost again," she replied. *Don't patronize me,* Steve thought as got into his car. *If I just retrace my steps, maybe I'll be able to figure this all out.* He backed the car out of the driveway and headed north on Prospect, toward the supermarket, as he did before this all began. As he drove past Grove Street, he noticed that the road was completely paved. *That was a quick repair,* he thought.

Steve continued driving until he crossed Maple Avenue. Then an idea hit him. He pulled into a driveway, made a U-turn and headed south on Prospect. At Grove Street, he saw the same yellow cones and detour sign with an arrow facing left onto Grove Street. There were no construction workers in front of him, nor was anyone else nearby. *What the hell???* he thought. *I just drove by here moments ago. How could this construction site have appeared so soon?*

Resisting the urge to follow the detour sign, he proceeded around the yellow cones and onto the broken asphalt pavement, confident that his trusty Volvo station wagon would handle the rough road in front of him for two blocks without sustaining any damage. *After all,* Steve thought, *it's a Volvo. That's why I bought it!*

Steve held the steering wheel firmly as the wagon jostled along for the next two blocks. Once he reached the end of the gravel portion and returned to solid pavement, Steve pulled over to check for any possible damage to his pride and joy. Finding none, he proceeded to drive home. His Volvo hummed along as if it had never been driven through the jagged and rocky construction site. He parked in the driveway, turned off the motor and sat in the car for a few moments. He pressed the automatic garage door switch on his visor and watched as the garage door opened normally. Entering through the garage, he called out to Eileen, "Honey, I'm home."

"What?" Eileen said. "You just left two minutes ago. Did you forget something?"

Steve stood silently for a moment. "What did you just say?" he asked.

"I asked you if you forgot something," Eileen said, smiling. "Your wallet, perhaps?"

Reaching into his back pocket, Steve replied, "No, I have it."

"Then why did you come right back, the store wasn't closed, was it?"

"Is Jerry here?" Steve asked.

"Jerry?" Eileen responded, puzzled by Steve's question. "Of course not. Why would he be here? He's probably at work. Why do you ask?"

"I don't know." Steve responded.

"You know," Eileen continued, "I haven't spoken to Jerry in a few days. Which reminds me, I should call him and see how Alice is feeling. She's been bit under the weather lately. So, are you going back to the supermarket to get what you need for dinner tonight?"

"Maybe I'll just order a pizza for delivery," Steve said. He paused and then walked slowly into the den and stood in front of the liquor cabinet. He glanced to his right at the three road rally trophies on the shelf, all of which reflected the setting sun's gleam through the window. Each trophy was decorated with one of Eileen's scarves. He opened the liquor cabinet and took a cut crystal glass from the top shelf. Eileen had purchased a set of them at the Waterford factory when they vacationed in Ireland five years ago. He poured himself a glass of Chivas Regal and glanced up at the family portrait hanging on the wall. His four children, their spouses and six grandchildren all were smiling at him.

Steve stared again at his trophies. He stared at the books on the built-in shelves. He stared again at the portrait, making sure to notice Jerry and Alice. Finally, he glanced at the glass in his hand. He walked into the living room and sat in his favorite recliner.

"Well, mister man of leisure," Eileen said, as Steve appeared to be relaxing comfortably, "What's on your mind?"

"Nothing," he replied, as he sipped his drink, enjoying the smooth feeling of twelve-year old Scotch as it trickled down his throat. "Nothing much."

They Answer Our Prayers

RONALD MOUNTEBANK awoke from a pleasant dream in which he was playing racquet ball against the top player at the Beacon Hill Athletic Club. Ronald was ahead and was about to win the set when he was jolted into reality by the shattering clang of the seven o'clock alarm bell on the corridor wall of the Logan Avenue Men's Shelter. This was Ronald's current residence, not far from Boston's affluent Back Bay Area. Ronald tossed back his forest green blanket and sheet and sat up at the edge of the bed. He dropped his head into his hands as he did each morning, and stared at his surroundings. He assessed the meager 6 x 8-foot space that was his allotted living area. In the space was a small, three-drawer dresser. In a 6-foot by 12-inch gray metal locker hung his woolen coat on a wooden hanger, a shabby brown cardigan sweater dangled from a metal hanger, and a pair of pants hung on a hook. The upper shelf held his personal items: a toothbrush, bar of soap, drinking cup, comb, and stick deodorant. A towel lay in a heap at the bottom of the locker. Inside the door, masking tape held the daily schedule of chores that were assigned to each resident.

Ronald glanced at the wall clock. It was indeed 7 am, another day to experience homelessness and contemplate how he arrived at this place and this time of his life. He was only 40 years old.

He awoke hungry as he did every morning. He had only 15 minutes to finish getting dressed, wash, and make his bed before going downstairs to breakfast at 7:15. Chores began at 8:00. A final glance at the list of chores indicated that it was his day to sweep the floor in his section of the dormitory. Watery oatmeal and weak coffee were on the menu this morning. Yesterday it was steam-table scrambled eggs. Tomorrow it would be dry pancakes or French toast. That was the cycle repeated every three days: scrambled eggs, oatmeal, pancakes. He could have coffee and toast whenever he wanted.

As Ronald began his chores, he scanned the 40 x 60-foot room he shared with seven other homeless men. His living area was identical to the others – the same bed, locker, and dresser. There was a small bathroom at the end of the hall which he shared with the other men in the dormitory. Each of them took turns cleaning it on a rotating schedule. He didn't mind that so much, but what he could not get used to was the sour odor of the place and the stench of urine that lingered in his nostrils. It reminded him of his childhood, living in poverty. The acrid smell of chlorine bleach reminded him of the times his mother used to clean their small bathroom.

He put on his sweater and, reaching into one of the pockets, pulled out seven one-dollar bills. His corduroy pants pocket contained $6.75 in loose change. Thirteen dollars and seventy-five cents were yesterday's panhandling proceeds. Heaving a heavy sigh, he recalled more productive days, but sometimes he returned to the shelter with less.

It was September in the new millennium and Ronald was not

looking forward to another chilly fall season, followed inevitably by a cold and harsh New England winter. He stood at the door of the shelter, wondering what today would bring out there on the streets of Boston.

Ronald's childhood was not particularly pleasant. His parents loved him, but were not in a position to provide much else for him. Although they were poor, they always tried to make sure he had enough to eat. He dressed mostly in hand-me-downs, worn by his older cousins, but his mother occasionally bought his clothing at Goodwill. He had few toys and even fewer friends. But Ronald had dreams. His incessant prattle about how he would become rich alienated the few friends he did have, and they often tried to avoid him. He was, for the most part, a lonely little boy. He was so lonely, in fact, that Ronald created the only true friend he had – his imaginary friend, "Giant Billy Boy."

Giant Billy Boy would appear whenever Ronald called him. He would play games with him, keep him company in his lonely room, and would whisk him away to far off places on his magic carpet, places that Ronald had only seen in the pictures of his grade school geography book. Giant Billy Boy was Ronald's savior. But as he got older, Ronald came to the realization that Giant Billy Boy was only a figment of his imagination, a temporary measure to distract him from loneliness. Eventually, Giant Billy Boy would have to be put aside – faded into a pleasant memory from his childhood.

Ronald's dreams of success and wealth never faded. He became determined to pull himself out of poverty and obtain those riches he saw others enjoy. He was resolute in achieving this goal by any measures he could muster, even if it meant shoving others out of his way to get what he wanted. Ronald stayed mostly to himself during high school and studied hard to obtain good grades. His parents could not afford to pay for college, but because of his excellent grades, he was awarded a college scholarship. That, and his pay from a part time job, helped him earn his degree with a major in business and finance.

Ronald became a smooth talker who could persuade others easily. Capitalizing on this talent, he landed a job in the finance department of Tenacity Chemical Company in Boston. Ronald immediately convinced one of Tenacity's vice presidents to become his mentor. It did not take long for Ronald to rise quickly to the position of senior budget analyst. He was given his own office and shared the secretary with the budget manager.

By the age of thirty, Ronald was promoted to senior financial planning analyst, poised to become department manager when his boss retired the following year. From where he sat, Ronald knew the ins and outs of the company, their business plans, and their clients. He was well liked by upper management and because of his financial acumen, his advice was eagerly sought and accepted.

Many of his co-workers, however, considered him an opportunist who would stop at nothing to get ahead. There was very little they could do about it, though. Speaking out against Ronald could hurt their own chances for advancement. Ronald had the ears of top management, those who could propel his career. He gave no thought to his peers, often maligning them behind their backs. He would furtively sabotage their work in order to enhance his own position. What was good for Ronald was all that mattered – all others be damned.

Ronald seemed to have everything he wanted. He was good-looking, had a great job as the budget manager at Tenacity, and owned a 3,000 square foot home in Newton. He was married to Sara, a beautiful but high maintenance woman. Ronald especially enjoyed his new favorite toy, a red BMW convertible. He liked to brag that he drove *The Ultimate Driving Machine,* often to the point of being obnoxious, just as he did as a child.

In spite of his outward successes, Ronald was not satisfied. His craving for money, more toys, more everything became an obsession. To maintain his expensive lifestyle, he ran up significant debts. Ronald didn't care though; he was enjoying the good life. His childhood dream was becoming a reality. Sara also had an appetite for the more luxurious things in life. So long as Ronald could satisfy her desire for furs, high fashion clothes and jewelry, Sara seemed happy. That, in turn, made Ronald happy. Ronald was intent on keeping Sara happy.

For the next three years, Ronald zoomed up the ladder at Tenacity. Once he was promoted to budget director, he continued to indulge the good life on Sara, while at the same time sinking deeper into debt. But he appeared happy. That was until the day he received a phone call from Frank Dexter, Tenacity's executive vice president.

"I'd like to see you, Ron." Frank said. "Come to my office immediately." At that moment Ronald's world at Tenacity Chemicals, as well as his career, came crashing down. "Explain this to me," Dexter said, handing Ronald a letter that he had received from the president of Vinyl Products, one of their leading customers. It was from Singapore Chemicals, Tenacity's competitor, who were offering raw materials to Vinyl Products at 20% less than Tenacity's own selling price. The letter from Singapore Chemicals was signed, "Ronald Mountebank, Sales Manager."

Ronald stood in front of Frank Dexter's desk, silent in is new Armani suit, sweat building on his upper lip and under his arms, his mouth becoming dry as if stuffed with cotton balls. Nausea began overtaking him. In a futile attempt to maintain his composure, Ronald insisted it was a forgery. But it was in vain. There was no mistake. It was Ronald's distinctive and unambiguous signature at the bottom of the letter. Frank Dexter stared at Ronald for what seemed an eternity. Then Frank's face turned threatening.

Frank Dexter had suspicions that Ronald was up to something devious. Arnie Wilson, the company's credit manager, told Frank that Ronald had been pressing him about specific product pricing. Arnie, who had never liked Ronald, informed Frank that his adversary may have been attempting to undermine the company's sales. The letter confirmed it. Before Ronald could even begin to fabricate an excuse, he heard Frank say, "You betrayed my trust. Clean out your desk. I want you out of the building in an hour." Frank raised his hand and silently pointed to the door.

Ronald turned without saying a word and walked out of Frank Dexter's office. Quickly and quietly Ronald returned to his office and without saying goodbye to those who stood watching in silence, packed his personal items in a cardboard box and left Tenacity Chemicals' office building for good.

Despite Ronald's six-figure salary, his personal debt far exceeded his income and credit. So, he devised a scheme to undercut Tenacity's prices. Once he persuaded Arnie to confide the selling prices of Tenacity's products to him, he convinced Singapore Chemicals to offer Tenacity's customers the same products at a lower price. Ronald was to receive commissions from Singapore. Who would be the wiser? Indeed.

Word of Ronald's unethical and, possibly criminal, actions spread like wildfire. It wasn't long before he was blacklisted by almost every major firm in the industry, making it virtually impossible for him to find a new position. He was fortunate that Tenacity chose not to press charges against him. After struggling unsuccessfully to find work and depleting his remaining funds, he had to sell the house to reduce some of his debt. Sara left immediately and filed for divorce. His beloved BMW was repossessed and he eventually filed for bankruptcy.

To make ends meet, Ronald found a part time job as a clerk in a local hardware store. Once again, using his ability to mislead, Ronald was hired after falsifying his job application. Still struggling financially, however, he was caught stealing small items from the store and was terminated. With no one to turn to, he found himself homeless on the streets of Boston. In utter desperation, he moved into the Logan Men's Homeless Shelter. Dejected and depressed, and to break up the monotony, he spent most of his days roaming the streets, panhandling.

Ronald often met up with Brenda and Andrew, two other homeless people he befriended during his daytime wanderings. Ronald occasionally saw Andrew at the Logan Men's Shelter, where he also stayed.

Brenda Johnson had actually been quite pretty as a young woman, but these days you'd hardly know it. Although she tried to keep herself as clean as she could, dirt often settled in her now wrinkled skin making her look much older than her forty years. She hid her unkempt hair under a red bandana, like those worn by cowboys. She wore a long denim skirt that reached almost to her ankles, underneath which she wore a pair of torn jeans. What was once a fine leather jacket was now ragged, with several tears along the seams. She wore fingerless gloves and carried a large burlap tote bag in which she kept her odds and ends plus a small bottle of brandy, or whatever bottle of liquor she could scrape up the money to buy – or steal. But brandy was indeed her beverage of choice.

Brenda was not the sharpest knife in the drawer. She dropped out of high school when she became pregnant at the age of sixteen, not really knowing who the father was. She gave birth to a beautiful baby boy, and upon leaving the hospital, put the swaddled newborn into a peach basket that she stole from a fruit stand. Quietly sneaking into a church, she left the baby at the altar hoping that the priest would find a home for him. After moving back into her parents' small apartment, Brenda slept on the pullout sofa bed in the living room. She was hired as a clerk the local Walgreen's but was fired within three months for stealing money from the cash register.

Brenda bounced from job to job for the next few years with no prospects for a future. Her parents died within a year of each other, and Brenda stayed in their apartment until her money ran out. Broke and desperate, she wandered the streets of Boston, getting arrested several times for prostitution. At a bar one evening, Brenda met and soon married an older man whom she believed would take care of her. He turned out to be a drug addict and alcoholic who abused her repeatedly. She fled to a women's shelter but wound up spending most of her time on the street with no place else to go. Whenever she felt she could get away with it, she turned a few tricks in order to get some quick cash.

Andrew Bogue's first words to Ronald were, "Please do not call me Andy. I prefer Andrew." Andrew always thought he was smarter than anyone he worked for. He would argue constantly with every employer, and would subsequently be fired regularly. When he tried to set up his own business, he learned a desperate lesson: he wasn't as smart as he thought he was. The only thing he was successful at was convincing others to back him in a shady business scheme. Not only did the business fail, but because of his fraudulent practices, he spent a year in prison. During that time his wife filed for divorce.

At the age of fifty, but with a white beard that made him look much older, Andrew was virtually penniless. Having no other family, he moved into the Logan Avenue men's shelter. Like Ronald, Andrew lived off handouts he begged for on the street. One of his favorite places to sit with his blue and white Olympia Diner paper coffee cup was on the two-block stretch designated Restaurant Row, around the corner from Salem Street. When he was hungry, he'd sit near what used to be his favorite upscale steak and seafood restaurant, Leonardo y Josefina's. He would sit just far enough away from the front door so that he wouldn't be chased away, but close enough to be seen by some of the more liberal-leaning patrons who would either bring him leftover food or make a donation to his paper cup.

Andrew always had his cardboard sign with a string looped around his neck. The sign had three lines. The first line read: "Homeless Vietnam Veteran." The second line read: "Please Help," and "God Bless" was on the third line. He drew pictures of the American flag around the edges. Andrew was a habitual liar. He never served in Vietnam. Nor was he even in the military.

Ronald, Brenda and Andrew would often hang out in the alley near L&J's kitchen door where they would wait for handouts. They were now a triumvirate of vagrants, calling themselves *The Three Musketeers*. They found solace sharing their thoughts and problems with each other. Late one afternoon, while the three sat in the alley behind L&J's, Ronald began the conversation.

"I'm so tired of this existence. I've been in the Logan shelter for over a year, and I don't think I can take it anymore."

"Sure, smart guy, but what are you going to do about it?" said Brenda. "You have no family, no friends, no money. Where are you going to go?"

"I know exactly what you're saying," Andrew piped in. "We're all in the same boat."

"Oh yeah?" Brenda quipped. "Try being a woman out here on the streets. It's worse."

"I hear you, Brenda," said Ronald. "I wish I could go back in time, get my life back. But I realize that isn't going to happen so easily."

"Easily?" said Andrew. "Try never."

The Three Musketeers just sat quietly leaning against the wall. Toward evening the temperature began to drop. Ronald broke the silence. "Did you ever wish you were someone who actually made something of himself? I thought I had it all. Good job, nice house, car, beautiful wife. The works. But I blew it all by being greedy. And stupid."

"We all want to be someone else." Brenda responded. Andrew nodded in agreement.

"No, seriously." Ronald said. "Didn't you ever wish that you *could* be someone else, somewhere else, and that you never had to worry about money again?"

"Come on, Ronnie boy, get real. We're here, we're bums, and this is our life. I'm tired of it all, too," Brenda lamented. "Sometimes, I think of climbing up to the top of the Tobin Bridge and jumping into the Mystic River. At least that will end my misery."

Ronald looked at his companions and said soberly, "Didn't you ever wonder how your life would be different if you had been born someone else? I mean, like, if you never had to work hard for a living. If you were born wealthy?"

"C'mon, man, who in our situation hasn't thought of that?" Andrew replied. "Sure, I've often thought how nice it would have been to be born into a rich family that owned a big business, where you'd become the boss, giving the orders. You'd be the one living the high life, sipping champagne, and munching on caviar at the country club, rubbing elbows with the other rich guys and having a beautiful woman at your side." He paused and then said, "Back to reality. This is our life now, and it sucks big time."

"Andrew," Ronald responded, "That was me. I used to think about a different life all the time when I was a kid. My folks never had money. I always wanted to be one of those other kids in school who had so much more than I had. Even when I thought I was moving ahead in the business world, there was always someone who got ahead faster, always had more than I had. I wanted a bigger piece of the pie. I did what I thought would get me ahead faster. And I thought I had it all."

"So, you blew it, eh Ronnie?" Brenda chimed in.

"Yes, I blew it big time. I cheated and it came back to hit me in the face. My wife always demanded more of me, more money, more things that I struggled to provide. I made one big mistake and my career came crashing to an end. I was over my head in debt, went bankrupt, lost everything – my house, my BMW, everything. The bitch left me and I wound up on the street."

"My wife left me, too," Andrew responded, "And she got it all in the divorce. Come to think of it, most all of it was hers anyway. Whenever I think about it, I get more depressed. Maybe Brenda has the right idea about jumping into the river. I don't think there's any other way. I'm just biding my time, day by day, struggling to survive and waiting to die, hoping it won't take too long to happen or be too painful when it does."

"I don't want to end it that way," said Ronald. "At night, in the shelter, I still dream of getting out of this life and becoming rich again. Then I wake up to my 6-foot by 8-foot world. But I did it once and I can do it again."

"You're not making any sense, Ronnie boy," Brenda said.

"I was lonely as a little boy," Ronald continued. "But I had one true friend, Giant Billy Boy. He was only my imaginary friend, but he used to take me away from the sad life I had. He was my savior.

"Giant Billy Boy?" Andrew mocked. "Are you serious?"

Ronald closed his eyes, lowered his head, and clasped his hands together, as if in prayer.

"Please, Giant Billy Boy," Ronald began. "Come back to me. Don't forsake me, Giant Billy Boy. Take me away again on your magic carpet."

Andrew and Brenda looked at each other in disbelief, snickering at Ronald's nonsensical utterings.

"You're delirious, Ron," said Brenda.

"Okay, Ronnie boy, here's a reality check. You sound like a nut," Andrew scoffed. "There are no magic carpets to carry you away to a magical land, my friend. Or even back to the land of the living. We are dead ended. This is it. Come on Ron, Giant Billy Boy, really???"

"You may think I'm nuts," Ronald replied, "but lately I've had this feeling that I can make my wish come true. It's already the second week in September and it's getting colder. I don't want to end my life jumping into the river with Brenda."

Brenda and Andrew stared at Ronald, wondering if he had lost his mind. He turned to Brenda and said, "I'm dying for a cigarette. Look in that tote bag of yours. Do you have any?"

"Ronnie," said Brenda, "stop your foolish fantasizing. Wishing and praying, it's all a waste of time, believe me. I've tried it all my life. It doesn't work that way. There's no Giant Billy Boy who's gonna come and rescue you. Ain't nobody gonna come and save you. Grow up! Besides, you should be careful what you wish for. There's a saying I heard once: *When the gods want to punish us, they answer our prayers.* Think about that for a while. And no, I don't have any damn cigarettes."

As the sun slowly started to set, The Three Musketeers noticed an unusual orange glow appearing on the horizon. "Look at the sky," said Brenda.

"Yeah, that is strange," Andrew said. "Let's go out front and get a better look at it."

Once on the street, they observed a large white chauffeur-driven Mercedes Benz stop in front of Leonardo y Josefina's. The chauffeur opened the rear door, allowing a tall man of large stature to exit the Mercedes. He wore a fedora and a long black overcoat with a shiny silk collar, like gangsters wore in movies of the 1940's and '50's. His coat was unbuttoned, and the three vagrants could see that he was also wearing an expensive suit. He was accompanied by a beautiful blond woman wearing a white sable fur coat. Ronald could not help staring at the woman's legs. The man, Daniel Peacock, appeared to be extremely wealthy.

"Hey, hey," Brenda remarked. "Look at that guy going into L & J's. He seems rich enough to own half the city of Boston. And get a load of that Mercedes. With a chauffeur, no less. I'll bet he's the kind of son-of-bitch you used to be, eh, Ronnie boy? Looks like he's got it all. Maybe his world is your fantasy land."

"And would you look at the broad he's with?" Andrew chimed in. "Perks of being rich, right Ronnie?" That's the guy you wanna be. But you just keep on wishing my friend. Why not ask your friend, Giant Billy Boy, to come and take you away to his world? Meantime, I'm going back in the alley to see if L & J is getting rid of some leftovers."

"Yeah, you do that," Ronald retorted. "And do me a favor would you, see if you can find some cigarettes back there while you're at it. I really could use a smoke."

Daniel Peacock was a wealthy man who inherited his family's trash collection business. His grandfather, Hermann Pfau, emigrated from Germany in the early 1900's. Pfau started off as a garbage collector in Boston. Daniel's father anglicized the name to "Peacock" and followed in his father's footsteps, adding scrap metal to his collections. Eventually, he became involved with the Boston underworld and, with their help, he took over the much of the trash collection business in Suffolk County. He became wealthy as well as beholden to Boston's criminal element. Daniel continued to expand the business in connection with the same cast of characters, "The Mob," as they were called by many.

Daniel demanded loyalty from anyone who worked with or for him. His only reason for helping others was to make them feel obligated to him. Because Daniel kept his workers in line by paying them more than adequately, they put up with his abuse.

Jimmy Larson, Daniel's chauffeur, was a handsome young man of thirty, whose mother worked in Daniel's organization. Jimmy had been in jail for selling drugs when Daniel attained an early release for him through some of his political connections and by promising him full time employment. Daniel wasn't a generous man; there was a method to his madness. Daniel needed someone to handle the "less than clean" projects that helped him enrich himself. Jimmy fit the bill. He was trying to straighten his life out and was grateful to Daniel for the opportunity. But after working for Daniel for a while, he had little respect for him, as did many of the people who worked for Daniel. Jimmy felt trapped. He was afraid that if he didn't follow Daniel's orders, he'd get thrown back in prison.

Melissa, Daniel's trophy wife, twenty years his junior, had been a salesgirl in the glove department at Loro Piana, one of Boston's most prestigious stores. Daniel was in the store to purchase a pair of gloves for his second wife, Olga. Seeing Melissa at the glove counter, he became infatuated with her beauty. They began an affair that ultimately ended his marriage to Olga.

Two months later, Daniel and Melissa were married. Attracted to Daniel initially and impressed with his wealth, Melissa soon learned of Daniel's darker side, his bigotry and insensitivity towards others less fortunate than himself, including anyone who worked for him. But having come from a poor background, Melissa chose to sacrifice some of her dignity in favor of the life of luxury that Daniel offered. She would take pleasure in living a life she had only dreamed of as a child.

"Make sure you're right here when we're finished inside, Jimmy. I don't want to have to wait for you," Daniel snapped, and escorted Melissa into the restaurant.

"Welcome Señor y Señora Peacock," said the Maître D' as he escorted them to their usual table and handed them each a menu. When the waiter approached, Daniel ordered his usual Glenlivet on the rocks and a Chardonnay for Melissa.

"I'll have the filet mignon, rare, and my wife will have the broiled scallops. That's okay with you, Melissa, right?" he said.

"Whatever you say, dear." Melissa responded, deferring, as usual, to her husband's wishes. The waiter was quick to return with the drinks, as he was well aware of Daniel's impatience.

"I don't know if you can appreciate it, Melissa, but that deal I closed this afternoon was one of my best negotiations," Daniel gloated as his savored his favorite Scotch. "Those guys didn't know what hit them and who they were dealing with. This move will put another fifteen million in my pocket within six months. You're one lucky gal, Melissa. I'll bet you never thought you'd be with a guy like me, did you, coming from that hand-to-mouth family of yours? Don't you forget it, either." Daniel sipped his drink, then said irritatingly, "What the hell is taking that waiter so long to bring our dinner? I'm damn hungry."

"You know you can't rush the chef, darling," Melissa said.

"Whaddaya talking about," Daniel grunted in disdain. Melissa turned away and looked at the paintings on the wall, avoiding Daniel's scornful looks.

The waiter arrived with their dinners. "Bon Appetit," he offered, politely. But before the waiter could walk away, Daniel scowled.

"Hold it right there. I want to check this steak first." He cut into the center of the steak and scowled once again. "What's the matter with you?" he barked. "I said I wanted my steak rare! You call this rare? I call this shoe leather. Take this back and tell the chef to get it right, dammit."

Recoiling, the waiter responded, "My apologies, sir. I'll have another one for you right away."

The waiter picked up Daniel's plate and scurried back to the kitchen. Having observed this scene, the Maître D' quickly brought another drink to Daniel. "I apologize, Mr. Peacock. Please accept another Glenlivet on me for your inconvenience."

"Yeah, well, all right," Daniel replied. "It's okay now. I'm actually in a good mood this evening. Closed a big deal today, so not to worry."

"I may have come from a poor family," said Melissa, after the Maître D' departed, "but at least I was taught to have compassion. Why do you always talk to people like that? They have feelings, too."

"Really?" Daniel retorted. "People get what they deserve. If that guy had any other talents, he wouldn't be just a waiter. Look, after my father died and I took over the business, I had to figure out for myself how to keep it running and make it more profitable. No one taught me anything. I not only maintained it but edged out my competitors and took control of the market. That was me who did it. Me. My father was letting it slide. You can't be successful by feeling sorry or having pity for people. You have to think of yourself above everyone else; take advantage of the situation whenever you can. You have to outsmart them all. That's the system, sweetheart."

The waiter returned with Daniel's steak and said, "Is the steak to your liking sir?"

Daniel cast a disdainful look at the waiter, slowly picked up his steak knife and methodically cut into the center of the steak. This time it was exactly as Daniel had ordered.

"Yeah, it's fine," Daniel responded, and with one hand, waved the waiter away. He then ate his steak in silence. Finishing his dinner, he lit up a cigarette, sat back in his chair and took a long drag.

"Don't you remember what that the doctor told you about smoking and eating all that red meat?" said Melissa. "It's no good for your cholesterol, not to mention how bad it is for that heart of yours? When are you going to quit?"

"Dammit, Melissa," Daniel fired back. "I'll eat what I want, when I want, and how much I want. And I'll smoke when and where I want to. Screw what the doctor said. What the hell does he know anyway? I think he actually got his degree in Guatemala or Honduras or somewhere down there. I feel just fine. No one tells me how to live my life. No one, hear me? Just finish your own dinner."

"Please, Daniel, put out the cigarette. You know you can't smoke here," Melissa pleaded. Daniel took another puff and blew the smoke into the air, as many of the other patrons watched in disgust.

The Maître D' approached Daniel cautiously. "Please, Mr. Peacock," he said. "It's against the law to smoke in a restaurant. I could lose my other customers as well as get fined by the state." Daniel glared up at him. Without saying anything, he dumped his cigarette into his glass of water. The Maître D' quickly removed Daniel's glass and said, "I'll get you another glass of water immediately, Mr. Peacock."

As Daniel and Melissa continued their meal, Jimmy approach the table

"Boss, I parked the car right out in front, like you told me," Jimmy said. "You want me to stay with the car? The cops told me to move it."

"Jimmy, you don't come in here while we're eating! And yes, dammit, I want you to stay with the car. Just move it around the corner. And while you're waiting, polish the damn fenders. We'll be out in fifteen minutes. Make sure you're right in front of the restaurant so we don't have to wait, understand?"

Nodding his head, Jimmy responded, "Sure thing, boss."

Melissa watched as Jimmy scurried out of L & J's and then said to her husband, "Daniel, don't you have any feelings for anybody? Why do you treat Jimmy like that? He's not stupid. He's a person with feelings, too."

"I'll talk to anyone the way I want to," Daniel replied disparagingly. "Remember who's in charge and who pays the bills. Besides," he said with a smirk, "it's just Jimmy, the ex-con."

"But you can still treat him with some sense of decency, can't you?" Melissa begged.

"Look, I've known Jimmy for a long time. He was a small-time crook and now he's a dumb ex-con. I got him out of jail, cleaned him up and gave him a job. No one else would've been willing to hire him. He owes me for that. I keep him on the straight and narrow. He's got to learn what it takes to be on the up and up, not the bum he used to be. So, yes, I can talk to him any way I damn well please. And that goes for anyone else who works for me, too."

Melissa sat silently for a moment, recoiling at her husband's responses. "Oh, Daniel, do you know how cruel you sound?" she finally said.

"Melissa," said Daniel, "you're my wife. Am I really cruel to you? No, I'm not," he said, answering his own question. "I'm good to you. I take care of you and buy you all sorts of nice things, don't I? Of course, I do. You gotta remember that I didn't work my way up to the top by being Mr. Nice Guy. You gotta be tough when you're in charge. Otherwise everyone tries to get away with something. They all just wanna hang on and feed off me. Well, that's not gonna happen while I'm still on top. Now where the hell is that waiter with our check?"

Melissa toyed with her food, moving the vegetables side to side with her fork, barely eating during Daniel's rants.

"What's the matter with you, Melissa? Why is it taking so long for you to finish eating? Come on, finish already. I want us to get home 'cause I got something special for you. And me."

As Daniel added that last "And me" Melissa looked up from her plate and noticed Daniel's leering smile and wink. She knew what he wanted and was not too thrilled about the prospect of making love with her husband.

"I have a slight headache," Melissa responded.

"Don't worry, my dear. You'll take a couple of aspirins and you'll be fine. I even bought you something I know you'll like," said Daniel, another licentious grin lifting the corner of his mouth. Daniel then reached into his inside jacket pocket and produced a rectangular box wrapped in bright red paper tied with a silver ribbon and bow. As Melissa stared at it, expressionless, Daniel opened it to reveal a magnificent diamond studded bracelet.

"Oh, how lovely," Melissa said, trying desperately to show some semblance of gratitude and enthusiasm. She was tired of pretending to be excited about Daniel's gifts. Resigned to what Daniel had in mind for later in the evening, Melissa said, feigning enthusiasm, "Okay, let's go already."

Daniel signaled the waiter to bring the check. Suddenly, he became distracted by a strange orange glow in the sky through the restaurant's front window, alternately flashing bright and dim. Outside the restaurant, The Three Musketeers noticed the same orange glow again.

"Hey," said Brenda, will you look at the sky. There's that orange glow again, just like we saw a while ago. This time it seems even stronger than before."

The intensity of the orange glow increased dramatically, so much that the three of them had to shield their eyes from it. As quickly as it appeared, the orange glow suddenly vanished, giving way to the evening sky. The sun was setting as before, reflecting its pink glow on the remaining clouds.

As Daniel sat at the table perusing the check for errors, he was overcome with a strange sensation. It felt like pins and needles from the top of his head to the tips of his toes. His body began to quiver and he felt goosebumps on his arms and legs. Then his head slumped forward and his chin rested on chest. At that exact moment, Ronald Mountebank felt the same sensations as he stood on the sidewalk outside the restaurant. He quivered, then became motionless as if in shock, while Andrew and Brenda watched incredulously. Daniel and Ronald had been transformed – one into the other.

⊶ ‹‹●›› ⊷

Daniel/Ronald slowly lifted his head. He looked from side to side, up and down. He focused first on his expensive suit, the rings on his fingers, the table, the fan on the ceiling, and the artwork on the walls. His eyes fixated on the beautiful woman sitting across from him. He continued to stare at Melissa. Calmly he began to speak. "You know, I feel good. I mean exceptionally good. I really like my suit, don't you? My god, you are beautiful, you know that?" He continued to sit motionless, smiling at Melissa.

"What's come over you?" asked Melissa. "Are you all right? You said you were in a hurry to go home, didn't you? Next thing, you're acting strange. Are you okay now? Let's get going already."

Ronald/Daniel relaxed as the sky returned to normal. Brenda and Andrew stared at Ronald, who remained motionless. Then he began to flail his arms. He realized he was standing in the street, wearing tattered old clothes. He saw two homeless people staring back at him. He began to panic. "Oh my god, oh my god" he screamed. "What just happened? Where the hell am I? What's going on? What's going on? Oh, my god!!!"

Brenda and Andrew continued staring in amazement at Ronald, who seemed to have become possessed, as if a demon had taken complete control over his body.

"Ronnie," they both yelled at him simultaneously.

"What's wrong, Ronald?" Brenda implored.

"Ronnie, are you okay?" asked Andrew. "What's the matter?"

Ronald just stared vacantly, at both of them. Then he blurted out, "Who the hell are you? Who the hell is Ronnie? What the hell is going on? Why am I dressed like a bum? Why...? How did this...? I'm insane!!! Leave me alone!!!"

Ronald turned and immediately burst past his two friends, like an Olympic track runner toward the finish line, into the street and the oncoming traffic. They heard the blast of a car horn, a screech of brakes and then silence. Andrew and Brenda followed him in a panic, wondering what had gotten into their friend. By the time they turned the corner, they saw Ronald lying in the street, motionless, his left leg at a ninety-degree angle to the rest of his body. Blood was seeping out of his mouth and ears. A taxi driver was standing over him sobbing,

"The guy just ran out in front of my cab like a maniac. There was no way I could have stopped in time. He just ran into me. It wasn't my fault. Somebody please call 911."

The police and ambulance arrived in less than five minutes. The EMTs checked his heart and pronounced Ronald Mountebank dead at the scene. Dumbfounded, Brenda and Andrew walked away from the scene in shock. "I can't believe he just ran out into the street like that," Brenda said. "And right into traffic no less. What could have happened that made him do that? One minute he was dreaming about being someone else, the next minute he went crazy."

"I just can't believe he's dead," Andrew responded as they walked back towards the restaurant.

"At least he's out of his misery," Brenda grumbled.

"No need to rush, my dear," The transformed Daniel said to Melissa, adoringly. "I'll be in your tender hands, looking forward to a lovely evening of passion with you."

"Yes, you said that," said Melissa. "Let's go already."

Daniel helped Melissa with her coat and, as Jimmy met them at the door, Daniel spoke to him differently than he had previously.

He actually sounded civil. "Thank you so much, my good man." He then took Melissa's arm, politely, and said, "Shall we, my dear?"

Puzzled at Daniel's new behavior, Melissa stared at Daniel quizzically while he turned toward Brenda and Andrew, who were still in shock over Ronald's death.

"Just a moment, my sweet," said Daniel, "I'd like to help these unfortunate people." He walked over to Brenda and handed her a $100 bill. "Buy yourself a new coat, Brenda."

Turning to Andrew, he said, "Some new clothes for you, too, Andrew," handing him $100. "Perhaps one day your wishes will come true, too."

Stunned, Andrew looked in Daniel's eyes and saw a certain sparkle. "How did you know my name? Wait a second...Ron...Ronald, is that you? It is you, Ronnie, isn't it? You did it! Oh my god, you did it. I can't believe it. How can that be? How did you do it?"

Daniel turned and escorted Melissa into the Mercedes, as Jimmy held open the car door.

"Oh my god," said Brenda as she spun towards Andrew. "Oh my god, they answered his prayers."

"Giant Billy Boy!" Andrew exclaimed.

Jimmy stopped the white Mercedes Benz in front of the luxury brownstone that Daniel owned.

"Park the car and then take off for the evening," Daniel ordered. "Pick me up tomorrow morning at the usual time."

"Yes sir, Mr. Peacock," said Jimmy. "Have a pleasant evening."

"You have one, too, Jimmy," said Melissa.

In anticipation of his amorous plans for the evening, Daniel had given the housekeeper the night off. The house was quiet. Melissa turned on the floor lamp and removed her coat, tossing it casually on a chair in the foyer. She then helped Daniel take off his coat and placed it on top of hers. She strolled over to the living room coffee table and picked up the exquisite 24-karat gold trimmed glass cigarette case that Daniel had purchased during one of their recent trips to London. Selecting a cigarette from the case, she seductively placed it between Daniel's lips. She then took the matching gold cigarette lighter from the coffee table and lit his cigarette. Melissa then walked over to the liquor tray and poured a glass of Glenlivet Scotch for Daniel. As she handed him the glass, she said, "Why don't you sit and relax for a few moments while I make myself ready for you."

Ronald, now in Daniel's body following the transmogrification, looked around at his magnificent surroundings and wondered how this all had happened. Was it his friend, Giant Billy Boy, who made his wishes come true? Was it karma? Was this to be his true reward in life? Whatever it was that made this miracle happen, Ronald was finally happy. *I suppose I'll have to get used to the name 'Daniel' from now on*, he thought. *No matter. With this life, it'll be a breeze.*

Ronald gazed slowly around the room at the luxurious furniture and the exquisite furnishings; the imported artwork, the fireplace, the beautiful plush carpeting, the fabulous chandelier. It was all Ronald could do to avoid dancing in circles. *"I made it...I finally made it,"* he whispered to himself. Excited with where he was, he took two long drags on the cigarette, enjoying the feeling of inhaling that he had been longing for. Then, as he sipped his drink, he thought to himself, *it's been so long since I've had a drink and a smoke. This is the life.*

Taking a third drag from the cigarette, Daniel sat on the sofa anticipating a wonderful night of romantic pleasures, the likes of which he hadn't enjoyed for several years. What was her name again? *Melissa,* he remembered, and he was to become Daniel Peacock. The new Daniel leaned back and placed his feet on the coffee table, feeling relaxed and pleased with himself. After taking another puff on the cigarette, he felt a sudden tightness in his chest and a burning pain in his throat, as if it were on fire. He threw his cigarette on the coffee table, missing the ashtray. His body began to tremble uncontrollably, going into convulsions. His eyes shut tightly, and he experienced harsh flashes of light, after which he collapsed on the sofa. His glass fell to the floor with a thud, spilling his favorite Glenlivet Scotch all over the carpet.

Melissa, who had been hiding behind the bedroom door, heard the glass fall and walked into the living room. She placed the cigarette in the ashtray, then picked up the glass and put it on the coffee table. She placed her fingers on the side Daniel's neck. Feeling no pulse, she confirmed that Daniel was indeed dead. Daniel Peacock and Ronald Mountebank were both dead.

Melissa pressed autodial #3 on the phone. After two rings, the voice on the other end said, "Melissa? Is that you?"

"Hello Jimmy, you can come up now."

"Is it over, is he dead?" Jimmy asked.

"Yes, sweetheart, it's done. The miserable bastard is finally dead."

Melissa opened the door and invited Jimmy into her open arms and passionate embrace. "The cyanide in the cigarette worked, right? Learned it from a guy I met while I was, you know, away for a while." Jimmy said.

"Yes, my darling. As soon as he lit up. That was a clever idea you learned about putting cyanide in the cigarette. But now let's get on with our plan. Place this suicide note on his desk. Then let's get his body into his office and hang it from the ceiling fan. The step ladder is behind the door."

As Jimmy and Melissa together dragged Daniel's body from the living room, Jimmy asked, "What exactly did you write in the note?"

Melissa opened the envelope containing the suicide letter and read it. *Heart's no good. No more mountains to climb. No more places to conquer before my heart gives out. Wife said she's leaving me. I've always been the one calling the shots. I don't want the doctors calling them now. Had a good run, time to go. To hell with everyone else. See you on the other side.*

"The doctors knew that he had a bad heart," Melissa continued. "And with the note saying that I was threatening to leave him, they won't be surprised that he committed suicide. I'm sure they won't even think anything more about it."

"I know you hated him," said Jimmy. "I'm glad I was here to help get rid of him. You saw how hard I tried to go straight after getting out of prison, but I just couldn't take him treating me like dirt any longer. I hated him too, and now I'm glad he's gone. I've always been in love with you, Melissa."

"And I love you, too, Jimmy. But there were so many times I wondered what it would have been like if he had been someone else. What would our marriage have been if he had somehow been more compassionate, if he had been kinder, more gentle, caring and thoughtful. I'm sure you would have liked him like that way, too. Then again, if he had been different, we wouldn't have been together now, would we? But we are who we are. And, as they say, a leopard can't change its spots."

It wasn't easy hoisting Daniel's heavy, limp body up to hang from the ceiling fan. Jimmy was strong, having worked out on a regular basis. But the two of them were able to manage, and made it appear as if Daniel hanged himself. Jimmy looked at his watch and asked, "You've got the plane tickets, haven't you? What time do we leave?"

"I have them right here in my pocket book," said Melissa. "I confirmed our flight earlier today with American Airlines. We're on Flight 11 leaving for Los Angeles tomorrow morning at 7 am. We'll have to get to the airport around six. I can't wait to get out of here. We can begin a new life in California. I always wanted to go there, but Daniel never wanted to. He complained that it was too hot and there were too many earthquakes. Well, that's that. I closed out our bank accounts and we'll be set for a long time. Let's remember that tomorrow, September 11, 2001, will mark a milestone for us. We'll have a brand-new life together, away from all this. Now kiss me, darling."

Stay With Me

THE GRAY OVERCAST SKY was beginning to show its twilight face as Jack and Rita began the 300-mile, five and a half-hour trek (including a "pee stop," as Jack called it) on Route 81 from their home in Wichita, Kansas, to Jack's parents' home in Colonial Hills, a suburb of Lincoln, Nebraska. In order to avoid most of the Thanksgiving holiday traffic, they decided to leave early Tuesday afternoon and arrive in time for a late dinner. Jack's dad told them not to rush – that for dinner they'd order a couple of pizzas from Michelangelo's, Jack's favorite Italian restaurant in Colonial Hills.

Jack and Rita were looking forward to spending a few extra days in their hometown, hoping to visit some friends from high school. They had been high school sweethearts. Jack was the catcher on the varsity baseball team and Rita was a cheerleader. They began dating in their junior year and continued through college at the University of Nebraska in Lincoln. After graduation, Jack accepted a position as an accountant at a large CPA firm in Lincoln. Rita began working as an assistant to the bank manager of the Lincoln

Savings Bank. Five years later Jack's firm decided to expand and open a new branch in Wichita. Jack was regarded highly by the firm and was offered a promotion as manager of the new office. It was a decided step up for him. The salary was extremely attractive, and difficult to turn down.

Jack's parents weren't happy about their son moving so far away, but they were proud of him and recognized that the move would be good for his career. Rita's parents felt the same, but Jack and Rita convinced them all that they'd still see them as often as possible, and would call at least once or twice a week. So, their parents helped them pack and wished them luck as they moved to Wichita.

Rita quickly found a platform position in the Sedgewick County Bank without difficulty and, because of her experience and outstanding performance, was soon promoted to manager at one of the local branches. Now, both at the age of forty-five, they were doing well for themselves.

They took little time off from work, so they made the trip back to Lincoln only two or three times a year. Thanksgiving, Christmas and a few days during the summer accounted for the other trips. Their plan was to save and invest as much money as they could in order to secure their retirement. With Jack's accounting and investment acumen, their plan was right on track.

Jack's parents lived only three blocks from Rita's in Colonial Hills. They alternated hosting Thanksgiving dinners which were always joyful and festive with both families coming together. This year, Jack's father would take pride in carving the huge turkey. Jack's mom would have to extend the dining room table into the living room, even adding a bridge table to accommodate all the guests – fifteen in all. But she loved entertaining. The extra work never bothered her.

Andy, Jack and Rita's son, was in his junior year at the University of Nebraska. He usually joined them for Thanksgiving dinner but, to his parents and grandparents dismay, planned to stay with his girlfriend, Sally, at her parents' house for the long weekend. Besides, it was only a few miles away in Bishop Park, and he promised that he and Sally would spend the entire day with them Saturday.

Rita, along with her mom and Jack's mom, were looking forward to some early morning "Black Friday" bargains at Target and Best Buy at the Colonial Hills Shopping Mall.

Jack's twelve-year old blue Toyota Camry had logged over of 150,000 miles and was still in good condition. Jack had it maintained religiously at the dealer's shop and believed that with some TLC, it could easily last another 100,000 miles. Having achieved a comfortable financial stage in their lives, Rita wanted to upgrade to something more luxurious and reliable. She convinced Jack to buy one of the new Volvo models, the XC40 SUV with all the state-of-the-art safety features: driver lane assistance, adaptive cruise control – all that good stuff. This new model was in high demand and they would have to wait until mid-December for delivery. No matter; the Camry would be fine for another few weeks. And Jack felt he could still get a good price for it.

Daylight was fading rapidly. Rita turned back from watching the flat, bare scenery and, glancing at her watch said, "Will you look at that? It's five o'clock already. We've been on the road for what, three hours? What time do you think we'll arrive in Colonial Hills, Jack?"

Jack was deep in thought about leaving the office early that day. He had been advising a client on a business acquisition and hoped that his assistant manager would accommodate him until he returned after the holiday. With only one extra day out of the office, however, Jack felt the client would be all right.

He continued to stare straight ahead at the monotonous road with its hypnotic double yellow lines, a lonesome tree here and there whizzing by, and an occasional billboard detracting from the scenery. The moon danced in and out of the clouds in an attempt to illuminate the road as best it could. Exhaling a yawn and rubbing his eyes with one hand, Jack replied, "I dunno, maybe another two and a half hours. You know, this two-lane road isn't as fast as the freeway. How are you doing, you tired?"

"I'm fine," Rita responded, "but you must be."

"Nah, I'm okay," said Jack, as he yawned once again. "Let's make a pee stop soon and we can stretch our legs. Maybe get a cup of coffee. It's getting dark already."

"Yes, that's a good idea," said Rita as she stretched her arms over her head and yawned also.

"I'm looking forward to getting back to Lincoln for a few days," she continued. "It'll be so nice to see our folks. I hope the weather stays nice. I heard the forecast is for a beautiful and clear Thanksgiving holiday, although they said it'll be a bit cold. But cold and clear is better than snow, right?"

Jack turned to Rita and yawned again. Rita reached into her handbag, pulled out a roll of LifeSavers and popped one into her mouth. Green, her favorite. "Do you want one?" she asked Jack. "Maybe it'll help."

"Thanks." It was a red one, Jack's favorite. "Ah, the old home town," he said. "But did you ever notice how every time we go back there something changes? I heard that they're going to tear down one of the grammar schools in Colonial Hills. They're also planning to combine the middle school with our high school into a single building. Gotta save money, I suppose. Fewer kids in the area, I imagine. That's progress."

"Speaking of high school," Rita said, "I was just thinking of Mel and Dee."

Mel had been a pitcher on the baseball team with Jack, and Dee was on the cheerleading squad with Rita. Like Jack and Rita, Mel and Dee had been high school and college sweethearts. They were married right after graduating from college and stayed in Colonial Hills. Mel worked at his father's Chevrolet dealership while Dee became an English teacher in the Colonial Hills Middle School.

"Remember how the four of us were inseparable back then?" Rita continued. "The Gang of Four, they called us. I tried calling Dee yesterday but couldn't reach them. I hope they'll be in town while we're there. I haven't spoken to Dee in over six months. I feel guilty not having called her. But she could have called me, too. I'll try to reach her tomorrow morning, or maybe even after we arrive this evening. I really miss them."

"I miss them too," said Jack. "Let's not wait until tomorrow. Let's call them tonight. You have their phone number, right?"

"Right here in my phone," said Rita, fumbling in her purse for her cell phone. "Aha, I found it," she said. "Jack, are you sure you're okay, not too tired to drive? I saw you yawning a few times back there. Do you want me to take the wheel for a while?"

"No, I'm good," Jack insisted.

Jack tried to maintain his focus on the long, straight road, which had now become dark except for the Camry's headlights. He let out another huge yawn, during which his head tilted back into the head-rest. In that brief moment, Jack failed to detect that the Camry was swerving across the double yellow line into the southbound lane. Rita did notice the car veering and screamed, "Jack, Jack, you're drifting!"

Jack jerked his head back and struggled with the steering wheel, relieved that he was able to recover control of the Camry and steer it back into the northbound lane. He pulled off to the shoulder and turned off the engine. He shook his head and rubbed his eyes. "You okay, Rita? Oh my god, that was close. Are you all right?"

"If a car had been coming," Rita sobbed, "we could have crashed. Been killed, even. Thank God we're all right. Look, my hands are still shaking." She began to cry uncontrollably.

Jack put his arms around her shoulder and nestled her head against his chest to console her. "It's okay, Rita. We're all right, we're fine now. Don't cry, I'm so sorry. No damage done. Take your time. Just breathe and relax. I promise to stop at the very next place we see. There's no rush. We'll have some coffee and get refreshed."

They sat still for a few more minutes, staring through the wind-shield as darkness was creeping in. Rita took a handkerchief out of her purse, wiped her eyes and said, "I'm all right now, Jack. Let's go." She turned to him, hoping to reassure him. Then, with a sigh, she added, "Please, Jack, be careful. I'm still a little shaky."

Jack cranked up the Camry, looked in the rear-view and side mirrors, then pulled back onto the road slowly and carefully. A mile farther down the road Jack noticed a billboard that read, *Pete's Borderline Café – 2 miles ahead.* "Look at that sign, Rita. It'll take us less than five minutes. I'll stop there. And look, there's the *Welcome to Nebraska* sign, right after the sign for Pete's Café. We're less than two hours from my folks now."

Jack made sure to maintain the 55-mph speed limit. Rita watched the clouds retreat, unmasking a beautiful, bright full moon. She gazed at the Man in the Moon who, it appeared, was winking directly at her. Then she closed her eyes and thought about enjoying a cup of coffee at Pete's Borderline Café.

— ‹‹ ● ›› —

Jack turned the Camry into the gravel driveway of Pete's Borderline Café and parked near the front door. The café was one of those old-fashioned railroad car diners with quilted aluminum siding. The sign on the roof that read, **Welcome to Pete's Borderline Café** surrounded by flashing lightbulbs, like those on an old theater marquee. "Wow," Rita remarked, overwhelmed by nostalgia. "Would you just look at this place, Jack! It reminds me of one of those diners from the fifties. I'm so glad we stopped here."

"Yes, that it does, Rita," said Jack. He slowly stepped out of the car and stretched his arms over his head, yawning once more. "I could really use a good cup of coffee, maybe even some pie to go with it. To hell with my diet," he added with a chuckle.

Rita had been pestering Jack to shed a few pounds. She often told him that he was inflating his spare tire. They held hands, walked up the steps to Pete's Borderline Café and opened the stunning mother-of-pearl door handles. The interior was just as they would have expected it to be. The counter was accompanied by a row of red vinyl swivel stools. Above the counter were posters of the different breakfast, lunch and dinner specials, including the ubiquitous "Blue Plate Special" for $14.95 that included dessert and coffee. One sign behind the counter read, *"Occupancy by more than 120 persons prohibited."* The rest of the café was decorated with 1950's posters of James Dean, Marilyn Monroe, Jane Russell and a number of Chevys and Fords from that era. "This place is adorable," Rita exclaimed. "How come we never noticed it before?"

A sign on the chrome stand in front of them said *Please Be Seated.* Jack observed that the café was about half occupied. At one end of the counter a man was seated quietly enjoying his *Blue Plate Special.* Three other patrons were seated at the counter drinking coffee. Several of the booths were occupied. Two waitresses were busy attending to customers. They wore white uniforms with cute half-aprons bordered with pink ribbons.

As they looked for a table (Rita always preferred a table to a booth – never the counter), they saw a familiar-looking couple seated at the last table. The man stared in recognition and then jumped to his feet. "Jack? Rita? Is that really you?" he called.

The woman he was with, turned with a start and, "Rita, Oh my God. Look Mel, it's Rita and Jack."

Jack and Rita stood in amazement. Recognizing their old high school pals, they were overcome with emotion. Mel and Dee ran towards them with open arms. The four hugged each other like schoolchildren, laughing. "What are you guys doing here?" Rita asked excitedly. "We were just talking about the two of you not thirty minutes ago. We're on our way to Jack's parents' house for Thanksgiving. We were even going to phone you this evening to see if we could all spend some time together this weekend if you were in town. We felt it would be a good idea to rest a bit and get some coffee before heading up to Colonial Hills."

"Talk about coincidence," Mel replied. "We were on our way home. We stopped here once before at Pete's Borderline and loved the place."

"It's charming, isn't it?" Dee added. "Come, sit with us," she beckoned.

"Peter has the best peach pie in Nebraska. No, in the world," Mel continued. "You have to try it. My treat. I'm so glad to see you guys."

As soon as the foursome were seated, a man approached wearing a white apron over white trousers. A white cap covered the bald spot on his head. His short-sleeve shirt had the name "Pete" embroidered on the pocket. A ball-point pen was clipped to the inside of the pocket, which also held a small menu pad. A white dish towel trimmed with red piping was slung over his shoulder.

"Typical diner, isn't it?" Jack said. "I bet that's Pete, himself."

"Yup, that's Pete all right," Mel said. "You could tell by the name on his pocket." Jack let out a small embarrassing chuckle. "Order whatever you want. But I especially recommend the peach pie. And remember, it's on me."

"Welcome to Pete's Borderline Café. What'll it be?" Pete smiled, as he took a pen and pad from his shirt pocket. "Would you like to see a menu or hear today's specials?"

"No thanks, Pete," Jack replied, looking up at him. "We'll both have a cup of coffee and some of that peach pie my friend, Mel here, raves about. Is that okay with you, Rita?" Rita, nodded, and reached across the table to hug Dee again.

"No problem, Jack," Pete replied. "My peach pie can't be beat."

As Pete returned to the counter, Jack said, "I'm so impressed that he knew my name."

"So, what have you guys been up to lately?" Rita asked. "We haven't seen you in, what is it now, Jack, two or three years?"

Jack held up two fingers, then added, "It's been way too long, Mel. What's the latest?"

"Oh, quite a lot has happened," Mel replied. "I guess you didn't hear about the fire."

"What fire?" Rita asked with a troubled look.

Dee glanced at Mel, then turned to Jack and Rita. "It was all over the news. Our whole house burned to the ground about four months ago after we had gone to bed," Dee lamented. "We lost everything. I'm so glad Jeremy was away at school when it happened. He's at UCLA, you know, studying Biology. He's a junior, just like your Andy at Nebraska. He was a mess when he heard about it, but he's back at school now."

"All over the news, huh? Gosh, no, we didn't hear about it," said Jack. "We don't get local Nebraska news in Wichita, and my folks didn't tell us about it. They're getting on in years so I'm really not that surprised."

"But you guys are all right, now, aren't you?" asked Rita.

"As I mentioned," Dee said trying to maintain her composure, "we lost the house and everything. Nothing was salvageable. But," she continued, "where we are now is really nice. We're at peace with it all and happy now. The views are so beautiful, absolutely divine, really lovely. The people we've met are truly wonderful. Mel and I are enjoying ourselves and don't think about what happened anymore. What's done is done. Have to keep moving forward, right?"

Pete returned with their order. "Hope you enjoy the pie," he said, as he placed two large cups of coffee and two huge pieces of peach pie, both with dollops of fresh whipped cream, in front of Rita and Jack. Leaving the check on the table, he added, "Let me know if you want anything else."

Mel quickly grabbed the check and said, "I got this, remember?" Then turning to Pete, said, "Hey Peter, I heard you're expanding the café. Is that right?"

"Yeah. We have to accommodate a growing clientele, so I'm working on it. I'm working on it. Will that be all?"

"That should do it, Pete," Mel nodded.

"Don't be strangers," Pete said. Then he turned and disappeared behind the counter and into the kitchen.

"He's working on it," Mel said, repeating Pete. "I Hope he doesn't shut down during the expansion. Dee and I love coming here." Mel turned to Jack and then asked, "So, are you staying with your folks in Colonial Hills or at the Marriott?"

"They want us to stay with them, even though it'll be a little cramped. Andy is staying with his girlfriend, Sally. But it'll still be tight."

"Jack's brother and their two kids will be staying there, too." Rita added.

"But it's my folks, you know," Jack said. "I suppose we'll manage for four days."

Dee and Mel shared a knowing smile.

"I have a great idea," Dee said. "Why don't you both stay with me? We have loads of room at our new place. You'll love it and we'll have fun being together again."

"Yes, please," added Mel. "Come on, be our guests. Stay with me, Jack."

"Thanks, Mel," Jack replied. "That's a wonderful offer, and even though I think it would be terrific, my mom's expecting us to stay at their place."

"Oh, Jack," Rita implored, "let's do it. Let's stay with Mel and Dee. Please? I mean, I appreciate how your parents might feel but, as you said, we'll be cramped there. It'll be fun at Mel and Dee's. We can call your folks and explain. We'll still be at your folks for the whole day on Thanksgiving, and again on Saturday when Andy and Sally come over. I'd really love to take Dee up on their offer, what do you say?"

"Come on, Jack, stay with me. You'll be happy there," Mel pleaded.

"Let's do it Jack," Rita pleaded. "Let's call your folks right now and tell them we're going to stay with Mel and Dee. They'll understand."

"Mel, let's not pressure them," Dee said. "If the timing isn't right, it's not right." She then turned to Jack and said, "We really must be going, so please give the matter serious consideration. I understand your dilemma, but call us just the same. Here's our new phone number."

Rita pulled her phone from her purse and entered Dee's phone number. "Got it now," she said, waving her phone at Dee.

"We want you to come, but whatever you decide will be fine with us, won't it, Mel?"

Mel continued the invitation. "C'mon, stay with me."

Dee continued. "We love you guys and want you to be happy with your decision. In any event, I hope we'll see you over the weekend."

The four of them exchanged hugs and kisses again. Jack and Rita watched Mel and Dee leave the café, and then sat down again to finish their coffee and pie. Jack scooped the whipped cream off his pie and piled it on top of Rita's. "Gotta watch my weight," he said.

After a moment, Rita looked at Jack and said, "I don't want to sound like a nag, Jack, but I would really, really love to stay with them. Wouldn't you? We'll be so much more comfortable there. We'll have fun, and I'd love to see their new place."

Jack remained silent, continuing to gaze ahead, in deep thought. He lifted his coffee cup slowly, took a sip, and put the cup down. Then he cut a piece of pie with his fork. As if in slow motion, he ate it savoring the wonderful flavor of fresh peaches. Rita stared at him without saying a word. She was not used to seeing Jack ponder for so long. Finally, Jack broke his silence. "It would be nice to spend time with Mel and Dee, but I'm not sure we should stay with them. I'd hate to disappoint my parents. Let me think about it some more."

"All right, Jack. You think about it some more. But I, for one, want to stay with Mel and Dee. Think about that, too," Rita said.

Traffic along Route 81, just south of the Nebraska border, slowed to a crawl. Police officers, with the aid of flashing red lights, directed traffic around the 18-wheeler that was stopped in the road. Thirty yards north of the truck two EMTs were performing CPR on the side of the road on the two crash victims – a man and a woman in their mid-forties. They had been pulled from their car after sideswiping the huge truck. Their smashed blue Camry had flipped over twice and landed upside down just off the shoulder.

"It was horrible, just horrible," the truck driver told the police officer who was taking notes at the scene. "I was heading south when all of a sudden this car starts to swerve across the yellow lines into my lane. It was coming right at me. I hit the brakes immediately. I thought they were going to hit me head on. I think the driver tried to swerve back into his lane, but he couldn't make it in time. He hit the side of my cab pretty hard, and in my side mirror I could see the car flip over twice and land on its roof. It wasn't my fault, really, it wasn't my fault. I feel so terrible."

His interview with the Kansas State Troopers finished, the truck-driver ran to the shoulder where the EMT's were attempting to revive the crash victims. "How are they doing? Are they going to be all right?" he asked the EMT's.

"Well, the woman didn't make it," the EMT said. She's DOA. What a shame, right before the holiday." Then, addressing the other EMT, who was still vigorously continuing CPR, she asked, "How's the guy doing?"

"I'm working on it. I'm working on it," he responded, without breaking his rhythm. "He might make it. His vitals are there, but he's borderline." Then he said to the victim, "Stay with me, mister. Come on fella, stay with me. Just stay with me."

Forever Friends

MARY JOSEPHS WAS A PLEASANT GIRL – polite, respectful and obedient. She was no beauty, but neither was she unattractive. Mary's mother died due to complications soon after Mary was born. Her maiden aunt Olivia, her father's older sister, accepted the burden of caring for Mary, while her father went to work.

Mary adored her father and wanted to spend as much time as possible with him. Together, on weekends, they would go to the park, the movies, or to the zoo. Each evening, her father would tuck her into bed after reading her favorite books to her and kissing her gently on the forehead.

When she was only twelve years old, tragedy struck again. Her aunt Olivia had the task of relating the news that her beloved father had died in an automobile accident on his way home from work. Hearing what had happened to her father, her champion, the light of her life, drove Mary into deep depression. She wouldn't eat, couldn't sleep and neglected her appearance. Mary became convinced that God was punishing her. She had lost any feeling of self-worth.

Most folks living in the small town of Woodland Grove knew that Mary's aunt Olivia was what they called a "difficult person." Olivia had never married. No man was ever good enough for her. She was seventy years old at the time of her brother's death and resented having sole responsibility for the needs of a twelve-year old child. Olivia was smart enough, however, to have Mary treated by a professional. Mary slowly improved with the help of counseling and medication, but the weight of low self-esteem was more difficult to cast off.

Olivia was a strict disciplinarian, often punishing Mary harshly for minor offenses, such as leaving her bed unmade, not hanging her clothes properly in the closet, and forgetting to put the cap back on the toothpaste. In response to her aunt's demands, Mary developed a compliant and submissive personality which, to Olivia, was ideal.

While Mary was a freshman at Woodland Grove High School, she sat next to Joan Darcy in home room. Joan was gregarious and sociable, pretty and popular with the boys. Unlike many of the other girls in her class, she was more compassionate and understood the value of friendship. Joan and Mary had known each other in elementary school, but they weren't close friends back then. Now, as young adults, Joan took Mary under her wing and tried to help her come out of her shell, becoming Mary's only true friend.

In the spring of their first year in high school, Joan convinced Mary to go with her to the freshman dance. Reluctant at first, Mary finally surrendered to Joan's persistence.

"Are you sure you even want to go to the dance?" Aunt Olivia asked. "Shy as you are, who do you think will even ask you to dance? What are you going to wear?" she continued.

Despite her aunt's negativity, Mary tried her best to maintain her composure. She searched her closet for something appropriate to wear, finding only her gray dress that, although two years out of style, fit her comfortably. Joan, on the other hand, sported the latest fashion: colorful, short, and revealing. Many of the boys' heads turned when they saw Joan entering the school gym. Mary felt invisible.

Mary and Joan took seats alongside the other girls against the gym wall. Immediately, a boy approached Joan and asked her to dance. "Just wait," Joan said to Mary. "It'll be your turn soon."

It wasn't until the fourth dance of the evening that a tall, gawky youngster wearing a plaid shirt and striped pants approached Mary. The aroma of his cheap cologne reached Mary before he did. He extended his hand towards Mary and said, "My name's Arnold. Would you like to dance with me?"

Mary recognized Arnold from fifth grade. He was one of the "nerdy" boys who was chosen last for any softball or basketball game during recess. She still thought of him in that way. "I suppose so," Mary responded shyly. She took Arnold's hand as he escorted her to the dance floor. Mary felt awkward, never having learned to dance. But she tried her best to follow the ungainly boy's lead on the dance floor. Arnold thanked Mary for the dance and walked back to the opposite side of the gym and took a seat alongside some other boys. He was the only boy who had asked Mary to dance. She sat quietly on a folding chair against the wall for the remainder of the evening, watching Joan dance with several boys, hoping for the evening to come to an early end. "How was it? Did you have a good time?" asked Joan.

"It was okay," Mary answered. "I got asked to dance by Arnold. You remember him, right? From elementary school? He's still kinda goofy," Mary chuckled. "He didn't know how to dance any better than me, either. And it was probably the first time he ever wore cologne because it was overpowering," she continued, laughing, "but it was worth a try."

"Be patient," Joan told her. "It'll get better with time. I promise you," she continued.

"How?" Mary said, puzzled.

"Well," Joan responded, "first we have to lighten you up a bit. We'll have to give you a new hairdo. Something a bit more stylish. Then we'll add some make-up. And you can wear one of my more colorful dresses. I'll bet your old Aunt Olivia doesn't buy you new clothes, does she?"

"It's been a while since I've had anything new," Mary said. "Only when I outgrow something."

"I knew it," Joan said. "You know what? I have some things you can pick out to borrow for a while."

"But I'll still be...well, me," Mary insisted.

"Oh, Mary. Stop being a fuddy-duddy," Joan said. You just have to come out of your shell."

"You're such a good friend," Mary said. "I'm so lucky to have you."

"That's what friends are for," Joan replied, and gave Mary a hug. "Friends forever, right?" she continued.

"Forever friends," Mary replied, wiping the tears from her eyes. "It's late," Mary added looking at her watch. "I've got to get home or Aunt Olivia will howl like a banshee."

"Oh, to hell with her," Joan said. "Why does she treat you so poorly?"

"It's just her way. I think I deserve it sometimes," Mary said as she hugged her friend again and waved goodbye as she turned to go home.

"You don't deserve to be treated badly," Joan said, frowning.

"Think positive. I'll see you in school. Love you."

At 11:15 pm, Olivia began pacing the living room floor. *Where is that child?* she muttered under her breath. *She's already fifteen minutes late.*

Olivia stood in the hall, frowning, with her arms crossed as Mary walked in at 11:30. "Where have you been? Olivia scowled. "You're a half-hour past curfew. I told you to be home no later than eleven. I'm tired, and I don't like waiting up for you. Now get on up to bed," she ordered as if she were a drill sergeant. "You're lucky I don't ground you. As long as you're living in my house you will obey my rules, young lady." Olivia followed Mary up the stairs, muttering under her breath, *Damn brat. I can't wait until she finishes school and gets the hell out of here and out of my life.*" Olivia went directly to bed and didn't hear Mary crying herself to sleep.

Olivia's domineering control over Mary continued. She was not prepared to handle the temperament of a teenage girl whose hormones often affected her behavior. Olivia often struck Mary for the slightest infraction, leaving welts on her arms, back and legs. But she was careful to minimize striking Mary in the face. Those marks might arouse suspicions of child abuse. All the while, Mary succumbed to Olivia's cruelty without responding. She accepted the abuse quietly, retreating to her room and crying herself to sleep. Her only salvation was her deep friendship with, and love for her friend, Joan.

Mary's social life remained stagnant throughout the remainder of high school. Joan continued to help Mary with her clothing selection and make up, and she did receive a few more offers at the school dances. She was happy that Arnold wasn't at many dances. And when he was, he didn't ask her to dance. Once in while she and Joan double-dated, but none of Mary's dates resulted in any relationships.

Mary's excellent grades throughout high school afforded her a scholarship to the local Community College where she majored in chemistry. Mary loved working with chemicals and excelled in her lab work. She became so focused on her studies that she seldom thought about boys or dating. She and Joan maintained their close friendship, spending many of their weekends together. Occasionally, Joan would convince her to go to singles dances where Mary was asked to dance but, as in high school, nothing ever developed. Joan, on the other hand, was always on the dance floor. "Don't worry, Mary," Joan would often say. "The right guy will come along and make you happy. You'll see. Don't give up."

"I'm not so sure about that," Mary would respond.

During Mary's second semester at college, she was offered an internship with the local police department's forensic laboratory. Woodland Grove's CSI lab was small, but was the only one in the area, serving several neighboring small towns. Mary enjoyed working with, and accompanying crime scene professionals on a variety of cases. She assisted in dusting for fingerprints, post mortems and, on a few rare occasions, death scenes. Mary decided that she wanted a career in forensics.

Olivia died of an apparent heart attack one month after Mary completed her first year of Community College. She inherited her aunt's house and a bank account of over one hundred thousand dollars. At her aunt's funeral, Mary expressed relief to Joan that she was no longer under Olivia's thumb. Furthermore, Olivia had finished paying the mortgage on her home, so Mary owned it free and clear. In celebration of Mary's good fortune, she treated Joan to a lobster dinner immediately after the funeral. They drank a full bottle of Sauvignon Blanc, toasting with each glass to their friendship, Aunt Olivia's passing and Mary's new-found freedom.

After completing her Associates Degree in Chemistry with High Honors, Mary was offered a position as a forensic lab technician in the Police Department. She especially enjoyed working with the coroner, conducting autopsies and determining causes of death. The position suited her, as she was still a bit of an introvert, and was able to keep to herself most of the time.

Mary's life consisted mainly of working at the police lab, reading romance novels, keeping her house clean, and going out to dinner at least once a week with Joan. Sometimes they'd go to the movies, walk in the park together or spend hours just talking on the phone.

Joan convinced Mary to attend a singles dance sponsored by the Woodland Grove Rotary Club early one spring. Dressed in a tailored pinstripe black suit, white shirt and red tie, Daemon Talbot approached Mary and Joan, who were seated together. He looked at Joan and winked, but then turned toward Mary, extended his hand

and, in the most gentlemanly fashion said, "Hi, my name's Daemon. May I have this dance?"

Daemon Talbot was handsome, muscular, witty and debonair – the kind of man that women flocked to at parties. He had the aura of a celebrity. He appeared in Woodland Grove one month prior to the Rotary Club's single dance. No one knew exactly where he had lived before his arrival, but there were rumors. Given his suave image and bearing, some suggested that he came from a big city, such as New York or Chicago. Some folks said that they heard he had been in prison. Some even suggested that he had been a gangster and was in the witness protection program. No one knew for sure, nor had they the nerve to ask him. Despite the well-dressed and sophisticated air he displayed in public, Daemon was only a counter clerk in the Woodland Grove lumber yard. He managed to keep a low profile, however, attempting to fit in to life in this small rural community.

Joan nudged Mary with her elbow, arousing her out of her stunned silence. Mary stood up without saying a word and took Daemon's hand as he escorted her to the dance floor. "And your name is...?"

"Mary. Mary Josephs," she replied, trying unsuccessfully to hide her crimson cheeks. Unlike Arnold, the gawky teenager who had asked her to dance in high school, Daemon's charm was intoxicating.

"I've been watching you for the last ten minutes," said Daemon. "I think you're just the kind of girl I've been searching for."

"Really," Mary responded, still blushing. "Why me?"

"I just got a certain vibe from you," Daemon said, pulling her closer. Mary could feel the warmth of Daemon's body and delighted in the subtle aroma of his cologne. *I must have died and gone to heaven,* she thought. They continued to dance together for the rest of the evening, stopping long enough only for Daemon to go to the punch bowl and return with two glasses, handing one to Mary.

"Here's to us," Daemon said as he clinked Mary's glass.

"I'll drink to that," Mary acknowledged. "Will you wait for me for a few moments while I run to the little girl's room?" she said. With a nod of his head, Daemon watched her approach Joan, who had been leaning against the wall. As the two of them walked into the Ladies' Room, Joan asked, "What have I just been witnessing? Who is that guy?"

"His name is Daemon Talbot," Mary replied. "Isn't he something?"

"He looks like he's really into you," Joan said, rather puzzled herself.

"What if he wants to take me home?" Mary said. "He hasn't asked yet, but I think he will. Is it okay with you? You have your car."

"Hey, go for it," Joan said. "I'm fine with it."

"I love you, Joan," Mary said excitedly as she hugged her friend. "You've been such a good friend for so long, helping me and all. Maybe this is what all your help and advice was for."

"I love you, too. Be careful," as she kissed Mary's cheek.

"I will," Mary responded as she returned to find Daemon standing by the punch bowl.

"Ready for another dance, Mr. Talbot?" she asked.

"Ready for only you," he responded as he led her back onto the dance floor. "Tell your friend that I'm driving you home," he whispered into Mary's ear as he held her tightly in his arms. The aroma of his cologne aroused her once again.

"I already did," Mary chuckled.

Daemon parked his car in front of Mary's home and, turning

toward her said, "I had a wonderful time, Mary. I'm glad we met tonight." He leaned towards her and, to Mary's surprise, kissed her on the cheek.

"May I see you again?" he asked.

"I'd like that," Mary replied. She opened her purse, removed a tissue and jotted her telephone number with her lipstick. She turned to open the car door, but then turned back toward Daemon, leaned over and kissed him. She watched him drive away, then went inside the house and lay on her bed. Instead of crying after coming home from a dance this time, she smiled. This was the happiest day of her life.

Mary and Daemon continued to date every week for the next two months. She was ecstatic when he proposed. *Of all the girls he could have chosen, he chose me. How lucky I am*, Mary thought.

After the wedding ceremony, a small reception was held in the local VFW hall. The only guests were Joan, Mary's Maid of Honor – who had arranged the decorations, and some of Mary's colleagues from the police department. No one from Daemon's side attended. He didn't have much money, so Mary paid most of the cost. She didn't mind. She could afford it. Besides, she was in love with Daemon. The guests danced to the music from Joan's CD collection and enjoyed an Italian buffet dinner, accompanied by wine and liquor. Daemon drank a lot, staggering a few times, but managed to stay on his feet. Joan drove them home after the reception.

Daemon insisted on postponing their honeymoon until he could afford to pay for it himself. Mary offered to pay for it, but Daemon refused. Meanwhile, he settled easily into Mary's house as her husband. During the first three months of their marriage he took her to restaurants, bought her jewelry and gifts. Mary became more relaxed and confident than ever before. But her feeling of happiness ended abruptly when Daemon came home from work one evening later than usual. The overwhelming stench of liquor coming from his clothing and his breath made Mary reel. She knew Daemon liked to drink occasionally, but had never witnessed him totally inebriated.

"Where's my dinner, bitch?" he mumbled as he staggered through the door, throwing his coat on the floor.

"Daemon, what happened to you?" Mary said, startled by his behavior. "You're drunk."

"None of your damn business!" Daemon blurted out, shoving Mary so hard that she banged her wrist on the kitchen table as she fell to the floor.

"It's all your fault," he continued. Then he took a step back, stumbled into the living room, sank onto the sofa, and passed out.

Mary lay on the floor in shock. Her right wrist throbbed with pain. At first Mary thought it was broken. But since she could bend it, she realized that it was only a bad sprain. She picked herself up, stunned. She sat in the wing chair opposite the sofa, where Daemon lay in a drunken stupor, snoring loudly. She put her head in her hands and cried.

This was new to Mary. She was experiencing a new and different kind of pain, the pain of betrayal. When she stopped crying, she went into the bathroom, wrapped her still aching wrist in an Ace Bandage and downed two Advils. Her low self-esteem began to reappear. *What did I do wrong?* she wondered. Mary cried herself to sleep, as she had done so many times in her life.

The next morning Daemon was nowhere to be found. Confused, and with her wrist still in pain, Mary was too upset to go to work. First, she called in sick. Then she called Joan.

"Are you busy at work, right now?" she asked.

"It's okay," Joan replied, a bit startled by Mary's unusual call. "What's the matter?"

"Daemon came home late last evening, totally drunk. I never saw him like this before. He was mean and nasty. He even knocked me to the floor. Then he passed out on the sofa. When I woke up this morning he was gone."

"Jesus," Joan blurted. "What the hell happened?"

"I don't know," Mary sobbed. "What should I do?"

"Are you home right now?" Joan asked.

"Yes," Mary replied, "I took a sick day."

"I'll take an early lunch break and come over in about an hour," Joan said. "We'll talk more when I get there. Don't worry, I love you."

"Love you, too," Mary said, as she hung up the phone, her eyes swollen with tears. She took a tissue from her bathrobe pocket, dried her eyes and put up a pot of coffee. Mary tried to figure out why Daemon, who swore he loved her, acted the way he had. He said it was her fault. But why? Maybe she was at fault, but for what? Still baffled, Mary got dressed and waited for Joan to arrive.

"Tell me what happened, in detail," Joan said as she and Mary sat at the kitchen table. After Mary had related as much as she could remember about the night before, Joan said, "Mary, you can't let this happen again. Maybe Daemon thought he had a good reason for getting drunk, but that's no excuse for his outrageous behavior. And for hitting you. Physical abuse is never okay, for any reason."

"He once told me that he was beaten by his father as a child, but he's an adult. And his father's dead. I have no idea what might have set him off last night," said Mary.

"You have to confront him tonight," Joan insisted.

"You're right," Mary responded. "But I'm scared."

"I know, I know," Joan said, consoling her. "But you can't let this go on."

Mary and Joan sat together, holding hands, until Mary calmed down.

"I have to get back to work," Joan said. "Please let me know how it goes with Daemon tonight. Keep your phone in your pocket. Call me if he gets rough again."

"I will," Mary responded, drying her tears once more.

Daemon walked through the door at 6 pm carrying a bouquet of roses. He stood silently, his head bowed, as Mary stared at him, also in silence. "I am so sorry, Mary. Can you ever forgive me?" he pleaded.

"Before I'm able to forgive you, you have to let me know why you did what you did. Why did you get so drunk?" Mary demanded.

"Some stupid thing at work set me off," Daemon attempted to explain. "I promise it will never happen again. I love you."

"And I love you, too. But why did you blame me?" Mary asked.

"I was stupid. I wasn't thinking straight. It had nothing to do with you. Please say you'll forgive me."

Mary rushed into his arms.

"I'm taking you out to dinner tonight," Daemon said.

Mary changed her dress while Daemon called the Venetian Gardens, their favorite Italian restaurant, to reserve a quiet table for dinner. Daemon downed two Scotch and sodas and then rambled throughout the meal about how things were going to change at his job, how successful he was going to be and that he was expecting a raise soon. Mary remained silent during dinner, nodding her head occasionally but remaining skeptical. She did not want to allow herself to be swayed by this one apology.

Later that evening Mary reported in to Joan. "He said there was a problem at his job, but he worked it out and that things would be better."

"I pray that's so," Joan said.

"Me, too," Mary responded. "Talk again soon. Love you."

For the next two weeks Daemon appeared to have overcome his problem. That is, until he came home drunk again, staggering through the door, slamming it behind him. Mary ran down the stairs to the sounds of a living room lamp crashing on the floor, and her Aunt Olivia's expensive Royal Delft blue vase and bowl hurled against the wall, smashing them to bits.

"Mary, where the hell are you?" Daemon yelled. He had been fired that afternoon for verbally abusing, then losing a major client that cost the firm thousands of dollars.

"Stop it, stop it! What are you doing?" Mary yelled.

"You don't deserve all these things," Daemon screamed. "You

women are all alike. All you do is take. And you, Mary, you're nothing, that's why I married you." He grabbed Mary by the shoulders and shook her like a rag doll. Then he slapped her across the face knocking her senseless. Mary tumbled onto the kitchen floor, striking her head. The pain felt like bullets shooting through her skull. He stood her up and raised his fist to strike her again. Instinctively, Mary reached for the cast iron skillet that was sitting on the stove and swung it blindly at Daemon, striking him in the forehead. Daemon staggered and fell to the floor, unconscious.

Tears streaked down her cheeks as Mary stood, hysterical, over his motionless body lying on the kitchen floor. She suddenly became aware of the heavy weight that she still held in her hand – the weapon that stopped her husband in his tracks. Releasing her grip on the skillet, she barely heard the dull thud as it dropped onto the floor, cracking one of the tiles. Regaining her composure, Mary rushed to the telephone and called Joan. "Come quickly," she said.

Joan arrived within ten minutes and tried her best to console Mary.

"Daemon was at it again," Mary said. "He came home drunk and really hurt me. I honestly thought he would kill me. I was just trying to protect myself."

Joan looked at Daemon's body on the floor. "Is he dead?" she asked.

"No, he's unconscious and still breathing," Mary said. "but I wish he were dead." Joan hugged Mary and the two sat in silence as Mary cried again in Joan's arms. After a few moments, Mary looked into her friend's eyes and said, "Joan, I need your help."

"Anything for you," Joan said.

"Grab his arms and help me move him to the cabinet near the

sink." Daemon's limp body was heavier than they expected, but together they were able prop him against it. Joan held Daemon's body still while Mary retrieved a funnel and a length of tubing from her pantry. "Joan, go the liquor cabinet and bring me a bottle of Scotch, please," Mary said. Joan returned with the liquor to find that Mary had inserted the funnel and tubing into Daemon's throat while he remained unconscious. Mary proceeded to pour the Scotch into his mouth through the funnel, slowly, so as not to cause him to gag. She successfully emptied two-thirds of the bottle into his stomach.

"Joan, take off one of his shoes and sock," Mary instructed. "I have one more thing to do." Mary left the room and returned with a syringe and a small brown bottle of liquid.

"What's in the bottle?" Joan asked.

"I took this from the lab," Mary responded, "right after that first episode. I kept it in a box in the back of the pantry. I was hoping never to have to use it, but I guess I was wrong. We're going to make certain that he's dead. It's hydrogen cyanide."

"Are you sure you want to go through with this?" Joan asked.

"It's the only way, Joan. We have to do this."

"All right, then," Joan sighed, holding Daemon's foot still. "I wouldn't do this for anyone but you."

Mary inserted the syringe into the bottle, pulling the plunger back to fill the tube. She injected the full amount from the syringe into the space between Daemon's big toe and second toe and said, "Daemon will never harm me, or anyone, ever again."

"How do you know about injecting the poison between his toes?" Joan asked.

"You hang around the police, you learn stuff," Mary responded with a smile. "Junkies do that when the veins in their arms can no longer take the needle. Rarely does anyone look at their toes, and I'm quite certain that no one will look at Daemon's toes."

"You're the expert," Joan said, as she put Daemon's sock and shoe back on. They put his jacket on him and, making certain no one outside the house was watching, dragged him from the kitchen to the driveway. Mary opened the door to the back seat of Daemon's car and they pushed his limp body inside. Mary drove the car three miles down the highway that led through a wooded area while Joan followed in her own car. When they reached a secluded area, Mary drove the car off the road, smashing it against tree. Joan parked her car on the shoulder of the road and proceeded to help Mary drag Daemon's body out of the rear of the car and into the driver's seat. They carefully leaned his forehead against the steering wheel, matching it with the bruise caused by the skillet.

"I'll call the police in the morning," Mary said, "and tell them that Daemon didn't come home tonight. When they find him here, they'll say he was driving drunk, ran off the road and was killed in the crash. They'll think it was an accident."

Pleased with the success of their plan, they drove silently back to Mary's house in Joan's car.

"You're sure the police will buy it?" Joan asked.

"Yes, they will. The evidence is obvious," Mary stated confidently. "I work in the forensic lab, remember? I know how the process works."

When they were back inside the house, Mary turned and held her arms out to Joan, who rushed into them. They hugged each other tightly, both of them sobbing.

"Thank you so much for helping me," Mary said. "You are my best friend in the whole world. Will you stay with me tonight?"

"Of course, Mary, there's nothing I wouldn't do for you," Joan smiled back.

"I have some extra night clothes you can wear," Mary said. "Now I need to take a shower."

Mary went to her bedroom, took off her clothes and proceeded into the bathroom. She stepped into the shower and felt all the ugliness of the evening, as well as her marriage to Daemon, wash away under the warmth of the water as it streamed over her naked body. As she stood in the tub, savoring the water cleansing not only her body but her soul, the shower curtain opened. Joan, completely naked, stepped into the tub alongside Mary.

"Joan, what...?"

"Mary," Joan said, "I've loved you since we were in high school."

"Oh, Joan," Mary cried, reaching out to Joan, "I love you, too."

Mary and Joan embraced, clinging to each other, experiencing the tingling and joy of their warm, naked bodies up against each other. When they kissed, Mary felt a sensation throughout her body she had never known.

"Friends forever," Joan whispered, as they snuggled under the covers in Mary's bed afterwards.

"Forever Friends," Mary responded as she kissed Joan passionately. Mary had discovered the kind of love she had been searching for since childhood. She now believed that the child that was growing inside her womb would be raised in a loving and tender environment, by two people who truly loved each other. Joan lay alongside her best friend, and now, her lover. Mary laid her head back on her pillow, closed her eyes and, for the first time in a long while, fell into a deep and peaceful sleep.

Epilogue

The police located Daemon Talbot's car late the following afternoon in the woods, just as Mary and Joan had left it. "Cause of death: DUI," the police report indicated. The autopsy confirmed the cause of death, just as Mary had predicted. Fortunately for Mary, the coroner never performed an autopsy on her Aunt Olivia's body years earlier. Olivia's death was due to natural causes, the coroner's report stated.

Hell of a Time

PASTOR GREGORY SMILED with regal pride as he gazed out upon his Sunday morning flock. He was considered evangelical royalty in the small heartland community of Humble Creek. He not only led the townsfolk in prayer, but it was Pastor Gregory from whom the town's populace sought advice on all the religious, and many of the personal decisions in their lives. *"Am I devout enough?" "Should I forgive so-and-so for...whatever," "Must my wife obey me?" "Should I let my son date so-and-so's daughter?"*

Pastor Gregory gladly dispensed his wise counsel to his parishioners. Standing at over six-feet tall with closely cropped white hair and sporting the kind of beard worn by Amish elders, he was an impressive figure who reveled in the true power given him in his pulpit.

It was unseasonably hot for the first week in June. The temperature was already ninety degrees at 10 am. Many of the women were trying

to cool themselves with home-made paper fans. Men had loosened their ties and opened their collar buttons. Everyone was suffering in the heat. The church building committee had not yet installed the upgraded air conditioning system due to limits already realized in their budget. The old system was straining to pump out cool air at full capacity, barely managing to lower the temperature in the chapel.

The small church was filled to capacity. The congregation eagerly awaited the guest speaker. Old and young alike had come to hear the noted author and lecturer, Ms. Lucy Dickens, speak about the relationship between God and Satan.

Behind Pastor Gregory and slightly to his right, Lucy Dickens sat with her legs crossed. The curve of her long calves was visibly apparent. She wore a red dress with long sleeves and a white bow at the neck. The dress was cinched at the waist with a shiny black leather belt. Black patent leather shoes completed her outfit. An alluring smile decorated her lips, the color of sweet red wine. Her nails were colored with the identical bright shade of red. Her long black hair was pulled back into bun. One might call her pretty; another might say she was a handsome woman, with a bearing and attitude of culture and refinement. She displayed no jewelry that would distract from her beauty save one cornucopia-shaped pin that was attached to the collar of her dress.

The fact that her most recent book, *Satan's Journey Home,* had been one of the top ten on *The New York Times* Best Seller List for the past three weeks was not that much of a draw, since barely anyone in town read *The New York Times* – that biased, left-slanted newspaper of the "Liberal Elites" on the East Coast. Most had never heard of Lucy Dickens, let alone read any of her work. No, it was Pastor Gregory's encouragement and their love for him that inspired the townsfolk to attend in such numbers on this hot Sunday morning. He had not read the book itself, only a brief synopsis of *Satan's Journey Home* on the *Christian Life* website. The reviewer hadn't given the book a critique one way or the other. However, because of Pastor Gregory's fascination with the Devil, he was inspired to invite Ms. Dickens as a speaker. And Lucy Dickens was happy to make a small diversion from her planned book tour route to accommodate his request.

"And as we all know," Pastor Gregory beamed as he ended his sermon, "God in Heaven above, who controls all things in the universe, who created the Earth and all its inhabitants, who created each one of us in His own image, who has a divine plan for us, will always see to it that goodness will always triumph over evil."

Cries of "Amen, brother," "Hurrah," "God be praised," "Praise the Lord," and, "We love you Pastor," were shouted repeatedly from the congregation as they stood in unison and applauded his sermon. Pastor Gregory stood with his head bowed and arms extended. He motioned all to take their seats and return to the quiet calm of Sunday morning worship. Once they were seated and decorum restored, he spoke again.

"And now, my children, it gives me pleasure to introduce a woman who has studied our beloved Bible, the concept of good and evil, God and the Devil. She has written a book that, some say, could possibly change forever the way we perceive Satan himself. Or at least, that's what I've heard the *New York Times* critics say. I haven't read the book, but personally, it makes no difference what any book says." Pastor Gregory raised his arm and displayed his Bible to his flock.

"The Bible is the only truth," he exclaimed.

Shouts of "Amen" and "Hallelujah" resounded with zealous enthusiasm from the congregation.

"But I'm always willing to hear what others think," Pastor Gregory continued. He glanced at the notepad he took from his inside pocket, then put on his reading glasses. Pastor Gregory stood proudly at the lectern and introduced Lucy Dickens. "Our guest speaker is a Bible scholar, having studied at The Sorbonne in Paris. She earned her Master's degree in Bible and Religious Studies from Baylor University and her Ph.D. from Pepperdine. So, it appears she may know something about the Bible." Some chuckles were heard coming from the flock of worshippers. "And now, please welcome Ms. Lucy Dickens, author of the best-selling book, *Satan's Journey Home*."

Lucy Dickens rose slowly with a decided air of confidence. Cordial, but muted, applause greeted her as she approached the lectern. Immediately, two flashbulbs went off from the back of the room. Pastor Gregory had notified the local newspapers of this morning's event. They were also eager to hear what she had to say. No doubt this would garner major headlines in this area of the Bible Belt.

Lucy was in no hurry. Her eyes moved deliberately from one eager face to another. Then she began. "Pastor Gregory, thank you for inviting me. It is an honor to visit this beautiful town and speak to you in this lovely church."

Everyone noticed how poised she appeared, pronouncing each word distinctly with quiet self-assurance. "What do we know about Satan?" she continued. "Has anyone here ever actually seen the Devil? Or, ever confronted Satan himself?"

The congregants looked around to see if anyone would respond to Ms. Dickens' question. No one did. She seemed to have created a hypnotic effect on the townspeople. No matter where anyone was seated, everyone felt that Lucy Dickens was speaking directly to them.

"Interesting," she commented. "Then how do you know he exists?"

There were rumblings and mutterings from all the pews. "Wait just a minute," said a man jumping up, shouting. "We know he exists. The Bible says so. And who do you think accounts for all the evil in the world?" He sat down to the applause and cheers of the crowd.

"And the Bible is God's truth," called out a woman seated behind him, accompanied by multiple shouts of "Amen," "Praise the Lord," and more applause.

Lucy Dickens continued with her questions. "And what, dear friends, does the Devil do? What is his role in our lives?"

"The Devil is pure evil," called out another woman, "he must be shunned." Applause and shouts of "Amen" followed.

"What if I were to tell you that the Devil, Satan, Beelzebub, Lucifer or whatever name you assign, just wants to be loved in the same way that you all love God?" Lucy asked. "And that if you loved him, all your wishes, dreams and hopes would be granted."

"What are you talking about?" called out a man from the front row. "Love the Devil????" he continued, shaking his fist at the speaker. Lucy Dickens stood, while maintaining her cool and calm composure in spite of the rising temperatures both outside and inside the church.

The belligerence increased as the crowd became more restless. "Let me give you some new insight," Lucy continued, above the murmurs of her audience. "As you know, if you've studied the Bible as I have, Satan was an angel created in perfection and beauty. Angels, just like all of you and everyone else on Earth, have free will. You can choose to do good or you can choose to do evil. God doesn't cause you to do good, and Satan doesn't cause you to do evil. It's your choice. You make the decision. Satan just wanted to exercise his own free will, granted by God. If God were truly just, He would have allowed Satan to remain in Heaven. But how can one exercise free will if one must follow whatever God says?"

Many in the crowd rose from their seats, lifting up their bibles, hollering, "Damn the Devil, Praise the Lord." Lucy Dickens continued unfazed, "There's the paradox, my friends. And, being a jealous God, He punished Satan by casting him and his followers out of Heaven. As the title of my book states, Satan just wants to go home, back to Heaven on high, and sit with the other angels."

"You're spouting nonsense," yelled someone from the back of the room. "Blasphemer!" shouted another.

Amid the commotion and disruption going on throughout the assembly, Pastor Gregory stepped forward. "Please, brethren, please quiet down," he implored. "Stop shouting. Show some respect for our guest. You may not agree with her, but please allow her to explain herself before you condemn her," he pleaded again, waving his arms up and down, trying to restore decorum and encourage his flock to take their seats.

Throughout the attack on her presentation, Lucy Dickens remained calm and composed, with a slight hint of a smile on her dark red lips. "I fully understand your concerns," she articulated, holding her arms up to her audience as they reluctantly began to take their seats. "Please let me ask you another question," she continued. "You claim to be God-fearing, righteous, religious, and basically good people, am I correct?"

"You bet your sweet life, we are," a woman shouted.

"You all follow God's commandments as well as the laws of the land, do you not?" Lucy responded.

"Yes, we do," the same woman answered. "What's your point?"

"Here's my point, madam," Lucy retorted, her eyes staring down directly at the woman who began to cower in her seat. Her pleasant composure faded. She was no longer smiling. As she focused her gaze directly towards that specific woman, every person in the room felt Lucy's gaze burning directly into their own eyes. They sat glued to their seats, unable to move, unable to speak or to turn away from Lucy's eyes. It was as if everyone had been immobilized by the intensity of her glare.

"You, all of you and the others like you, have chosen of your own free will to follow evil. It was not Satan who forced you, but it was your own dark hearts that made you decide to enslave others, to denigrate those whose faces or skin color was not like yours, whose belief systems were not yours, whose pleas to alleviate their burdens and pains were disregarded, whose requests for asylum remained unheeded. You made the decision to turn them away, while at the same time claiming to be righteous and God fearing."

As the throng sat motionless and silent, fixed to their seats, Lucy raised her arms above her head to the roar of thunder. She grew taller and taller until her head reached just below the inverted boat-shaped church ceiling. Her face elongated into a grotesque rectangle, and her ears extended unnaturally to reveal their true pointed configuration. Her skin turned the color of rusted metal. Her eyes, which were now yellow, oval, and catlike, looked piercingly at all who remained transfixed with fear. Insects of all shapes and sizes flew out of the cornucopia brooch on her dress and began to circle the flock of horrified congregants, biting and stinging wherever they found a victim. The crowd was in a panic, howling with fear and pain as they were brutally attacked, and yet could not move out of their seats. "You are the sinners! You are the blasphemers," she bellowed. "You don't deserve free will any longer."

Amid another clap of thunder, a black cloud appeared above the church. The entire building quaked and creaked, collapsing in on itself, falling into an enormous hole that opened beneath it, swallowing the building and its inhabitants into oblivion.

Within moments, the gigantic hole that had appeared out of nowhere sealed itself. The dark cloud disappeared and the sky returned to a robin's egg blue. White clouds that looked like cotton balls appeared. The sun shone on an otherwise beautiful late spring afternoon. Birds sang in the trees, crickets chirped and frogs croaked in a nearby pond. The aroma of newly mown grass filled the air.

Lucy Dickens stood alone in an empty field, dusted herself off and strode over to her bright red Mercedes. "What a lovely day this has turned out to be," she reflected. Before starting the engine, she opened her planner, took out a Mont Blanc pen and ticked off the name of the church that once occupied the location one hundred feet from where she was parked.

"Let me see," she said, checking her calendar. "It looks like I'm scheduled to speak at Congregation Beth Israel next week in Borough Park, Brooklyn. I must call Rabbi Pincus to confirm my appointment." She sped away, leaving behind a desolate, empty lot in a cloud of dust.

Visions of Lorelei

FROM THE TIME he was nine years old, Max Steinberg loved playing Little League Baseball in Fair Lawn's All-Sports Association. A lefty, Max was a star pitcher as well as a superb center fielder with an outstanding batting average. He loved being on the baseball diamond, with the aroma of newly mown grass and the breezes in the outfield. His focus on the game was so intense that he didn't even notice how much the polyester jersey made him sweat in the mid-August heat.

Max was one of twenty boys selected out of more than one hundred boys and girls to play in Fair Lawn's summer travel team league. During July and August, the travel team competed against teams from towns in northern New Jersey – North Bergen, Jefferson Township, Pequannock, Montville, and others that were sometimes close to an hour's drive during rush hour.

Max's mother, father, and older brother Todd, made it a point to be at every away game to watch him compete. The games commenced at 6:00, so Max's family often had to forego a home-cooked dinner in order to get to the games on time. They'd pack folding chairs in the trunk of their Buick, stop at a local deli on the way to the ball-field, and eat their evening meal while sitting on the sidelines. They were happy to change their dinner schedule because it was their Max who played in every game. Each time Max made a spectacular play, whether hitting two home runs in one game or running with the speed of Secretariat to chase down and catch a fly ball in center field, his fans cheered. Many of them patted Max's parents on the back to show their appreciation for his achievements. Max's family were often embarrassed by this display, but it was difficult for them to hide their pride.

At the age of fifteen, Max was selected to play on the freshman baseball team at Fair Lawn High School, known as *The Cutters*. He was excited to be a *Cutter* and proud to wear the name on his jersey. Max was in the starting pitcher rotation. Whenever he didn't pitch, he played another position or was a pinch hitter. Max's play continued to be outstanding and he even contemplated pursuing a career in the major leagues. It wasn't long, however, until Max realized that he'd be better off with a more stable family lifestyle than he would have with a career in baseball. With a solid B+ average, he wanted to become a successful history teacher like his uncle Mitch. Max admired and was inspired by his uncle, who was highly respected by his colleagues and loved by his students.

It was during his first year in high school when Max began experiencing recurring dreams. At first, he thought nothing of it, but after having the same kind of dream several times a month he was puzzled by their similarity. Most of the time, Max's dreams consisted of what many normal fifteen-year old boys dream about:

sports, driving fast cars, wild adventures in far off-lands, love and, of course, lots and lots of sex.

The first of Max's recurring dreams came on a Monday night after having spent the weekend playing with his friends, riding his bike, and doing the usual things that fifteen-year olds do. In that dream he was playing baseball with his 9th grade classmates at Memorial Field. Max was pitching against their arch rivals from Saddle Brook. His team had a slim one-run lead in the top of the seventh inning. At Max's level, the game consisted of seven innings. There were two outs. Bases were loaded. The count was full: 3 balls, 2 strikes. Sweat poured off Max's forehead. His heart was pounding. The fans were chanting, "Strike him out, Max. Strike him out." Max leaned forward, staring down the batter.

Suddenly, Max noticed a girl standing behind the backstop at home plate. *Why is that girl standing behind the backstop?* he thought. *No one is supposed to be there. She should be in the stands.*

"Come on Max, put 'er right here," the catcher, Ernie Collins who was Max's best friend, hollered as he pounded his mitt. "Strike him out. You can do it!"

Max tried to focus on the batter, but he could not take his eyes off the girl behind the backstop. She appeared to be about his age, but he did not recognize her as a classmate. He seemed to be the only one to notice her. Max was one of the more popular boys in his class and he knew most every girl in his grade. *Maybe she's new*, he thought. Most of the girls wore jeans and sneakers to the game. She wore a floral print dress with a ruffled collar and ruffles at the end of her short sleeves. Her long, strawberry blond ponytail was tied in the back with a big blue bow. It was unusual to see a girl dressed this way at a baseball game, let alone standing in plain sight behind the backstop. She reminded him of Olivia Newton-John who played the role of Sandy in the movie, *Grease.* Ever since seeing *Grease,* Max had developed a crush on Olivia Newton-John. Seeing this girl made his heart beat a little faster.

"C'mon Max, strike him out," the crowd chanted again.

Turning his focus once more on the batter, Max took his windup, hurled the pitch and, as the umpire raised his right arm with the call, *strike three,* Max felt a thrilling sensation of pleasure run through his body. The home crowd roared with delight. Max awoke suddenly and sat up in bed, not being able to get the image of the girl with the blond ponytail out of his mind. The bright red numerals on his clock-radio read 1:30. It took him over an hour to fall back to sleep. Try as he might to continue his dream, the girl did not reappear that night.

Max thought of his mystery dream girl while eating breakfast. He thought of her while walking to school. He thought of her in math class, in English class, most of the day in fact. He thought of her that evening while lying in bed, waiting to fall asleep. *Please let me see her again tonight,* Max begged his brain, but to no avail. His dreams Tuesday night were the usual ones.

The following Monday night, Max dreamt that he, Ernie Collins, and some other boys went camping in Bear Mountain State Park. After they had pitched their tents, gathered firewood, and lit the campfire, Ernie began strumming a guitar and they were all singing.

Strange, Max thought, *Ernie plays like Bruce Springsteen. I didn't know Ernie could even play guitar.* In fact, Ernie could not play guitar or any other musical instrument. But in a dream, of course, anything can be possible, so it was not unusual that Ernie played the guitar like a professional.

As the boys sat around the campfire toasting marshmallows, Max glanced off to the side. There she was, the girl from his baseball dream, leaning against a sycamore tree. He recognized her immediately by her beautiful smooth skin and long blond ponytail. It was 'Sandy' again, from *Grease*. This time she wore a pink sweater and flowered capri pants. Arms folded, she stood there watching the boys sitting around the campfire. Ernie noticed that Max had stopped singing and was staring off to the side. He stopped playing the guitar and said,

"Max, what are you staring at?"

"She's here," Max replied. "Over there, leaning against the tree."

"Who's here?" Ernie responded.

Before Max could answer, he awoke with a start and sat up in bed. He glanced at the red digital numbers on his alarm clock radio. It was 12:30 am. He stared at his bedroom wall for a few moments before falling back to sleep. Although he tried and hoped, he could not recreate the dream. The next day at school, Max couldn't concentrate. His attempts to focus on his studies were interrupted by the thought of the blond girl. Difficult as it was, Max eventually forced himself to stop thinking of his dream girl and concentrate on his classwork.

That evening, he wondered whether or not he would dream about the blond girl again. He wanted to go to bed as early as possible. After dinner, he completed his homework and, at 10 pm told his parents he was going to bed.

"Tired already?" asked his mother. "It must have been a busy day at school."

"Yeah," Max replied.

He kissed his mother and father, then went upstairs to prepare for bed. It didn't take him long to fall asleep. He had several different dreams, one about driving a race car, another about his mother and father dancing in front of the fireplace while he ate popcorn. But no mystery girl appeared in his dreams that night. Nor the next night, nor the night after that, nor the week after that.

As the mystery girl drifted to the back of Max's mind, she appeared in one of his dreams one month later. Max was rowing a boat on a mountain lake. The lake was serene. On the shore, the bright green leaves rustled in the trees, and birds chirped. A few wisps of puffy clouds dotted an otherwise deep blue sky. Suddenly, there she was – the pretty blond girl with the ponytail – right there in the rowboat. She was close enough for Max to reach out and touch her. This time she was wearing a short-sleeved blouse, short pants and tennis shoes.

Max wanted to speak with her, but he couldn't. He felt his mouth moving, but no words came out. The girl continued to stare into his eyes. Max was enthralled by her pretty, smiling face. He tried to row the boat to the shore, but it didn't move. The next moment, the image changed to him and Ernie on Safari in Africa photographing lions.

Lorelei Golding was enjoying her typical Saturday morning break-fast; eggs, stewed tomatoes, toast and a cup of tea with milk. She looked up at her mother and asked, "Mum, have you ever had a recurring dream?"

"What's that, luv?" her mother replied, in her prominent Mancunian accent.

"You know, the same dream over and over," said Lorelei. "I've been having a lot of them."

"Tell me about them," her mother inquired.

"Well," said Lorelei, "about a month ago I had this strange sensation that I was in another country, America, I think it was, watching some boys play cricket, only it wasn't cricket. I was in a large field with lots of other people, mostly young like me, who were watching and cheering."

"That's a game called baseball," her mother explained. "They play that game in America. It's a bit like cricket."

"Maybe that's what it was," Lorelei continued. "Don't you think it's funny that I should have dreamt about that game, since I've never seen it before? Anyway, I was standing behind a huge wire fence and was looking at this very handsome lad who hurled a ball at the batter. The batter swung his stick and missed the ball. All I could think of was how cute the hurler was."

"Was that the entirety of your dream?" asked her mother.

"That's all it was that night, but the same boy appeared in my dream a week later."

"Go on," urged her mother.

"In my dream it was late evening. The sun had already set. I was leaning up against a tree watching a group of boys sitting around a fire, roasting marshmallows on sticks. One boy was playing a guitar, quite well, in fact. They were all singing a song I never heard before. All of a sudden, there was that cute boy again. You know, the one who was hurling the ball in my first dream. He turned and looked at me, almost as if he knew me."

"How curious," her mother said.

"Wait, mum, that's not the end of it." Lorelei said. "Two nights ago, I saw the boy again in my dream. We were in a rowboat on a beautiful lake surrounded by mountains, just the two of us, together. Then the dream stopped. What do you think?"

"If I were you, luv, at your age, I'd concentrate on my school work and not think too much about the meaning of dreams. And boys, too, for that matter."

"Face it, Max," Ernie said, laughing, after Max confided in him about his recurring dreams on their way to baseball practice. "You're in love with Olivia Newton-John. She's that girl in your dreams. Ever since we saw *Grease*, you've been drooling over her. Don't worry, though. All the guys are in love with her – Jimmy, Tony, all of us are. Me too, even."

"Yeah, I get that," Max admitted. "But I think there's something different going on here," he continued. "I don't know what it is, but I think it may be more than just my crush on Olivia Newton-John."

"Well, forget about it for now," Ernie said. "We've got baseball practice in fifteen minutes. If we want to make the varsity team, we have to be in top shape."

Max and Ernie were both chosen to play on the varsity squad. With Ernie as his catcher, Max had a 10-1 record as a freshman pitcher. Ernie had an impressive .350 batting average. They were an imposing battery.

During his sophomore and junior years in high school, Max was too consumed with his school work and varsity baseball to give much thought to the blond girl with the pony tail in his dreams. Once in a while, he would see her during a REM fantasy, but they occurred infrequently and for too short a duration to make him think that they were anything but remnants of his earlier nighttime experiences about her.

After six month's absence from Max's dreams, she appeared again. It was during his senior year at FLHS, one month before graduation. Max had completed a no-hitter against the Saddle Brook High School team and was on top of the world. It was a late Friday afternoon game and the team went to the Land & Sea Diner to celebrate. The party was filled with Max's teammates and friends. Some of the other customers even offered congratulations. Everyone was happy.

After the celebration, the team went to Ernie's house to continue the party in his finished basement, which Ernie's mom and sister had decorated with red and white streamers – Fair Lawn High School's colors. Baseball posters adorned the walls. At 11:30 pm, Ernie's parents announced that it was time for everyone to go home. Max and Ernie gave each other high fives and a big hug.

"Good night, Mr. and Mrs. Collins," Max said as he left Ernie's house. "Thanks for the party."

Mrs. Collins gave Max a kiss on the cheek. "You are very welcome, Max. Give my regards to your parents and have a wonderful weekend."

Max returned home overtired, but happy. "I don't know how I'm going to sleep tonight," he told his mother.

"Take a long, hot shower," Max's dad suggested. "Then have a glass of warm milk. That'll help you fall asleep."

Max followed his father's advice. He took the hot shower and drank the warm milk. He kissed his parents, went to bed, and was fast asleep within five minutes. Several hours into a deep sleep, Max experienced a number of different dreams, each lasting briefly.

It was well into the night when Max found himself walking through a wooded pathway lined with tall trees covered with leaves as bright as a hundred shamrocks on St. Patrick's Day. He watched squirrels jump around on the ground and scamper up the trees. He heard birds chirping and the rap-tap-tap of a woodpecker somewhere high in the canopy. The sweet smell of fresh wood bark was in the air. As he neared the end of the path, it opened up to a pristine lake with a wooden dock leading to a rowboat moored at a post halfway down the dock. Max noticed someone seated at the back end of the rowboat. As he approached the dock, he recognized the girl, wearing a yellow blouse and white shorts. Her long blond ponytail was tied in the back with a blue ribbon. She was smiling at Max as he neared the boat.

"Hi," she said invitingly. "Where've you been all this time? I missed you."

Max's heart raced as he stood motionless, staring at her as if she were a painting in a museum. After a moment, he uttered, "May I join you?"

"Please do," said the girl, extending her arm toward the oarsman's seat. "Come on aboard."

Max stepped cautiously, not wanting to rock the boat. He sat down facing the girl, his heart beating more rapidly than before. He wondered whether she could see the pounding in his chest through his shirt.

"I can't believe we're actually talking to each other," Max said, with wavering excitement.

"Yes, it's been three years since we first saw each other at your cricket match," the girl said. "I'm glad we're finally meeting face to face. My name is Lorelei, Lorelei Golding."

"Max, Max Steinberg. Actually, it's Maximilian, but all my friends just call me Max," he replied. "I was named after my grandfather. And it's called baseball, not cricket," Max said.

"My parents named me after my grandmother, Leah, who died in Poland," Lorelei said. "My mother loved the Lorelei legend, you know, the siren on the rock in the Rhine River. She had a beautiful voice that lured sailors close to her so that their ships would crash. I like the name, but I don't like the story that goes with it. You know, being responsible for wrecking all those ships and killing the sailors. Not to worry, though. I can't sing a note," she said as her face lit up with another beautiful smile that nearly bowled Max over.

My God, Max thought, *she is an angel.*

"I guess I'm not up on those kinds of legends," Max said. "But I'm glad you told me about it. Please tell me more about yourself," he continued as he began to row the boat out towards the middle of the lake.

As Lorelei began to speak, Max thought, *Am I still dreaming?* Without skipping a beat, Lorelei said, "We're both dreaming, aren't we, Max?"

"Did you just read my thoughts?" Max asked, puzzled.

"Of course," Lorelei responded with a knowing smile. "It's a dream, remember. Anything is possible. But this dream could also end without warning. We could both vanish in a flash. So, let's make the most of it," Lorelei said. "Kiss me."

Max moved off his seat carefully so as not to capsize the rowboat. He stood up in the rowboat and took a step towards Lorelei. The boat rocked as he approached her, but he made sure to keep his balance. The last thing he wanted to do was tumble into the water. As their lips were just about to meet, a bright light suddenly appeared, as if the sun went nova, causing Max to cover his eyes.

Max awoke with a start as the bright sunlight attacked his bedroom through the unshaded window, jolting him out of the dream. Being so tired the prior evening, having reveled in celebration of the Cutters' win over Saddle Brook, he neglected to pull down his window shade. His clock radio read 11:15 am. He had slept for more than ten hours.

"Damn!" he said.

"Mum," Lorelei said to her mother at breakfast. "Remember I told you my dream a while ago about a boy I saw playing a game like cricket? I think you called it baseball, right?"

"Yes, I remember," her mother replied.

"Well, I dreamt about him last night again."

"The very same boy?" asked her mother.

"Oh, yes, mum. It was him all right. I remember him distinctly. His name is Max Steinberg. He was just about to kiss me when I woke up."

"Kiss you, did he?" asked her mother.

"Almost." Said Lorelei.

"Max Steinberg, did you say? So, he's Jewish, is he?"

"I suppose he is. I wonder if I'll dream about him again. He's really cute," Lorelei sighed.

"Remember, Lorelei, it was a dream, not reality. All right now, luv, eat your breakfast. I want to get the house ready before your father gets back from shul."

"You're from England, aren't you?" Max said to Lorelei in his dream the following Wednesday night. They were sitting alongside each other on the dock after having moored the rowboat.

"You have deduced correctly, Mr. Sherlock Holmes," laughed Lorelei. "Manchester, in fact. Derby Street (she pronounced it 'Darby'). And where in the colonies, I presume, do you reside?"

"I'm from New Jersey, a town called Fair Lawn," Max replied. "I'll be graduating from high school in a couple of weeks. I'll be going to Montclair University to study history and education. I'm going to be a teacher. World history. I play baseball on the varsity team, and am a B+ student. What else would you like to know?"

"Do you have a girlfriend?" Lorelei asked, her cheeks blushing.

"No, not right now," Max replied. "Only you, in this dream of course," he said, and reached to hold Lorelei's hand. As he touched it, Lorelei turned slowly toward Max and caressed his cheek with the palm of her other hand. She moved her mouth close to his and kissed him on the lips. Max was in heaven, their mouths together for the first time. He put his arms around her to pull her closer to him. Just as he felt her body touching his, he awoke. His eyes opened and he stared at his bedroom ceiling. *Jeez!* He thought. *Well, at least this time we actually kissed.* He sat at the edge of his bed and savored the last few moments of his dream.

"I kissed him, the boy in my dream," Lorelei said to her mother. Her mother was focused on her ironing and responded to Lorelei without looking at her.

"Again with your dream boy?" her mother said. "Are you certain you're not making this whole thing up?"

"Mother, look at me," Lorelei demanded. "I told you that I've been having this recurring dream with Max. That's his name, remember? I told you last week. Mum, this same dream has been going on for about three years now. I don't understand why, but I think it's a sign or something."

"Lorelei, sweetheart," her mother said as she rested the iron on the hot plate. She turned and placed her hands on her daughter's shoulders. "Darling," she continued, "I don't know what this is about. Many people have recurring dreams. I've had them, your father had them, and I'm sure your brother has had them as well. In your case, it's been a few years. That doesn't mean anything, really. Maybe your dreams have something to do with a boy in school that you fancy, and you've created a story substituting this boy in your dream for him. Don't fret about it. Now please carry those clothes I've ironed upstairs while I finish the rest of my ironing."

"All right, mum," she sighed. "I'll be going next door, then, to spend a while with Audrey," Lorelei said.

Audrey Cohen was Lorelei's best friend. Her family had moved into the flat next door to Lorelei's when they both were six years old. Audrey and Lorelei became fast friends immediately, spending as much of their time together as possible. They played together, walked to school together, often borrowed each other's clothes, and shared secrets.

"Why hello, Lorelei," Audrey's mother said, welcoming her into the house. "Audrey is upstairs in her room. You can go right on up."

"Thank you, Mrs. Cohen," Lorelei said, politely.

Mrs. Cohen was extremely fond of Lorelei and was happy that she and Audrey were best friends. "Have fun, you two," Mrs. Cohen called as she returned to her housework.

Lorelei scooted up the stairs to Audrey's bedroom. "Remember I told you about the recurring dream I've been having about that boy for the past three years?" Lorelei said excitedly. "Well, in my dream last night, we finally kissed. It was a *real* kiss, too." she said, blushing. "He told me he lived in America, which I figured out for myself, anyway. In New Jersey."

"After three years, it's about time you kissed," Audrey laughed. "You know, Lor, she continued, "I'm sure you've become infatuated with this boy in your dreams, but luv, you have to remember that it's only a dream. You're not a child. You have a real life here, with real people. And there are real boys out there who can give you real kisses. They could be right here in Manchester. Or at least on this side of the Atlantic. You don't have to go all the way to America to find a boyfriend. Did you know that Benjamin Blume likes you? He gawks at you in history class."

"I know you're right, Audrey, about the dream, that is," Lorelei sighed. "And, yes, I've caught Benjamin staring at me. But he doesn't *gawk*. He just looks and smiles, that's all. Maybe he does like me. And yes, I do think he's cute, too."

"I think he's going to ask you to the junior dance at school next month," Audrey said.

"Well, if he does, perhaps I just might go with him."

"Ernie, she kissed me," said Max Thursday morning at school.
"Who, Isabel?" Ernie asked quizzically.

Everyone in the senior class knew that Isabel Furman had a crush
on Max. Isabel was a member of the Lacrosse team. When her team
was not competing, she attended all of Max's baseball games. Ever
since they were freshmen, Isabel couldn't hide her infatuation with
Max. Although they went to the junior prom together the previous
year, Max never felt any sparks between them. To him, they were
just good friends.

"No, not Isabel," said Max. "You know there's nothing between
us. It was Lorelei, the girl in my dream."

"Oh, she has a name now, does she?" said Ernie, with an air of
sarcasm. "When did you find that out?"

"I dreamt about her again last night. Ernie, something strange is
going on in my dreams with her. Each time I dream about her, the
dreams seem to be getting longer with a lot more detail in them. She
even told me her last name, Lorelei Golding. She lives in Manchester,
England. We were sitting on a dock at a lake, the same one that I
dreamed about before. She touched my cheek then moved in to kiss me.
Ernie, it seemed so real. I could feel lips. I actually felt her kissing me."

"Okay, Max," Ernie said. "Way too much information."

"Ernie, what do you think's going on? Am I going nuts? I know
it's a dream, but why is it so real? Why do I keep dreaming of her
over and over again?"

"Ya got me," Ernie replied. "Why not just enjoy the dreams?"

"Yeah, maybe you're right. But I've been dreaming of her for three years," Max said. "How much longer can this go on? Maybe I need to see a shrink."

"I think you should forget about your dreams and focus on playing ball this summer. It'll be our last travel team together. Let's enjoy it," Ernie said.

That summer Ernie continued to inspire Max as his catcher, while Max had an amazing season with seven wins and no losses. Ernie was no slouch either, achieving an impressive .360 batting average. Before they could say 'Jackie Robinson,' the summer was over. Ernie went to Rutgers; Max went to Montclair. They saw each other as often as they could, but mostly only on weekends and during breaks.

Max's recurring dreams continued throughout his college years. He dreamed about Lorelei at least three times each month. And Lorelei dreamed about Max. Three weeks before graduation, Max returned to his dorm room after studying all day for his last round of final exams in the library. Exhausted, he fell asleep immediately.

That night, in another of his seven-year stretch of recurring dreams, Lorelei said something that stopped Max in his tracks. Max and Lorelei were sitting on folding beach chairs, the old-fashioned canvas kind that are so hard to set up, watching some ducks land on the lake that so often was the setting in his dreams. "I won't be able to see you anymore," Lorelei whispered.

Max felt his jaw drop. His eyes opened as wide as saucers. It took several moments before he was able to respond. "What?" he said, stunned.

"Max," Lorelei said. "I know that you and I are both dreaming this at the same time. I don't know how it happened or how it's even possible. It seems real, but it can't be, can it? You must have thought that too, haven't you?"

"I never knew what to think," Max replied. "The thought crossed my mind, but I only wanted to keep on dreaming about you and me together. Lorelei, I first started dreaming of you when I was fifteen. I'm twenty-two now and I've been in love with you ever since then. Why can't we continue?"

"We can't be in love, really," Lorelei responded. "We have real lives to live. We can't just dream them away."

"But..." Max began to interject.

"Max, I'm going to be married soon. In real life. You'll find someone to love in real life, too. I know it." Lorelei leaned over and kissed Max on the cheek. "Goodbye, my dearest Max."

"Wait, Lorelei. Who you going to marry? Are you really in love with him?"

Max awoke with a start, the sun peering around the corners of the Venetian blinds, greeting the beginning of a mid-April morning.

What just happened? he wondered. Max sat up in bed, rubbing his eyes and shaking himself awake. It was 7:30 am. His class began at 11:00. Still trying to recover from the dream, he washed, dressed. and went to the cafeteria for breakfast. He sat, staring at his plate of scrambled eggs, thinking of Lorelei and the last thing she said to him. He kept hearing her voice whispering, "Goodbye, my dearest Max," over and over in his head.

With his mind still in a fog, Max continued sitting by himself, sipping his coffee. He picked up his phone and dialed his best friend.

"It's 8:30 in the morning," Ernie said. "What's up? Anything wrong?"

"You're gonna think I'm nuts. But you know those recurring dreams I told you about, the ones I've had since we were fifteen?"

Ernie took a deep breath, then let it out. "Go on," he said.

"I think they're over with," Max said. "Last night in my dream, Lorelei – you remember, that's her name – well, she told me we can't see each other anymore. She's getting married. The last thing she said was, 'Goodbye, my dearest Max.' That's when I woke up and got the feeling that my dreams of her would never come back. That I'd lost her forever."

"Come on, Max," Ernie said. "You know it was all in your head, right? Dreams are imaginary. Look," he continued, "I've got classes all day. Why don't I call you around nine tonight so we can talk some more, okay?"

"Sure," said Max. "Talk to you then. I appreciate it. Bye."

Max muddled through the day. He tried in vain to focus during his classes, but couldn't get the thought of losing Lorelei out of his mind. Later that afternoon, he just sat in his dorm room and spent the remainder of the day fixated on the last seven years of dreams – dreams of Lorelei. He realized how much of his life he had allowed to be absorbed by her. He went out for a walk, hoping some fresh air would help clear his head. At 9 pm his phone rang.

"Hi, Ernie," Max. "Thanks for reaching out to me. It's been a rough day."

"Look, Max," Ernie said, "You're my best friend, and I hate to see you like this. I know these dreams have been a big part of your life, and I hate to keep harping on this, but you have to get over this fantasy of yours. We all have recurring dreams from time to time. All right, maybe not for seven years like you, but I never told you about my recurring dream, did I?"

"You?" said Max, surprised.

"I've had these weird dreams about looking for a bathroom. Now don't laugh when I tell you this. Every toilet I find is either filthy, overflowing, or out in the open where everyone can watch me take a dump. It's the most frustrating of all my dreams. And it happens often."

"Disgusting!" said Max.

"Damn right," Ernie replied. "Hey, I told you not to laugh! But I know it's just a dream. Maybe it has something to do with the fact that my mother never wanted me to use a public toilet when I was a child. Who knows? But I got over it. I can use a public toilet now without wondering if it would overflow while I'm sitting there," Ernie continued, trying hard to hold back his own laughter. "You'll get over Lorelei, too."

"I suppose you're right," Max said. "Wanna get together Saturday for a few drinks? I could come down to New Brunswick."

"Sure," said Ernie. "How about meeting me at nine at Hub City?"

"See you then," Max said.

Max opened his economics notebook to prepare for next week's final exam. After one hour of studying, he became tired and went to sleep. The following morning all Max could remember about his dreams was that he played baseball. He experienced a few brief flashes where he was driving a car, and another one where he was sitting alone, in a rowboat on a mountain lake. But there was no girl with a blond ponytail. No visions of Lorelei in his dream that night.

When Max arrived at Hub City, Ernie was already seated at the bar, chatting with Jared Stevens, one of his friends from Rutgers. "Over here," he called to Max, who joined them and sat down next to Ernie.

"Blue Moon," he said to the bartender. Ernie introduced Max to Jared and they shook hands.

"Nice to meet you," said Max as Jared stood up and said, "You, too, Max. See you in a bit. I'm going to circulate for a while."

"Good guy, Jared," said Ernie. "He's a junior, also majoring in Education. I met him just this year. So," Ernie continued as he turned his attention back to Max, "you're going to teach world history at Fair Lawn High School."

"Yup," Max replied. "And you'll be teaching special ed in East Brunswick."

"Isn't it interesting how many of our gang will become teachers," Ernie said. "John's teaching phys ed, David will be teaching biology, and Susie will be teaching first grade in Milnes. Holy cow, this is amazing."

"Hey, we might never be rich, but we'll be making a difference," Max replied.

"And we'll have pensions when we retire," Ernie chuckled.

"I'll drink to that," Max replied, as he chewed on the slice of orange from his Blue Moon beer and put the rind back in the glass. Max and Ernie clinked their beer mugs, shook hands and then gave each other a bro-hug.

"What are you doing this summer?" Max asked.

"I'll be working as the pool manager at the Livingston Swim Club," Ernie said. "You have any plans yet?"

"Not yet," Max replied. "At least not for the full summer. My folks are helping fund a three-week trip to Europe right after graduation. I figure what with my teaching world history, it'd be a good idea to visit some of the historic sites that I'll be teaching about. I'll be leaving sometime in June and returning in July. I should be able to get a part-time job somewhere until school starts in September."

Max's European sojourn began with a whirlwind trip to Germany during the second week in June. Then he went to Poland, Prague, France, and Spain where he visited as many historic landmarks and museums as time allowed. He planned to spend the last five days of his trip in England, specifically, London and Manchester. Max realized that a trip to Manchester would be capricious, but he was determined to find out if anything in his dreams about Lorelei made sense. He didn't even know whether the name of the street she lived on, Derby Street, even existed. But if it did, wouldn't it be reasonable to find out if there were a Golding family living there? He would already be in England, so what did he really have to lose?

While in London, he Googled Derby Street in Manchester. If there were none, he'd return home directly from London. To his amazement, there was, indeed, a Derby Street in Manchester. His heart began to race. Could there possibly be a real girl named Lorelei living on Derby Street? Might there be some psychic power at work?

After two days of sightseeing in London, Max began to feel anxious about his upcoming trip to Manchester where he hoped to find out whether his dreams for the past seven years were more than mere fantasy. On the third morning he boarded a train at Euston Station and counted the minutes during the three-hour ride to Piccadilly Station. As soon as he disembarked from the train, he hailed a taxicab and asked to be taken to Derby Street (making sure to pronounce it 'Darby').

"What address, sir?" asked the cabbie.

"I don't know. Just any house on Derby Street," Max replied.

Derby Street ran for less than a mile between North Street to just beyond Waterloo Road. It was noon when they arrived at the corner of North and Derby. Max went from door to door for the next two hours asking if anyone knew whether a family by the name of Golding lived nearby. Reaching Waterloo Road, he was disheartened at his lack of success. He hailed a taxicab and asked to be taken to city hall, where he thought they would probably have records on file of the local residents. Max jogged up the stairs and into the main hall where he saw a directory on the wall that listed the various departments and their room numbers. Max noticed that the Office of Vital Statistics was in Room 104, just down the hall. He opened the door and saw a tall, thin man with thick, horn-rimmed eyeglasses. He was seated at a long counter, working on a computer. Behind the man were three rows of records stacks. At first the man did not notice Max standing in front of him. "Excuse me, sir," said Max. "Can you help me?"

"Oh, forgive me, young man," the clerk said looking up, just a tad startled. "I was so engrossed that I didn't see you standing there. We're trying to put all our records online. Have to keep up with the latest technology, right?"

"Yes, I suppose so," Max replied.

"How may I help you?" asked the clerk.

"I'm looking for a family by the name of Golding. I think they might have lived on Derby Street some time ago."

"Do you know the address?" asked the clerk.

"I'm not quite sure," Max replied. "I don't know whether they still live there right now. Perhaps they moved."

"Let me check the books in the stacks," the clerk said. "They're not on the computer yet."

"I really appreciate your help," said Max.

"No problem at all," said the clerk. "It's been a slow day. I'm glad to get out from behind the counter. You seem like a nice young man. I'm glad to help. Now what was that name again?"

"Golding," Max said. "Please see if there's a Lorelei Golding."

The clerk walked to the second row of stacked books, the ones beginning with the letter G. "Aha," he said, and removed a large book from the shelf and laid it on a table at the end of the row of shelves. The letters on the spine read 'GOF-GOM'. "If it's anywhere, it'll be here," the clerk said. After flipping through several pages, the clerk stopped at one with the heading, 'GOL'. "Should be on this page or the next," he said.

Max peered over the clerk's shoulder as he watched him run his finger down the page, column by column, until at last the clerk announced, "Here it is, Golding; Stanley Golding, 110 Cheetwood Road."

Max's heart beat with excitement as soon as he heard the clerk mention the name Golding. *Is it really possible?* Max wondered. "Nothing on Derby Street?" Max inquired.

"That's the only Golding I have listed near where you asked. Cheetwood Road is right around the corner from Derby Street."

"All right," Max said, his voice trembling with the anticipation of speaking to someone named Golding. "Thank you so much."

"You're quite welcome, young man," said the clerk. "Have a lovely day."

It was now almost 5 pm. Max decided to find a hotel before it was too late. He would contact Stanley Golding in the morning. "Oh, one more thing," Max asked the clerk. "Can you recommend a reasonably priced hotel in the area?"

"The Hallmark Inn's a decent place, and they serve breakfast, as well," the clerk replied. "I can look up the number for you."

"Thank you again," Max said, as the clerk handed him the phone number.

Max called the hotel and reserved a room for two nights. He hailed a taxicab, checked into to the Hallmark Inn, had an early dinner, and made his plans for the following morning to call on Stanley Golding. Max got little sleep that night. He tossed and turned for hours in anticipation of what tomorrow's meeting with the Golding family might bring. The next morning, he dressed quickly, bolted down breakfast, approached the desk clerk and asked, "Do you have a telephone directory?"

"Yes, we do. May I help you with a number?" the desk clerk responded.

"I'm trying to find a Stanley Golding on Cheetwood Road," Max said.

"Ah, here it is," the clerk said. He wrote the number on hotel stationery and gave it to Max.

"Thanks so much," Max said, and went over to the phone booth in the hotel lobby.

"Hello, Golding residence," said Betty Golding.

"Hello, my name is Max Steinberg. Is this the home of Stanley Golding?"

"Yes, who did you say you are?" Betty responded.

"Max Steinberg, from New Jersey. I'm looking for Lorelei Golding."

There was a long pause before Betty responded. "Let me put my husband on the phone," she said. "Stanley, there's a Mr. Steinberg here inquiring about Lorelei Golding."

Stanley Golding took the phone from his wife and said, sternly, "Who is this, and what's this about?"

"My name is Max Steinberg. I'm visiting from America, and I wondered if there were a girl by the name of Lorelei Golding in your family?"

"How did you hear of Lorelei, and why do you want to know?" Stanley said abruptly.

As the man mentioned Lorelei's name, Max's mind began to whirl. *Oh my god*, he thought, his heart racing, *she actually exists*. Thinking quickly, Max responded, "Friend of the family. It might be easier if I explained in person rather than on the phone. May I please come over and speak with you? Just for a few moments, please," Max pleaded. "I'm staying at the Hallmark Inn right now."

"Who did you say you are?" Stanley Golding asked. "Is this a joke?"

"Please, Mr. Golding, it's not a joke. My name is Max Steinberg from New Jersey, in the United States. I'm trying to find Lorelei Golding. May I please come over?"

"It's a gentleman from America, Betty," Stanley said after hanging up the phone. "He asked to come over, and I told him it would be all right."

"Why did you invite him?" Betty remarked. "You don't even know him."

"Well, he sounded like a decent sort. I'm sure it will be okay."

Max took a taxicab to the Golding's home on Cheetwood Road. He walked nervously up to the door, pausing for a few moments to calm his nerves. Then, as if in slow motion, he moved his hand toward the doorbell and pushed the button, hearing the ring inside the house. Max felt the tension mount. His heart once again began to pound as the door opened to reveal a man is his late seventies, accompanied by a woman of the same age standing in the threshold.

"Hello, I'm Max Steinberg," the young man said. "We spoke earlier on the phone. Thank you so much for allowing me to come. I won't take much of your time. May I come in?"

Stanley and Betty eyed Max up and down, from his hair to his face, to his Montclair University sweatshirt, to his shoes. Finally, sensing and hoping that the pleasant-looking young man standing in their doorway did not pose a threat, they invited him into their home. Although still a bit uneasy, they escorted Max into their living room and offered him a seat on the sofa. "Now what's all this about my Aunt Lorelei?" Stanley said.

"Your...aunt?" said Max, stunned at Stanley's saying "Aunt Lorelei."

"My aunt, Lorelei Golding. The woman you said you wanted to ask me about. Actually, that was her maiden name. Her married name was Blume. Why are you inquiring about her?"

Max immediately felt the blood rush from his head. His throat became dry and he thought he was going to pass out.

"Are you all right?" Betty asked. "You look as if you're going to faint." She brought him a glass of water. "Here, drink this."

"Thank you, Mrs. Golding," Max said. "I guess I'm in a bit of a shock." Max drank the water slowly, finally regaining his composure. "You said that Lorelei Golding was your aunt?" Max asked, his mind still whirling, trying to comprehend what he just heard about the young girl he had dreamt of for so long.

"Yes, she was my aunt," Stanley replied. "She died back in, let me think a moment, back in 1995 I believe, at age 90."

Once again Max felt a wave of lightheadedness. "May I have a little more water, please," he said, handing the glass to Betty.

"Of course, dear," Betty said as she went to the kitchen and returned, handing a full glass of water to Max, which he downed completely.

"May I ask, where is she buried?" Max asked.

"She's in Blackley Cemetery, over on Victoria Avenue. But again, why are you asking about her?"

In a fit of desperation, Max quickly devised the only logical explanation he could come up with. "My grandmother, Sadie, used to know her, but I don't know how they met." Max said, hoping his face didn't give away the lie. "My mother asked me to look her up when I got to Manchester, so that's why I'm here. She told me that Lorelei lived on Derby Street."

Satisfied that Max was on the level, Stanley responded, "She did live on Derby as a girl. Then the family moved to a larger home a few houses down, here on Cheetwood Road. After she married my uncle, Benjamin Blume, they moved to another house just around the corner on Broughton Street. It was nice that the family stayed in the same neighborhood. We were all very close. Come to think of it, I believe today is the anniversary of Aunt Lorelei's death, June 27th. Check that Betty, would you luv?"

Betty went to the bookcase and returned with a family bible. Turning to the back page, she said, "Indeed, here it is Stanley, June 27, 1995. Twenty-three years ago, today."

"Thank you so much for your time and hospitality," Max said as he stood and turned to leave. "I really must be going. I'm leaving day after tomorrow to return home to America. It was a pleasure meeting you both."

"You are most welcome, young man," said Betty. "It was a pleasure meeting you, too. We were glad to help you find your grandmother's friend."

"My thoughts as well, Max," said Stanley. "Interesting coincidence, now that I think of it. Max was also the name of my cousin, Lorelei's son. He passed on in 2012, at the age of eighty. Well, have a safe trip home, young man."

"Would you mind if I went to see her grave at Blackley Cemetery? I think my mother would appreciate seeing a picture of the grave stone. You know, with her name on it?" Max asked.

"Why no, not at all. I suppose that would be nice," Stanley replied. "Goodbye now."

Max left the house still in a daze. *How was it possible,* he thought, *that he and Lorelei shared dreams across the miles as well as the years. About 3,000 miles and 100 years. How could that be? What kind of mystical force could have been at work that brought them together, and why?* These thoughts continued to baffle Max beyond the point of curiosity. Max was convinced that something otherworldly was overriding all reason and sanity. It could not be explained, only accepted on faith.

Wait until I tell Ernie, was all Max could think about. He turned right on Derby Street and walked to Waterloo Road, where he hailed a taxicab to Blackley Cemetery. The taxicab driver left Max at the cemetery's administrative office, where he inquired about the location of Lorelei Golding's gravesite. The clerk opened his registry ledger and, after searching for a few moments, said that they did not have anyone by that name buried there. "Wait just a moment," Max said, "Check under the name Lorelei Blume."

"Ah, yes, here it is, Lorelei and Benjamin Blume. Just a short walk from here. Go out toward the rear of this building, up Cudworth and left onto Broomhall. Go through the arch of the Bishop Street Synagogue, Plot number A113."

"Thank you," said Max.

Max was glad that the weather was warm and pleasant on this late day in June. As Max entered the Bishop Street Synagogue gate and approached Plot A113, he noticed a young woman placing a bouquet of flowers on Lorelei's grave. The headstone read *LORE-LEI (LEAH) BLUME, Beloved Wife, Mother, Grandmother. 1905-1995.*"

Max approached the grave slowly and quietly. The young woman wore her long blond hair in a ponytail, with a scrunchie and a big blue bow. She turned to face him. He was stunned to see that she looked so much like the girl in his dreams.

"Hello. Who are you?" the young woman asked.

Still shocked at the girl's resemblance to Lorelei, he stammered, "My name's Max Steinberg, from America. Stanley Golding told me where to find Lorelei's grave. I think my family may have known the Goldings a long time ago. Anyway, I teach, or at least I will be teaching world history in the fall when I return home. I've been spending the last three weeks traveling in Europe to visit historic sights that I can relate to my students. I'm leaving day after tomorrow."

"Oh," the young woman responded, unfazed by Max's rambling and accepting his explanation. "Stanley is my uncle. Lorelei Blume was my great-grandmother. I always try to visit her on the anniversary of her death, which is today. I was named after her. Her Hebrew name was Leah; that's my name. You said your name was Max, right?"

Max nodded, silently, staring intently at Leah. He still could not believe the similarity to the young girl he dreamt about for so many years.

"That's curious," Leah continued. "That was my grandfather's name, too. Lorelei's son. But no one seems to know whom he was named after." After a moment's pause, Leah continued, "Some people in my family say I look just like my great-grandmama," she said pointing to the gravestone.

Max continued to nod, still marveling at the resemblance. "Do I know you from somewhere?" she asked. "Have we ever met? How long have you been in Manchester?"

"I just arrived here yesterday from London," said Max, unable to take his eyes away from Leah. They stood silently for a while, staring at the gravestone of Lorelei Blume. Then Max broke the silence. "Say, would you like to get a cup of coffee or something?"

Gazing intently at Max, Leah replied, "I think that would be nice. There's a pleasant tea shop out on Victoria Avenue, not too far from the cemetery. I usually go there after I visit great-grandmama. It's called Tea and Me."

"I'll go to the office and ring for a taxicab. I'll meet you at the tea shop," said Max.

"You know, I have a good feeling about you. We can take my car."

"Are you sure?" Max said.

"I'm sort of partial to chaps named Max," Leah said. "Let's get better acquainted."

"I'd like that," Max said. "I'd like that very much."

Leah and Max both searched on the ground for small stones that they could place on Lorelei's headstone, a custom they observed when visiting a cemetery. Then they left together to enjoy a cup of tea.

The Woods

LIVING "OFF THE GRID" in the woods gives me and my family the freedom to be ourselves to the fullest. No government intervention, no religious restrictions, and only the limits of nature in her beauty and grandeur to follow our hearts, minds and our own sense of morality and justice. Which, if I do say so myself, enables us to live in peace and harmony with our fellow woods dwellers who have taken up residence alongside us. We relish the outdoor aromas, living with the Earth, surrounded by nature. Our neighbors are close enough to share our feelings, yet far enough from our home not to infringe on our space. The only rules here are: live and let live. My parents chose this life, theirs before them, and even earlier generations recognized that civilization was no longer an option for them.

These woods offer scarce resources so we live mostly hand to mouth. But that's the choice we've made in this lifestyle. It's harsh at times, but we still have our freedom, despite the hardships. We have all learned to cope. We stay together as a family and maintain loyalty to each other.

Not having access to shopping malls and supermarkets, we have to depend on our own foraging skills to find food. As vegans, our family has succeeded in finding grains, seeds, nuts and other edible forms of vegetation. There have been times when pickings were slim, but we managed. Some of us have, out of necessity, ventured off to a house adjacent to the edge of our woods to scavenge some scraps of discarded food. I'm not too proud of having to have done that, but when times are hard, one takes what one can get. On balance, we believe it's worth it.

Normally, our days are filled with fancy freedom. We play, we wander at our own pace, wake up whenever we want, and go to sleep the same way. But each of us is aware of the existential dangers that we face daily. We have to teach them diligently to our children and to our grandchildren.

Summers are pleasant. Food is plentiful, water is available, and life is easy. But winters are worse. It's often difficult to harvest enough food during the summer and store it for the winter, since we don't have refrigeration. Streams are sometimes frozen, but there are places where the ice has broken so we can have sufficient drinking water.

Not long after the sun rose today, I stepped outside my home to take in the fresh air, to enjoy the forest breeze on my face and take pleasure in the glorious scent of pine coming from nature in the woods. Living in the woods imparts a heightened realization of one's senses in contrast to the noise, grime and pollution of what civilization has become. In the woods, natural aromas are intensified, hearing becomes sharper, food is more palatable. You feel so alive and in touch with the Earth.

No matter how free we profess to be, living our lives as we see fit, we are constantly scanning our surroundings for intruders who are determined to eradicate us, often through acts of extreme violence and just plain cruelty. If anyone senses the presence of one, they are quick to sound the alarm to warn the rest of us. We all depend on cooperation.

This morning I was one of the first to venture out and, because it was early and quiet at that hour, I was able to hear the sound of impending doom. My strong sense of survival kicked in instantly. I dashed between two boulders, crouched silently and held my breath, careful not to rustle the leaves around me or make a sound. The flying monster passed overhead without noticing me and, fortunately, did not return. My life was spared. That experience is our way of life in the woods. But, I fear, it's just as bad in the civilized world outside the woods.

As I related earlier, it's hardest in winter. We have to collect whatever we can find to sustain us virtually every day, even when the flying monsters may be watching and waiting for us. We try to avoid going out during daylight in winter and do most of our food gathering in the evenings, by moonlight. If we venture out to the edge of the woods, we have to be extremely cautious about the giants who take pleasure in killing us.

Giants, for the most part, live outside the woods. Often, they venture in, seemingly for the fun of it, or just to track us down and kill us. Flying monsters live high above in the woods as well as outside. Last week, we mourned the death of my cousin and, I'm sad to say, one of my own sons who fell victim to the flying monsters. A month ago, my sister, who lives just down the path from our house, became an easy mark for one of the giants. We're still mourning the losses to our family. But life goes on. We go on. We won't succumb to the tyranny of the civilized life outside the woods. The woods is our home.

Why do they hound us? I don't understand what we have done to incur their wrath. Taken a few scraps of food? Is that sufficient to warrant our deaths? The deaths of my friends and neighbors who mean them no harm? Apparently, the giants think it is. The flying monsters seek us out and snatch us away. So many of my family members and friends have been carried off to their deaths. Why? Are our beliefs and values so different from theirs that we must pay with our lives? Who declared this war on us, if that's what it is? I certainly didn't start it. I just want to live my life without fear of hunger, capture or despair. So long as there are giants and flying monsters, we must resign ourselves to the fact that they consider us inferior beings.

I always believed that all creatures were created equal, that no one creature is superior to another. That we have a right to live our lives in peace. So why were the giants and flying monsters created? And by whom? Do their size, strength or special ability to fly grant them dominance?

But now, all this philosophizing has stimulated my appetite. Let me put these thoughts aside for a moment while I search for something to eat. After that, I'll continue my story. I'm at the edge of the woods now. The light is fading so I think it might be safe to venture out a little farther. I don't see any flying monsters or giants in the area. Ah, I smell the aroma of peanut butter that someone has apparently failed to wrap tightly. I'll just...

SNAP!!!!

"Hey, honey. Looks like we've caught another one of those pesky field mice. I'll set another trap tomorrow."

The Flower Box

"IS EVERYONE HERE?" said Impatiens, as she fluttered her pretty red and white petals, shaking off the remaining fragments of potting soil after being planted. "I don't have all day, you know. We're here to make this flower box beautiful," she continued as she glanced at the other newly planted flowers in the box.

Mr. Man was proud of the special flower box he built on his deck to keep the deer away from "deer salad" that the local nursery manager called the flowers. Mr. & Mrs. Man would then be able to enjoy their beautiful flowers outdoors, since the deer couldn't climb onto his deck.

Impatiens continued to watch the other flowers who, like her, were still fluttering their petals and trying to settle into their new home. "All right," she said, "I'll start the introductions. I'm Impatiens."

"Oh, hi," Marigold piped in. "You can call me Mary. Don't I look nice and bright with my yellow and gold petals glimmering in the sunlight? You know, Mr. Man put me here to keep the deer away. They probably won't climb up onto the deck, but here I am anyway. Probably because I'm so pretty," she said, chuckling. "You know, I can also repel dogs, moles, voles, rabbits, racoons..."

"That will do, Mary," said Petunia. "We get your point," she said, sarcastically. "What a bunch of fuddy-duddies you all are," she continued. The other flowers glared at her. "Well, anyway, my name's Petunia. You know, like Porky Pig's cute girlfriend? Only I'm much prettier than a pig, and slimmer, as you all can see."

"And I'm Daisy," said her neighbor. "like the duck. Donald's girlfriend. So, you see, Miss Petunia, you're not the only one with a boyfriend."

Forget Me Not spoke up next. "Please don't forget about me," she said shyly, her blue petals reflecting her mood. "No one ever seems to remember my name. I'm a Forget Me Not. Please everyone, just call me..."

"Okay, ladies, I'll take it from here," the tall Snapdragon said in a loud voice, rudely interrupting Forget Me Not. "You all may notice from my snappy colors that I'm a snapdragon. But don't worry, I don't breathe fire, so you're all safe. I'll watch over everyone."

"Hey, you guys," said the last of the bunch. "I hope you all don't mind me sharing your box out here. I know I'm not as colorful and as pretty as you are, but I think that Mr. Man just likes to have me around."

"Yes, you are indeed different from us. What are you?" asked Impatiens. "What's your name, already?"

"Oh, please permit me to introduce myself. I'm Venus Fly Trap."

"You don't look like a flower," said Daisy.

"I'm a bit more of a plant," Fly Trap said. "I'm different from you vegans," he continued. "I'm a meat eater," he added proudly.

"A what?" asked Marigold. "Are you sure you belong here in the same pot with us?"

"Hold your horses, Mary," quipped Impatiens. "He may be a little different, but he's still one of us. Don't ever forget that we're all in this together. Let's just settle in and get comfortable with each other and keep Mr. Man's deck beautiful. By the way," she continued, "I could use a drink. Is anyone else thirsty? Where's the water? Has anyone seen whether Mr. Man brought water? What's taking him so long. I'm going to wilt."

"Take it easy, girl," said Petunia. "We're all thirsty. I saw Mr. Man take off his gloves right after he finished planting Mr. Venus Thingy over there and go into the house. I'm sure he was probably going to get some water for us."

"That's *Venus – Fly – Trap*, Miss Piggy, if you don't mind," he said, emphasizing each word separately.

"Whatever," Petunia responded.

"Let's not forget what Impatiens said, that we're all in this together. We have to get along," said Forget Me Not.

"For sure," added Marigold. "We all so pretty, each in her own way. And, of course, in *his* own way," pointing her leaf towards snapdragon. "No fighting, please."

"Do I have to take charge of you girls?" Snapdragon bellowed. "I mean, I'm the tallest one here and, if I wanted to, I could block out your sunlight. But I'm a gentleman flower and I promise to respect all of you. Let's not get our petals in an uproar."

"He's right, girls," said Forget Me Not. "Remember what I said before? We'll all last longer throughout the summer if we share everything from the soil. That includes the water as well as the sunlight. Let's be friends."

"What did you say your name was?" asked Impatiens.

"Well, I didn't really get a chance to introduce myself..." Forget Me Not started to say, when Snapdragon interrupted again.

"Hold on everyone," he said. "I can see Mr. Man returning with a watering can."

"Well, it's about damn time," Impatiens said, with her petals akimbo. "Hey, Mr. Man, over here. Water me first."

"Hold on, missy," said Petunia. "We'll all get water. Have you got ants in your pants already?"

"Ants? Did somebody say ants? Where? Where are the ants?" asked Fly Trap, starting to drool.

"Easy there, big fella," said Petunia. "It's just an expression. There aren't any real ants here. At least, not yet."

"Well," said Fly Trap, "If you do see any, just send them my way. For now, the water will be okay, but I could really go for some hamburger," he continued, drool running down his stem. "Maybe even a beer. Just kidding, water's fine. Looks like you're really enjoying your drink, Impatiens."

"Oh, I needed that," she replied. "I felt like I was drying up like a prune."

"I hope Mr. Man gives us some more water in the morning from now on," Daisy added. "Late afternoon watering can ruin our leaves."

"Daisy's right," Marigold said. "We could develop gray mold or attract aphids and other bugs. Yuck."

"Yuck is right," Petunia added. "I had a cousin that was infected with red spider mites. It was *horrible!*" she said, sobbing. Tears ran down her petals. "They had to dig her out of her bed and bury her."

All the flowers remained silent for a few moments, focusing on Petunia's sorrowful story. They thought of how each of them might be susceptible to such an awful fate. The silence was broken by Impatiens.

"Nope, nope, no way is that going to happen to me," she said. "I take care of myself, and you all should, too. I'm not going to let any grass grow under my stem."

"All right ladies, enough of that talk," said Snapdragon. "You're just going to upset yourselves and wilt. I'll keep watch over you. It's getting late and the sun's setting. Fold up and try to get some sleep."

One by one, the flowers bade each other good night and, folding their leaves, prepared to settle in for the night.

The bright sun invigorated the flowers the next morning. Marigold began to shake the dewdrops off her petals as she greeted the new day and her new friends. "Good morning, everyone," she exclaimed. "Y'all sleep well?"

Impatiens was the first to respond. "I had a wonderful night," she said. "I dreamt of moist soil, sweet fertilizer and a bright sunshine. I even dreamt that a honey bee was tickling my pistil. It gave me the shivers. I woke up bright and shiny this morning, over an hour ago; wanted to be first to welcome the dawn. It's so exciting being in this box, with all of you, I just love it here. Don't you all love it?"

Daisy complained that it took her a long time to fall asleep in her new bed. She awoke a little grumpy, rubbing her big yellow eye with her white petals. "Please don't use that word, 'love' so much, would you?"

"Why not, Daisy?" asked Petunia. "What's wrong with 'love?'

"Yeah," Forget Me Not piped in. "Don't forget that everyone needs love, don't they?"

"Look, Miss What's Your Name," Daisy said, infuriated. "My people have been victims of 'love' ever since we were created. How would you feel being torn apart every time some damn fool can't figure out for themselves whether someone loves them, dammit? 'She loves me, she loves me not.' It's murder, flowercide, plain and simple. What are we, fortune tellers? We just sit here, looking pretty, then they yank us out of bed, tear our petals off, slowly and painfully, one by one until all that's left is our one friggin' eye." Daisy's frustration morphed into tears as she continued, "Then they...they just toss us in the trash." She began to sob, after which her anger returned, "And they still can't figure it out. What's the point? Love sucks, big time."

The flowers shared glances, as they listened to Daisy's rant. Impatiens broke the silence. "You've got quite a case there, Daisy," she said, attempting to console her. "I, for one, would not stand for it. If anyone tried to pull off my petals for something as stupid as that, I'd spit in their face."

"What are you gonna spit with?" said Petunia, recognizing the futility of it all. "We flowers don't have any control over humans. Now if we were poison ivy, or that Audrey plant from *Little Shop of Horrors*, it would be different."

"Gee, I never thought of that," said Marigold. "I suppose I'm lucky to have so many more petals than you. If someone tried to play 'She loves me, she loves me not' using my petals, they'd probably be too old to do anything about it by the time they figured it out."

"Thanks for your support, girls. But it won't help. Just try to keep the deer away, Mary," Daisy sighed, her big yellow eye welling up with tears.

"Ladies, don't you think that's enough negativity?" Snapdragon bellowed. "Remember that we're all beautiful flowers, created to keep the world smelling sweet and looking nice. Let's not forget what 'What's Her Name' said about trying to all get along. We all share the same box. We either live together or we'll die together."

"That 'What's Her Name' is me," said Forget Me Not. And just look what's coming our way," her excitement growing. "The sun's not up a half-hour and Mr. Honey Bee wants to sample our pollen."

"Me first," shouted Impatiens. "I love when those bees rub their hairy legs all over my stigma. My pistil's getting excited just thinking about it."

"I've got a pretty good-looking pistil, if I do say so myself," said a confident Snapdragon. "You all know that I'm quite a guy, but you should also know that I've got a feminine side, too. With my height and all my fancy blossoms, I think that bee will come to me first."

"Screw the lot of you," Daisy said, bragging and all aglow. "He's on in me right now. That's it, honey boy, do your thing. Ooh, baby baby, do it right there. Don't stop." As the bee flew away, Daisy sat still for a moment. Noticing that the bee had gone, she continued, "What? Is that all you got? That's it? A quickie and then you're off to one of your other girlfriends? All right, go. See if I care."

Finally, Venus Fly Trap opened his mouth. "It looks like Daisy enjoys being deflowered. Come on over here, Mr. Big Boy Bee. I'm ready for you. Come and get a treat like you've never had before!"

"Come to me next, you sweet bee," coaxed Forget Me Not. "Don't you remember me from last time? It was only a couple of days ago at the village nursery. Don't tell me you've forgotten me already!"

Forget Me Not had a beautiful singing voice as well as a pretty face. The flowers all swayed back and forth, as she began serenading Mr. Bee with Beverly Bremers' hit song from the 1970's about unrequited love, *Don't Say You Don't Remember.*

Forget Me Not was in full performance mode when Venus Fly Trap interrupted. "Forget about Mr. Bee, girl. He's on his way over here. Come on, big boy. I'm waiting just for you."

Petunia watched Mr. Bee flit from one flower to the next, leaving each one without giving them a second look. "Oh damn, he's gone," she said, "Just like all those sons of bees." Her frown turned into a huge smile as another flying creature approached. "Wait, is that what I think it is? Yes. Yes, it is! A butterfly who's come to suck my nectar." Petunia spread her petals wide with delight and invited M. Butterfly in. To her delight, M. Butterfly landed on Petunia and extended his long proboscis into her center.

"Just look at that slut," Impatiens said, "Opening up like that, right in front of everyone. Has she no shame?"

"She thinks she's all that," Marigold piped in. "Just because she can spread those petals."

"Ohh, ohh, Oooooooooooh," Petunia finally moaned. "Come again soon," she called as M. Butterfly flitted away.

As calm returned to the flower box, the flowers straightened their stems and groomed their petals. A sudden outburst from Forget Me Not broke the silence and tranquil mood.

"Oh my god," she shrieked. "Is that what I think it is?"

"Oh crap," said Marigold. "It's a fly. An ordinary, common, disgusting housefly. Keep away from me, you filthy excuse for a life form."

"Don't even think of landing on me," yelled Daisy, covering her good eye with her petals.

"I don't want him near me, either," said Snapdragon. "Oh, god, he's headed my way. Ooh, he's on me. Get him off. Shoo fly, shoo!"

"Shoo him over to me," begged Venus Fly Trap. "I'm hungry. I already have my mouth open. Hurry."

Mr. Fly buzzed and hovered around the flowers, one by one, causing each of them to cringe in horror. Finally, Mr. Fly was lured by the sweet aroma of Venus Fly Trap's breath, as he kept his huge jaws wide open. Within a moment of Mr. Fly's landing, Trap's jaws slammed shut, beginning the digestion process that would result in the demise of Mr. Fly. Each of the flowers turned and watched in silent horror as Venus Fly Trap consumed the fly. After a short while, Fly Trap opened his mouth. "That was delicious," he exclaimed. "I'm up for seconds."

"Yuck," shouted Daisy. "How can you eat that crap? Do you know where he's been? He spends half his time in animal poop and doesn't even wash afterwards! It's disgusting."

"Flies, bees, caterpillars, ants, mosquitos – whatever. They're all my meat. I don't care where they play or what they stepped in. You gals can worry about the aphids, earwigs, or whatever bugs you. Send them to me; I'll eat them all," Venus Fly Trap responded with glee.

As the flowers shrugged their petals in disdain, Snapdragon admonished Venus Fly Trap, "You know Fly-Eater, you are one disgusting carnivore."

"Comes with the territory," Fly Trap explained. "We've all got our own thing. I mean, that's what I was created to do. Why don't you all just go back to standing there and looking pretty. I'll take care of the bugs."

"Let's forget about Venus Fly Trap for now, and enjoy the beautiful warm weather," said Impatiens. "We'll be dead at the end of the summer. That goes for all you: Daisy, Petunia, Snapdragon, Marigold, and What's Her Name over there."

"It's Forget Me Not," a meek voice chimed. "Why can't anyone remember my name?"

The flowers basked in the sunlight throughout the summer. They bathed in the warm rain showers, welcomed visits from the bees and butterflies, and even took pleasure watching the occasional fly give Venus Fly Trap his sustenance. Mr. Man watered them several times a week, and fed them special growth fertilizer every so often. As they flourished in the flower box, they enjoyed knowing that they were appreciated by Mr. and Mrs. Man who sat on their deck drinking Piña Coladas and Margaritas on warm afternoons.

As the summer months drifted into autumn, the flowers realized that the change in weather and temperature did not bode well for them. Some shivered, some began to lose petals, and they all fought the natural impulse to wither.

"Ladies," said Snapdragon, "it has been a privilege knowing and sharing this flower box with you. My beautiful blossoms have been attacked by spider mites, and my stems have been attacked by aphids. It's been a hard-fought battle against them and, now that we're coming to the end of our season, I'm tired."

"Most of my beautiful white petals have turned brown, and some have even fallen off," said Daisy. "I'm having a hard time sucking up water from the potting soil, and think I've about had it, too."

"Last night's near frost didn't help," said Marigold. "Fortunately, I've still got my pretty yellow and gold petals. But I feel like I'll be wilting soon."

"I'm going to miss visits from my favorite butterfly," Petunia lamented. "The way he unfurled that long thing of his into my center, sucking up my nectar. Oh, my god, did I love that. He's left now and my nectar is just about all dried up. I'm ready to go, too."

"I'll never forget you guys," Forget Me Not reminisced. "We had some good times together, didn't we? But I'll be gone soon as well."

"I still have trouble remembering your name," an embarrassed Impatiens added, "But I know that you're a real sweetheart. It's been a good run, my dear companions. I think we can all fade away happily now."

"Boys and girls," Fly Trap grinned, "it's been a real high sharing the pot with you. I think Mr. Man will be here soon to uproot you all and bury you in the backyard. Here's where I leave you, though. You guys are only good for this one season. I, on the other hand, can live on for up to twenty years or so. I heard Mr. Man telling Mrs. Man that he's taking me indoors for the winter. I think he said he's got an ant problem. Yum!"

The Double Dee Dee

The Double Dee Dee is a scary old bird
That lives in a mountain cave.
He does what he pleases,
He bothers and teases,
And is never the one to behave.

Watch out and beware
Of the Double Dee Dee,
He has twice as much as you.
Though his body is single,
His legs and arms mingle,
Because they are four each, not two!

Take care how you speak
To the Double Dee Dee,
He hears twice as much as you say.
With four ears in his head,
He can tell what you said
Before your mouth gets it away.

He has two eyes in front
And two in the back,
And this makes it easy to see
Each move you are making,
Each step you are taking,
And he never will let you go free.

He'll lure you inside his dimly lit cave,
And before you know what is what,
He'll have you all beaten,
And chewed up and eaten,
And where you once were, you are NOT!

A Hair's Breadth

September 2018

PHIL DAVIDSON examined the top of his head critically in the bathroom mirror, as he did each morning before beginning his daily routine: brushing his teeth, shaving and making an almost fruitless attempt at combing what was left of his rapidly thinning hair. He was only 38 years old, but he was going bald rapidly. Phil's father was completely bald by the time he was 39, as were both grandfathers by the time they reached their late-30's. Phil's baldness was right on schedule. All else considered, he was in good shape. At 5'-10" and 175 pounds with a 34-inch waistline, Phil always exhibited an air of confidence. Going bald, however, was agonizing. Phil exhaled a long sigh, after which he completed his bathroom routine and returned to the bedroom to get dressed for work.

Donna had just awakened when Phil returned. Phil loved the way she stretched and yawned when she awoke. Wearing only her Eli Manning #10 New York Giants jersey, her long auburn hair hanging down to her shoulders, Phil noticed that she was still quite sexy, even at seven o'clock in the morning. At the age of 35, he thought she was even more beautiful than the day he married her, ten years earlier. "Good morning, handsome," she said, her arms wrapped around her knees that she pulled up to her chest. She was still thinking about the fabulous evening of passion they shared the night before.

"You'd better make sure Billy is awake and ready for school," Phil responded. "While you're at it, please put on some bottoms. That Jersey's a bit short. Billy may only be eight years old, but he's not too young to know what's going on, if you know what I mean."

"That kid's too smart for his own good," Donna joked. "Matter of fact, he's already been asking me some very pointed questions. I told him that you'd have 'the talk' with him soon. Are you up for it, yet?"

"I suppose I'll have to be," Phil replied, as he began to get dressed. Switching to a more serious tone, he continued, "Sweetie, do I look like I'm going bald?"

"Bald, schmald, who cares? You're handsome, athletic, fit, and what's more important, you're mine and I'm still madly in love with you," Donna said, as she pushed the covers aside. She got out of bed, put on a pair of pink panties and headed toward Billy's room, giving Phil a long, affectionate kiss as she went by. Phil finished dressing and, while tying his necktie, glanced in the bedroom mirror once more, scrutinizing his balding scalp.

"Hey Donna, how would you feel if I went to one of those Hair Club Society places and got fitted for a toupee? Or if I just shaved my head? It's either the Mr. Clean look or a full head of fake hair. I'm not too crazy about this 'almost bald' look, whaddya think?"

"Stop it, Phil, you're perfect the way you are," she called back from the hallway. Peering into Billy's room, she said, "Billy, get dressed."

"I'm still tired, Mommy," Billy moaned.

"You better wake up fast then. School's not going go wait for you."

Billy sat at the edge of his bed, his feet dangling above the floor. He removed his favorite Thomas the Tank Engine pajamas. "What should I wear, Mommy?"

"You know what to do," Donna replied. "Pick out a shirt from the drawer. Then take your jeans off the hanger in your closet. You're old enough to know how to get dressed." Donna walked into Billy's room and kissed him on the forehead. "Hurry up. I have to go downstairs and make breakfast for you and daddy."

Donna loved the newly redecorated kitchen of their home in Summit, New Jersey. She especially enjoyed the butcher block table and island. She put up a pot of coffee, whipped up her perfect scrambled egg recipe, made toast, and poured a glass of milk for Billy.

Billy finally sauntered into the kitchen wearing blue jeans, high top sneakers with the Velcro closings, and his favorite NY Yankees logo tee shirt with the number 2 on the front and the name, "JETER" on the back.

Donna looked at him and said, "Good job, Billy, you look handsome, just like daddy. Now sit down and eat your breakfast."

As Billy took his favorite seat next to his father, Phil nudged his fingers through his son's thick head of blond hair and said, "How's my boy today?"

"Good," said Billy. He adored his father and loved sitting next to him at the breakfast table. He especially loved Donna's perfect scrambled eggs. Phil sipped his coffee, winked at Billy and said, "What would you think if I shaved my head like Mr. Clean, Billy? Or do you think I'd look better with a full head of hair?"

"I dunno," Billy replied. "Maybe hair."

"Will you stop this already?" Donna interjected, scowling. "It's no big deal."

"All right," Phil replied. "But I still want to think some more about it. Hey, buddy," he said to Billy, "are you ready for school?"

Billy nodded, downed the rest of his milk, wiped his mouth with his shirtsleeve, and got his jacket and backpack. He returned to the kitchen, kissed his mother and announced, "I'm ready, Daddy."

Donna wiped the corner of Billy's mouth where he missed some crumbs. She kissed him and said, "Use your napkin, Billy, not your sleeve. And have a good day at school." She kissed Phil on the cheek and said, "You have a good day, too, Mr. Clean." Phil returned her kiss and said, "We'll see. Love you."

"Love you more," Donna countered.

Phil drove Billy to the corner just as the school bus arrived. He kissed his son on the forehead and watched as Billy ran to get on the bus. Then he headed off to work.

Donna was in no particular hurry to clean up the kitchen as it was only 8:15. She didn't have to report to work until 10 am at the Summit town library, where she was head librarian. The drive took only ten minutes, so she had plenty of time for a second cup of coffee. She peered out of the kitchen window into the backyard, marveling at the orange and yellow hues of the tall maple trees that separated their backyard from their neighbor's. The morning sun glistening through the trees added a bright, sparkling ochre hue to the leaves. She thought to herself, *the leaves are so beautiful and look like they've been painted. It'll soon be time to begin raking them again."*

She put her empty coffee cup in the dishwasher, cleared the kitchen table, and went upstairs to make the beds before leaving for work.

Phil arrived at the Provident Savings Bank building on Ridgedale Avenue in Morristown, where he had recently been promoted to Vice President and Loan Officer in charge of corporate accounts. Phil was considered one of Provident Bank's rising stars, and was looking forward to moving even further up corporate ladder. He parked in his reserved spot and went into his office. He opened his computer to his daily calendar and, scanning his schedule for the day, realized that it would be a light one with no appointments scheduled, and only a few accounts to evaluate. He opened his bottom desk drawer and took out the coffee mug that Billy gave to him last Father's Day with the words, "World's Best Dad" printed on the side. In the employee's lunchroom he noticed that someone had generously brought in a box of Dunkin' Donuts. A note was taped to the side of the box that read, "Happy Birthday to Me – Enjoy a Donut." It was from Cheryl, the Assistant Branch Manager.

Happy Birthday, Cheryl, Phil thought, as he took one of the three remaining donuts (jelly) and returned to his desk with his coffee, black, no sugar. Sipping it slowly, he scanned the room, studying how much hair each man had. He continued this obsession throughout the day. It didn't take long to conclude that he had the least amount of hair, or so he thought. It was then that he made the decision. He wanted a full head of hair.

April 2015

Karl Dovshenkov was born in Rostokino, a suburb of Moscow, to a family of little means. His father had been a shoemaker who died when Karl was fifteen years old. His mother, a housemaid, worked long hours to make ends meet. They lived in a small rented house with two bedrooms, one of which Karl shared with his younger brother, Anton. The brothers slept together in one bed and shared a dresser that barely fit in the corner of the room. Karl vowed to create a better life for himself. He had experienced poverty and wanted desperately to become rich.

Karl studied diligently in school and was admitted to Moscow University where he excelled in electronics. But he saw no way of attaining wealth in Russia by following the rules. To achieve his goal, he sought and developed friendships with a number of shady characters who helped him become involved with the Russian Mafia.

By the age of 45, Karl was recognized as being shrewd and unethical in business. A tall, burly man with full head of thick, curly black hair, he demonstrated technical strength in the field of electronics, specifically miniature integrated circuitry, transistors and solid-state componentry. He was also an excellent salesman with the ability to cajole, persuade and manipulate people into buying almost anything he was selling, whether they were products or ideas. He was known as "the man who could sell ice to Siberians in winter."

Aleksei Malkovsky, one of Russia's most successful, wealthy and brutal oligarchs, had taken a liking to Karl, whose expertise in electronics helped Malkovsky enhance his unscrupulous business dealings and further his position in the Russian mob. Money laundering was a well-established practice in Malkovsky's organization. His plans to expand his empire outside Russia, particularly in the United States, involved sending Karl to America to establish a money laundering business for most of his illegal operations.

"You have a beautiful, thick head of hair," Malkovsky said to Karl, "and you probably take it for granted. Are you aware of how many men are bald, or going bald prematurely? I've noticed many bald men in America during several of my trips there. So, let me tell you, my dear comrade, what I have in store for you. I have decided to set up a toupee company in the United States that will help us "clean up" some of our money, as well as manipulate the foolish Americans to make us even richer. With your knowledge of micro-circuitry and sales ability, we can't fail."

"Just tell me what to do," Karl responded eagerly, excited to be selected by Malkovsky to head this new project, one that he believed would also add to his own personal wealth.

"Come with me," Malkovsky said. "Let us go to the electronics lab that you helped set up for me." An array of men's full-head wigs and toupees lay on the workbench. Each hairpiece was different, and was positioned according color, length, and style. Nearby, several bins contained a variety of miniature capacitors, transistors and other electronic componentry as well as some spools of extremely fine tungsten and platinum wires.

"I want you to develop an undetectable miniature circuitry system that can be attached to each toupee," Malkovsky instructed, "so that anyone who wears the toupee can be commanded to obey our orders and directions."

"To what end?" asked Karl. "You told me that it would help funnel the money through the American business, but what would you have those men do, once under our control?"

"Don't be naïve, Karl," said Malkovsky. "We can have them do anything we want them to do for our benefit. We could have them affect politics, manipulate stocks, even rob banks if we tell them. Once they've completed their purpose, we get rid of them."

"You mean kill them?" Karl asked, his eyes wide open in surprise. "Seriously?"

"If need be," replied Malkovsky. "One way or another."

"All right with me," Karl laughed.

"Okay, then," Malkovsky said. "You can get started developing the prototype first thing tomorrow morning. Let me know what assistance you require. And I want you to be ready to proceed within two months. I'd like to get this project moving as quickly as possible."

"I think I can do that," Karl replied. "I'll need an expert in electronics and telecommunications, and a specialist in human anatomy and physiology – someone who is also an expert in understanding brain waves."

"Recruit whoever you need," Malkovsky advised. "I don't want any mistakes," he demanded.

The next morning, Karl set about developing Malkovsky's plan. His first call was to Boris Klemkov, whom he had known at Moscow University, and who had become an electronic engineering superstar. Boris was excited about the idea of working with Karl and agreed immediately. At Karl's suggestion, Boris contacted a friend, Fyodor Padarofsky, a medical technician who had worked with several neurosurgeons at Moscow General Hospital. Both men were as greedy, unscrupulous, and as unethical as Karl, and were eager for the opportunity to work for Aleksei Malkovsky. The following afternoon Karl had his team in place.

Under Karl's direction, the three men worked tirelessly testing various electronic communication systems. After three weeks of sixteen-hour days, they developed a device that converted a voice signal into an electrical impulse that could be decoded by the brain and translated into command signals. It would work like a telephone dialed directly into the brain. They completed and tested the voice command system the following week, taking another two weeks to make it impervious to water, shampoo, perspiration and hair spray. After a total of six weeks, they felt that they had perfected the device.

Proud that they were two weeks ahead of schedule, they invited Malkovsky to conduct the final test phase in the laboratory.

"I am eager to see your demonstration. Which one of you will wear the toupee to show me how it works?" Malkovsky said. Boris immediately stepped forward with an air of confidence announcing, "I will wear the toupee, Mr. Malkovsky."

As Malkovsky watched with anticipation, Fyodor fitted a toupee on Boris' head. He adjusted the mesh net to a perfect fit, then combed the hair to make the toupee look natural.

"Boris, you are a handsome devil," said Malkovsky, "I want you to go into the anteroom outside the lab and sit with your back to the window wall, facing away from us."

Boris smiled back at Malkovsky and did exactly as he was told. Once seated in the anteroom, he could not hear or see what was happening in the lab.

"Here, sir. It's your call now," Karl said to Malkovsky, handing him a communication device that looked like a cell phone. "The communicator converts a voice command into an electronic signal, which is then forwarded to the microchip receiver implanted in the toupee's mesh," Karl explained. "The receiver then sends a signal to a micro-converter, also embedded in the mesh that, in turn, directs an electric impulse to the brain. Just give Boris a command and watch what happens," Karl said, proudly.

Malkovsky began his instructions to Boris. Karl and Fyodor watched in anticipation with their faces pressed against the window that divided the anteroom from the lab.

"Boris," Malkovsky instructed, "stand up and raise both hands above your head." Boris immediately stood and raised both hands above his head. Malkovsky nodded his satisfaction. "Boris," he continued, "hop up and down on your left foot three times, then do the same on your right foot."

Karl and Fyodor chuckled as they watched Boris dancing, clumsily, following Malkovsky's commands.

"Boris, come into the lab and face the workbench," Malkovsky instructed. Once again, Boris did exactly as he was told.

As he entered the lab, Karl noticed Boris' face was void of expression. "Boris," the big man said once more, "put one hand on the bench with your palm downward." Boris obeyed his leader's instructions, his face again expressionless. The lab workbench was crowded with toupees, mesh, spools of titanium and platinum wires, needle nose pliers, screwdrivers of various sizes and other miscellaneous laboratory tools.

"Boris," Malkovsky continued, "pick up a screwdriver from the table, lift it over your head and jab it down into the back of your hand as hard as you can."

As Karl and Fyodor gasped, Boris once again followed Malkovsky's command, and plunged the screwdriver completely through the back of his hand, making a dull thud as it hit the bench. Boris immediately screamed in pain as blood surged from the gaping wound in his hand, spilling onto the floor.

"I just want to see how effective your system can be," Malkovsky said with a bitter grin.

Karl and Fyodor ran quickly to their injured comrade. Karl pulled off the toupee, while Fyodor removed the screwdriver from the back of Boris' hand. "What just happened to me?" cried Boris as he reeled in pain and watched the blood gush from his hand. "What did I do? Why did I stab my hand?" They quickly escorted a sobbing Boris to a chair where they bandaged his wound.

"Shh, quiet down," said Karl. "You're all right. Just a minor incident in the test. You'll be fine."

"I'm pleased with what I've seen," said Malkovsky. "You're a week ahead of schedule so I want you to run some more tests, just to make doubly sure that we're all set. Then let me know if you think we're ready to proceed with the start up. Now take Boris over to the hospital."

"Whatever you say, Mr. Malkovsky," said Karl, as his leader turned and left the lab.

Fyodor took Boris to Moscow General Hospital, where a colleague with whom he had worked while on staff treated Boris' hand without asking any questions. "Boris will heal just fine," the colleague said. "He'll have some pain for a while, and maybe lose about ten percent of his hand's mobility, but he will be okay. Have him take one or two of these pills for the pain."

The next morning, Boris sat on a stool in the laboratory nursing his bandaged hand while Karl and Fyodor straightened out the laboratory bench equipment, wiping it clean of Boris' bloody hand print.

"How's the hand doing this morning?" asked Karl.

"It will be all right, I suppose," replied Boris. "But it still hurts. The pain killers they gave me at the hospital help a little."

At that moment a messenger knocked on the door of the lab and announced, "I have a special delivery for Boris Klemkov. Is he here?"

"That's me," said Boris, as he scrawled his signature on the receipt for the brown envelope. The envelope was from Aleksei Malkovsky. The note inside read: "My dear Boris, I appreciate your loyalty. Keep up the good work."

The envelope contained 66,000 rubles, the equivalent of $1,000.

"I really would have preferred not to have stabbed my hand," Boris said to his comrades, "But I'll gladly take the money."

The next few days were spent further perfecting the device. They created a variety of frequencies that could distinguish one toupee from another. The system worked like a telephone, assigning a 10-digit number to each toupee which allowed them to dial each toupee wearer so that the specific commands to be implemented. Boris and Fyodor both agreed to become guinea pigs and put on a toupee under Karl's command, with the proviso that he would not tell them to do anything that would cause them any further pain or harm.

"Please don't tell me to stab my other hand," Boris said, half joking.

"Not this time," Karl replied with a laugh. He gave Boris and Fyodor separate commands first and then the same command to each of them in tandem, testing whether the commands would work identically, which they did. Karl notified Malkovsky that the final series of tests were successful.

During several of his visits to America, Aleksei Malkovsky had spent some time in New Jersey with his business associates. He was fond of New Jersey and decided that this was where he would set up the new company headquarters of International Hair Associates. Karl would be the president, Boris the vice president of operations, and Fyodor the vice president of research. Malkovsky's international contacts proved invaluable in securing visas and work permits for the three men. Everything seemed to be going according to plan.

August 2015

Once he arrived in America, Karl Dovshenkov moved quickly to set the plan in motion. Malkovsky had given each man a substantial amount of money in order to find suitable living accommodations in Wayne, New Jersey, a town with a modest Russian population. Under instructions from Malkovsky, Karl, Boris and Fyodor took on the appearance of upstanding and reputable immigrants to the United States. They were cordial to their neighbors and kept a low profile. Each had established a working knowledge of English while in Russia, but also took ESL classes to become even more proficient.

Karl identified a suitable location for the company in Morristown. He opened a business bank account with Provident Bank, one of the largest in Morristown, with ample startup funds that Malkovsky wired from Moscow to the Ridgedale Avenue Branch. They established their office on the second floor of a professional building near the grassy mall area in the center of town. Within two weeks of acquiring the lease, they finished decorating it and were ready to begin operations.

Karl hired Jeanne Norman, an attractive, smartly dressed woman in her early thirties as the receptionist and hostess for their new office in Morristown. Each man had his own office, and there were two fitting rooms in the back. With Jeanne's help, Karl hired an advertising and public relations agency to run both print and television ads He joined the Morristown Chamber of Commerce in order to increase local awareness of his new business. They placed their first ad in the Morristown Daily Record, which also ran a *"Meet Our Newest Neighbor"* article for the newly established hair restoration company. Karl also advertised in *The Star-Ledger, The Bergen Record* and *The New York Times.* The local CATV station, *Morristown This Week,* invited Karl, Boris and Fyodor to appear for an interview. The publicity campaign worked amazingly well. Within a week, the company had received more than a dozen telephone inquiries. They were in business!

Karl knew that it was extremely important to determine which clients would be suited to their plans – which of them had significant access to huge sums of money. He realized that not every new client who wanted a toupee would qualify for their brain control scheme. Each prospective client was required to complete a legal form that contained a hold-harmless agreement, as well as a questionnaire containing personal information relating to their health, reason for obtaining hair restoration and, most importantly, their employment, job description, and financial status. As to the latter, Karl wanted to learn the client's ability to access cash. Those who met his criteria would have their toupees wired for control.

IHA's first three clients were a local butcher, a barber and a dress shop owner in Morristown – none of whom could access the amount of cash that Karl wanted. Accordingly, they were just fitted for regular toupees and sent on their way.

Steve Sheeran, their fourth client, became Karl's first test candidate. Steve was a 35-year old successful stock broker and financial advisor at the Charles Schwab office in Morristown. He owned a comfortable book of clients and managed a portfolio of several million dollars. His toupee would contain the microchip control device. Steve selected his new hair style, which Fyodor fitted with the controlling devices. He instructed Steve to sit in the reception area for a short while before leaving. The first test on an unsuspecting guinea pig was about to begin. Karl picked up the controller in his office and dialed the code assigned to Steve Sheeran's toupee.

"Steve, I want you to go to the magazine rack and select an issue of *GOLF Magazine*," Karl commanded. Steve rose from his seat, approached the magazine rack, selected *GOLF Magazine* and sat down to read it. Pleased with the initial successful command, Karl continued.

"Steve, put the GOLF Magazine on the floor then walk to the magazine rack and select *Better Homes & Gardens Magazine*." Following Karl's command, Steve dropped the *GOLF Magazine* on the floor, selected *Better Homes & Gardens* and started leafing through the pages unemotionally, paying no attention to the content.

"Steve, put both magazines back in the magazine rack," Karl ordered, "and return to your seat as you would normally." Again, Steve followed the instructions exactly as commanded. Fyodor and Karl came out to the reception area and approached Steve as he sat in his chair.

"How do you feel?" Fyodor asked him.

"Fine, I suppose," Steve responded. "Is there anything else I need to know?"

"I want you to come back in one week so we can check you over," Karl replied. "We want to make sure everything is in order and that you feel comfortable. Please make an appointment with Jeanne."

"Is 4:00 pm next Tuesday all right with you?" asked Jeanne.

"Perfect. See you next Tuesday afternoon at four," said Steve. He shook hands with Karl and Fyodor, then left the office. Karl and Fyodor returned to Karl's office and, with Boris, opened a bottle of Champagne to celebrate what appeared to be their first successful victim.

Steve Sheeran returned the following week promptly at 4 o'clock. His hairpiece was checked, tested and found to be acceptable. Steve was delighted with his new look. "My wife loves it," Steve said to Karl, who smiled.

The following morning, Steve Sheeran stole $2 million from his clients. He deposited the proceeds into his personal bank account, after which he withdrew the full amount in cash and put it into an attaché case. He drove to the bus terminal in Morristown and placed the attaché case in locker #39. Next, he went to Karl's office and handed the locker key to Karl. Steve Sheeran returned to his home in Florham Park, locked himself in the bathroom, filled the bathtub with warm water, undressed, got into the tub and slit his wrists with a sharp kitchen knife. His wife, Sheila, screamed as she found his lifeless body in a tub of crimson water when she returned home from work that evening.

During the ensuing week, a second victim, Larry Windon, was identified, fitted with his hairpiece, magazine tested, and sent on his way. Windon was a CPA for Nuodor Chemicals with access to the company's balance sheet and financial statements.

One month later, Larry Windon drove his Buick through the side guard rail of the Garden State Parkway overpass in Saddle Brook, killing himself as well as the two passengers in the car he landed on as his car crashed down on the roadway below. Two days earlier, Windon had embezzled $3 million in company funds that had somehow disappeared from Nuodor's books, and mysteriously into the hands of Karl Dovshenkov.

Three months after that, Bruce Woodmere leapt to his death from the Bayonne Bridge after robbing Resorts Casino & Hotel in Atlantic City, where he had been employed as the Head Cashier. Karl, Boris and Fyodor added yet another $2 million to their wealth, sharing it, of course, with Aleksei Malkovsky. Another bottle of Champagne was opened in celebration.

For the next two years, Malkovsky funneled illegal profits he made in Russia through the IHA's accounts. The company appeared to be highly successful, lining his pockets and those of the three Russian comrades in Morristown. By the middle of 2018, three years after opening the business, Karl and his cohorts had stashed away over $11 million. The newspapers reported a total of nine unexplained suicides and seemingly accidental deaths during that time period. The only similarity between them was that each had stolen or embezzled huge sums of money just before they died. Nothing was detected or suspected about each man wearing a hairpiece – at least, not yet.

October 2018

"Donna," Phil said at breakfast, "we have a client at the bank in the hair restoration business called *International Hair Associates*. They've been with us right here in Morristown for a little over two years. Their office is not too far from my office. I know you're not thrilled with the idea of my wearing a hairpiece, but lately I've been losing a lot more hair. They appear to be successful and I'd like you and Billy to come with me to see what they have to offer. I have an appointment at 10:30 am on Saturday."

"I see you haven't given up on the hairpiece idea. All right, if it will make you happy, I'll go," said Donna, unenthusiastically. "Might as well get it over with."

"Thanks, sweetheart, I really appreciate it."

Donna pursed her lips and glared at him, after learning that he had already made the appointment without consulting her. "What I do for love," she said. Phil kissed her and left for work.

Phil set his alarm clock for 8:00 Saturday morning. His plan was to take Donna and Billy out for breakfast at IHOP, Billy's favorite place for pancakes, then drive into Morristown to meet Karl Dovshenkov for his appointment. They arrived at 9:45 and were greeted by the Jeanne, the receptionist.

"Good morning, Mr. Davidson," Jeanne said, "Karl's expecting you. Please have a seat. He already has the application you filled out earlier this week. Wait right here while I go get him."

"You already filled out an application?" said Donna. "That was rather ballsy of you, before even discussing this meeting with me."

"Well," said Phil, "I sorta figured you'd go along. Please don't be mad at me. At least let's see what it looks like."

Donna breathed a long sigh. "Whatever," she replied, disappointed.

Karl entered the reception area from a door behind Jeanne's desk that was marked *PRIVATE*. He opened his arms wide and greeted Phil as if he were a long-lost family member. He was accompanied by Boris and Fyodor, who greeted Phil and introduced themselves to Donna. Karl then knelt down on one knee and shook hands with Billy.

"Hello, young man," Karl said, and offered him a Tootsie-Roll lollipop.

Giving her son a slight nudge, Donna said, "What do you say, Billy?"

"Red, my favorite, thanks," Billy responded as he retreated, shyly, behind his mother.

"These are my associates, Boris Klemkov and Fyodor Padarofsky," Karl said. "Shall we go back to our fitting room? You can try on several of our newest hair pieces and see which suits you best."

Karl was eager to acquire another financial client, especially one who worked in a bank. More easy millions would be on their way to Karl's coffers. Jeanne escorted the family to Fitting Room #1, where Fyodor had up several toupee samples for Phil to try on.

"These are some of our finest creations," Karl said to Phil as he pointed to five hairstyles that were arrayed on Styrofoam head-shaped dummies. As Donna and Billy watched, Fyodor assisted Phil as he tried on each one of them. Each time Phil put on a different hairpiece, he turned to Donna, "What do you think?" he asked.

Before Donna could answer, Fyodor piped in, saying, "Just remember, this is not how the toupee will look in its final position. We'll make all the necessary adjustments so that it will look completely natural. No one will even know the difference."

With each hairpiece that Phil tried on, Donna said nothing but merely shrugged her shoulders. When Phil asked her what she thought, she replied, "Sweetheart, I know how much you said you wanted hair. But I don't think you should make this decision right now. Can't we discuss this more at length, at home?"

"Is that really necessary?" Karl chimed in. "You look totally marvelous with any one of these pieces. Do you really need your wife to decide for you? You can make that decision yourself, can't you, Phil?"

Phil watched Donna recoil at Karl's comment and immediately responded, "Karl, my wife is right. I don't want to rush into anything without discussing it with my family. After all, this is an expensive proposition and I'd like their input before I make my decision. I appreciate your time and I'll get back to you first thing Monday morning."

Phil and Donna shook hands with Karl, Boris and Fyodor and left the office, leaving the three Russians disappointed and frustrated. "Let's go have some lunch and talk this over," Phil said.

"No honey, I'd prefer to go directly home and discuss it there," Donna replied, placing her hand on Phil's forearm.

"Sure, sweets" Phil said. "I understand your concern. We'll go straight home."

Upon arriving home, Donna led Phil and Billy directly into the upstairs bathroom.

"All right, Phil, look in the mirror," said Donna. Billy sat on the edge of the bathtub, watching.

"Phil," she said, "You're a damn handsome man who happens to be losing his hair. I love you, and I love the way you look."

"But Donna," Phil protested, "going bald makes me look older. I'm not so sure I feel comfortable this way."

"You don't look older," she continued. "I'd even love it even more if you shaved your head and grew a goatee. Actually, I would like the Mr. Clean look on you. So many men are doing it these days. And, it's extremely sexy."

She then turned to her son. "Billy, I'd like your opinion, too."

"What is it Mommy?" Billy asked.

"What did you think of daddy with those hairpieces on his head this morning?"

"Well, I kinda thought at first that daddy would look better with hair, but when I saw him with the fake hair, I thought he looked so different, a little funny sorta," Billy responded. "Daddy," he continued, "why don't you shave your head just like Johnny's daddy does?"

Phil bent down and lifted Billy into his arms, hugging him. Then Phil and Donna each planted a big kiss on Billy's cheeks. Phil put Billy down and studied himself in the mirror once again, tilting his head from side to side, examining what was left of his hairline. After a moment, he turned to his wife and said, "All right, Donna, let's do this. Hand me my razor."

Epilogue

Local authorities in northern New Jersey and New York became suspicious of the alarming number of suicides during the two-year period from October 2018 to October 2020. An investigation found that *International Hair Associates* had caused the deaths, mostly by suicide, of forty-eight individuals and had reaped nearly $100 million as a result of their mind control scheme. Further inquiries turned up irregularities in their income tax filings that opened the door to their money laundering and tax evasion tactics.

The FBI stormed the offices of International Hair Associates on the morning of October 5, 2020 and arrested Boris Klemkov and

Fyodor Padarofsky on charges of attempted murder, racketeering, money laundering and tax fraud. Karl Dovshenkov, who would also have been arrested under the same charges, was nowhere to be found. He had been called back to Russia by Aleksei Malkovsky to attend a Board of Directors meeting of IHA. Immediately following the meeting, Karl was taken to the outskirts of Moscow where Malkovsky's henchmen took over. His body was never recovered. Malkovsky had become aware that Karl, in his greed, had been skimming funds off the top from IHA, having pocketed more than $5 million.

Boris Klemkov and Fyodor Padarofsky were tried in U.S. Federal Court and were convicted of all charges. Each was sentenced to life in prison. Warrants for the arrest of Karl Dovshenkov and Aleksei Malkovsky remain outstanding.

Ten years later, at the age of twenty, Billy Davidson, like the men preceding him in his family, would experience major hair loss. In keeping with men's fashion of the times, he would shave his head and achieve the "Mr. Clean" look. His girlfriend would say, "That's what attracted me to him in the first place."

What in The World?

IT SURE IS QUIET HERE. Not to mention lonely. Where am I? Where is this place and how did I get here? When did I get here? I'm just here. Alone in the dark. By myself. Quite frankly, I think I'm becoming a bit bored. Like, there's nothing to do here. But wait, I think I hear voices off in the distance. They're singing, chanting almost, sweetly. I can't see who they are, but I'm certain that I can hear them. I must be in some kind of sensory deprivation chamber. Yes, that's probably where I am. But who, if anyone, put me in here? And why did they put me in here, completely isolated. I can't remember anything before being here. And it feels like I've been here for an eternity. Maybe that's why I can't recall anything about my past, or anything else for that matter. Do I even have a name? If I do, I can't even recall it. No matter, it'll probably come to me sooner or later.

So, here I am, alone with only my thoughts for company. Still a bit bored. And then there's those faint sounds of melodious voices somewhere out there, off in the distance. They do seem rather calming. Background music, so to speak. Speaking of my thoughts, perhaps my time here should be spent thinking, in contemplation, pondering right and wrong, good and evil. I should come up with some kind of philosophy. Yes, that seems like a good idea.

Let's begin with what's right and what's wrong. That is to say, is there or should there be an absolute right or an undeniable wrong? Seems to me like a good place to start. Is there a perfect good or an absolute bad? Or are they relative terms? Gives one pause, doesn't it? If I were in charge, if I had total control, in other words, if I were the quintessential judge, I think I might be able to define right and wrong, good or bad in absolute terms. Yes, that would give me total control, wouldn't it? I think I'd like that. Wait a moment. Total control over what? I'm still in this place, this void, if you will, with no sense of what's beyond this place. Or whether if there is anything beyond this place. Once again, without knowing where I am, how long I've been here, how long I'll remain here, what's outside of here, and with no sense of memory whatsoever, there doesn't seem to be any reason for thinking philosophically, does there? I mean, since I may have been here for an eternity, perhaps I'll remain here for eternity as well. Interesting speculation, if I do say so myself.

So much for philosophy, at least for now. Perhaps people should create their own individual philosophical precepts. Wait. People. Are there any people? I haven't heard anything from or about people for...I don't know how long. Those singing voices could belong to people, but I'm not sure about that. No, I think they're something else. I can't remember ever seeing people, come to think of it.

I really wish I weren't so alone, isolated and in the dark. If I could, I'd just walk over to the light switch and turn it on. But I don't have any sense of feeling that I could walk or reach out and actually touch something. It would be nice, though, if all I had to do was say, *"Let there be light!"*

Upon those words being uttered, a light with such indescribable intensity as never before, flashed with an immense *BANG*. The energy thus emitted was so powerful that the astronomical amount of matter scattered at unrecognizable speeds in every direction, unbounded, seemingly to infinity.

I must have had that power all along, thought the Voice. Perhaps I won't be so lonely from now on. My goodness, just look at all that matter going every which way. And so fast, mind you. Some pieces are even joining together to make larger pieces. Amazing, if I do say so myself. This is truly interesting. Before I do or say anything else, I should probably sit here and watch what happens, how things change and how they evolve. Yes, evolution. I think that's a good idea. Just observe and don't get involved. Maybe, just maybe, in a few billion years or so, there'll be people on one or more of those little rocks that are forming as a result of that big bang. That would be nice. And you know what? They'll probably develop their own philosophies, their own sense of right and wrong, good and bad. Some may attribute them to me, others may not. I hope they appreciate what I've done. If not, no matter. They'll figure it out by themselves. Maybe I'll drop by now and then just to see how it all turns out. But for now, I think I'll just hang around here in the dark and watch what happens. Perhaps I'll even find it amusing. At least I won't feel lonely anymore.

Lost in the City

Melvin and Shirley

MELVIN ADDLER awoke to a beautiful, sunny June Saturday morning, the first day in the new apartment that he and his wife, Shirley, had just moved into on 81ˢᵗ Street between Columbus and Amsterdam Avenues, on the Upper West Side of New York City. He yawned, that wake-up yawn that clears the head after a solid night's rest. He rubbed his eyes, then gazed at the woman lying next to him. She was still asleep, her long blond hair curled around her neck. He stared at her bare shoulders above the covers and the comely shape of her body underneath. *My god,* he thought, *how lucky am I to have found, let alone married, such a beautiful woman.*

Melvin and Shirley had always wanted to live in the city, close to theaters, museums, restaurants and within an easy commute to their jobs. Both worked in midtown Manhattan, less than thirty minutes from their apartment. It was an ideal location. They were happy to have found an apartment within their budget, especially having spent the first three months of their married life relegated to the spare bedroom of Shirley's parents' home out on Long Island.

Melvin got out of bed and went into the kitchen and brewed a pot of coffee. He then went into the bathroom, brushed his teeth and washed, but decided not to shave this morning. As he stared at yesterday's five-o'clock shadow in the mirror, he noticed Shirley approach behind him, one strap of her silk nightgown slipping down off her shoulder, and her long hair flowing down one side of her face, like Jessica Rabbit, the vixen from the movie, *Who Framed Roger Rabbit?* "Good morning, good lookin'," she said in her sexiest voice.

"Good morning yourself, gorgeous," Melvin replied, as he pulled her tightly towards him and kissed her passionately.

"Now that's the way to start the weekend," Shirley beamed.

"I'll show you an even better way," said Melvin, as he swooped her up in his arms and carried her back into the bedroom. After laying his wife down gently on the bed, he removed his New York Yankees tee shirt and, by the time he removed his plaid shorts, Shirley had already slipped out of her nightgown and was lying in wait for him, the bed covers tossed aside.

"Nothing's better than Saturday morning sex," she said after they made passionate love. She leaned towards Melvin and kissed him on the lips and then on the tip of his nose. "I'm hungry now," she continued. "Since you made the coffee; I'll scramble the eggs."

Breakfast finished, Melvin and Shirley decided to take a stroll through their new neighborhood. They stopped to say hello to most all of the local merchants who, in turn, greeted them warmly. They met Armando, the green grocer on the corner of 83rd and Columbus, then Gwen, the florist next door to Armando's. They introduced themselves to Ivan, who owned the newsstand around the corner on 82nd street. They continued to meander up and down the streets for the next two hours, introducing themselves to store owners, then on to window shopping and people watching, all the while holding hands and smiling at each other as newlywed lovers often do. "I'm so glad we decided to live here," said Shirley. "I think we're going to like it."

"I'm with you on that," Melvin responded. "How about a quick bite of lunch? Why don't we try that place right over there, across Amsterdam, the Apollo Diner?"

They crossed the street and entered the diner where they were greeted by Dimitri, the owner, a short man of about sixty. He had an olive complexion and long black curly hair. He sported a huge moustache, twirled and waxed at the ends making him look like he was an advertisement for a men's facial grooming product. He escorted them to a booth and handed them menus. Cathy, the waitress, followed closely behind Dimitri, deposited two glasses of water on the table and, smiling, said, "What'll it be, lovers?"

Melvin and Shirley ordered burgers and coffee. "I think we lucked out with this place," Shirley remarked.

"I'm liking this part of town more and more," said Melvin. "Feels more like a small town than a big city."

Shirley reached across the table and squeezed Melvin's hand. "I really do love you," she said.

Michael and Alice

"Honey," Alice Yang said to her husband, Michael, "We need to go over to Key Food for some groceries. Would you please get the shopping wagon out of the front closet?"

Alice always used a wire shopping wagon when she went to the supermarket on the corner of 44th Street and Fifth Avenue, only two blocks away from their apartment on 46th Street in the Sunset Park section of Brooklyn. It was Saturday, a beautiful spring day. Like most Saturdays, Alice and Michael took their four-year old son, Luke, with them to do their weekly food shopping.

Michael and Alice Yang enjoyed living in the diversity of Sunset Park, comprised largely of Asians and Hispanics, with somewhat smaller populations of Whites, African Americans, even Native Americans and Pacific Islanders. Notably, the majority of the neighborhood lived in harmony.

Both Michael's and Alice's parents had emigrated to America from China. Michael was two years old when they arrived; Alice was a first generation Chinese-American, born here. Both families settled in Sunset Park and met each other in the Brooklyn Chapter of the Chinese Consolidated Benevolent Association known as Chong Wa. The Yang family and Alice Tsai's family became friends almost immediately. When Michael and Alice were children, they played together at family outings and other social activities sponsored by Chong Wa. They particularly enjoyed swimming in Sunset Pool during the summer. Over the years, Michael and Alice became increasingly fond of each other, falling in love as teenagers and, to the delight of their parents, finally getting married. Their parents were thrilled when Michael and Alice remained in the same neighborhood.

Michael taught eighth grade math at Montauk Intermediate School in Borough Park, only a fifteen-minute ride on the Number 11 bus. Alice took the subway to her job in midtown Manhattan where she was the IT Manager for an insurance services company. Luke was a regular at the Sunset Park Day Care Center, only a few blocks from their apartment, and an easy walk to the subway station for Alice.

Together Alice, Michael, and Luke rode the elevator down from their sixth-floor apartment and walked to the Key Food Supermarket on 44th. As they strolled along Fifth Avenue, Michael kept a firm grip on his son's tiny hand because Luke often liked to chase a pigeon, or run after a dog.

Victor Romano, owner of the florist shop waved, along with a "Hi Mr. and Mrs. Yang" greeting. "Beautiful day, isn't it?" Michael was a frequent patron of Victor's establishment, often surprising Alice with a bunch of flowers for no special occasion. Sue Lee, the Korean owner of Sunset Cleaners, spotted them through her front plate glass window and waved as she lifted her head from hemming Mrs. Salvatore's new dress. Sue loved to watch people pass by, often waving to her favorite customers.

Alice, Michael and Luke enjoyed walking on the sunny streets on their way home from Key Food. Alice towed the shopping cart laden with four bags of groceries, and Michael carried a fifth bag in one arm while holding Luke's chubby hand with his free hand. Alice had made sure to buy cold cuts for the family lunch, which she prepared soon after they arrived back to the apartment. Luke especially liked bologna on soft rye bread with spicy brown mustard. After lunch, they walked the two short blocks to Sunset Park, where Luke loved to climb the monkey bars and use the swings in the playground. Alice and Michael sat alongside other young parents watching their children at play without a care in the world. They were also eagerly awaiting the opening of Sunset Pool. They planned to give Luke swimming lessons when it opened July 1st.

Zoey and Gunner

Mark and Carol Wiley lived in Rocky River, a quiet suburb of Cleveland, Ohio. Mark commuted the nine miles to work at Cleveland's Museum of Natural History where he was the Executive Director of the Cleveland Archeological Society. On Tuesday and Thursday mornings, Mark enjoyed teaching a course on archeology at Cleveland State University, combining his expertise on the subject with his love for teaching. As part of Mark's program, he would frequently lead a student group for two weeks during the summer to parts of the Middle East and Africa to participate in archeological digs. One of Mark's particular joys of these trips was uncovering a rare relic that he displayed at the museum.

Carol and their ten-year old twins, Zoey and Gunner, always looked forward to accompanying Mark and his students on these expeditions. Zoey always found something to add to her collection of "rare finds" as she called them, whether it was a small shard from a piece of pottery, a stone, or just a few grains of sand that she would keep in a small jar as a memento of her field trips. Gunner also collected souvenirs but was more interested in the dig itself, often handing his discoveries to his sister to keep in one of her jars.

Carol was a natural educator who adored children. She was the proud recipient of the *Teacher of the Year Award* as a mathematics teacher in Rocky River Middle School. She would often challenge her students to determine the fallacy in two math puzzles she threw at them. One was the algebraic problem showing that 2=1. Another, in geometry, showed that the hypotenuse of a right triangle was equal in length to one of the other sides. The students had to determine the fallacy by identifying the improper assumption at the outset of each problem. Carol enjoyed watching her young students attack each mystery. She was delighted when someone would actually identify the fallacy. The students loved her. At Christmastime, her desk was loaded with gifts.

When the twins were small, Carol instilled in them the love for logic and solving puzzles, whether jigsaw, arithmetic, brain teasers or any other kind of solution-oriented challenges. Zoey and Gunner were outstanding athletes in their own right and played on the same Little League baseball team. Gunner was a pitcher, and one of the best batters on the team. Zoey, the catcher on the same squad, could throw the ball all the way to second base on a fly, which was uncommon for a child her age. They loved to go bowling, watch Disney movies, and especially loved to play games.

On Saturday, June 17, a beautiful and warm day that spread from the Midwest to the East Coast, Zoey and Gunner celebrated their eleventh birthday. Following the Little League game they won that morning, Carol and Mark treated the entire team to a pizza party in a private room in the back of the local pizzeria. The team and their parents celebrated Zoey's and Gunner's birthdays as well as the team's 6-0 record. Upon returning home, Mark made both children bathe and put on fresh clothes before opening their presents. "Make sure you write down the name of each child and the gift they gave you, and get ready to send everyone a 'Thank You' note," their mother reminded them.

Among the many birthday presents that Zoey and Gunner opened, tearing the wrapping paper off each one with abandon, so unlike the meticulous and careful manner in which they would attempt to uncover artifacts while on one of their digs in Egypt or Turkey, they came across two small gifts, one for each of them, beautifully wrapped in gold and silver foil. The card on one gift simply read, "Zoey," the other read, "Gunner." There was no other information as to who had sent them. Every other gift could be attributable to a child at the party. "Where did these two gifts come from?" Mark asked. "Did any of you see someone drop them off?"

"Who cares who sent them," Gunner shouted, eager to open his.

"Yeah," cried Zoey. "I wanna see what it is!"

"Let me check them out first," demanded Carol. "It could be dangerous."

"Let's not go overboard," Mark asserted. "Just open them carefully."

Carol unwrapped the gift with Gunner's name slowly and deliberately, taking care to avoid tearing the foil wrap. "Perhaps there's a name on the inside," she said. But she could find none. Nor was there a message of any kind. "It appears to be some kind of puzzle," she said, handing it to Mark.

"This reminds me of the old fashioned Fifteen Puzzle I used to play with as a kid," he said. "Only instead of the numbers, this seems to be a cityscape with a series of street scenes that you can move around to create different neighborhoods. Looks like you could slide the squares around to rearrange them into different pictures."

"What fun!" exclaimed Gunner. "Will you show me how it works?"

"Wait just a minute," Zoey bellowed. "How about my present? It's wrapped the same as Gunner's. Do you think it's the same thing?"

Mark picked up the gold and silver foil wrapped present with Zoey's name and carefully opened it, also trying not to tear any of the wrapping. Examining it carefully, he said, "Nope, no name on the inside of this one either. It's another puzzle, like Gunner's – a cityscape but with a different set of street scenes."

"Let me have it, Daddy," Zoey pleaded.

"Okay," said Mark. "But let me examine them first. We don't know where they came from."

"This is strange," said Carol. "Who would leave gifts for the kids without leaving their name?"

"Maybe it was just a second gift from one of the kids at the party that got separated from their first gift," Mark suggested.

"You're probably right, but it's still peculiar."

"Kids," Mark continued, "put these puzzles aside for now until mommy and I figure out more about them."

Zoey and Gunner continued opening their presents, delighting in every one and writing the name of the giver on each gift. While Gunner and Zoey wrote all the thank you notes, Mark began to examine the mysterious slide puzzles. "One less thank you note to write," Gunner said, as both he and Zoey laughed.

"All I could come up with," Mark said, "is that they each appear to represent a four-square block area in New York City. One of them says NYC Upper West Side on the back, the other one says Brooklyn NY. There aren't any other instructions included."

"What do you do with them, daddy?" asked Zoey.

"Yeah, how do they work?" asked Gunner.

"Well, as far as I can tell," Mark began, "you start with the existing picture and move the pieces around to rearrange the streets any way you want. Then you try to rearrange them into their original positions. That seems about all there is to it."

Intrigued, Zoey and Gunner took their puzzles to their bedroom and began rearranging the small squares, moving them up and down, side to side, creating different street patterns. They were each fascinated that so many different street scenes could be created. "This is fun," Zoey said. "It's like being a city street planner." Gunner kept rearranging the streets on his puzzle until he was tired. Finally, they both set their puzzles aside and went off to slumberland, dreaming about being eleven years old.

At the stroke of midnight on Sunday, June 18th, Melvin and Shirley were jolted by a sudden rumbling that awakened them after just having fallen asleep. Their arms were still wrapped around each other as their bed shook. Pictures on the walls rattled, furniture moved slightly and the frying pans hanging from their racks over the kitchen sink clanged as they banged in to each other. The rumbling and shaking lasted no more than three of four seconds. "Did you feel that?" Shirley said.

"I think we just experienced an earthquake," replied Melvin.

"Right here, in New York City?" Shirley asked, incredulously.

"Who knows," Melvin said. "I think I heard somewhere that there might be a fault line or two running up and down the East Coast. Perhaps one of them goes through Manhattan. Are you okay?"

"Now that it stopped, I'm fine," Shirley replied. "I didn't hear anything fall over or break." She turned and kissed Melvin. "Go back to sleep. We can check things out in the morning."

"Okay," he replied, as he put his arm around Shirley's shoulder and went back to sleep.

The morning sun broke through the bedroom curtains as Melvin and Shirley awoke to another warm and sunny morning on the East Coast. Birds were chirping in the trees outside their apartment window. They embraced once more, as the newlywed lovers they were, kissed each other passionately before arising to greet another wonderful day as husband and wife.

"How's about we go down to the Apollo Diner for breakfast?" Melvin asked. "I noticed yesterday that they had breakfast specials until eleven."

"What time is it now?" Shirley inquired.

"Nine-thirty," Melvin responded, looking at the imported Swiss Swatch watch that Shirley had given him as a wedding gift. Melvin loved that watch, and especially the sporty brown leather strap. "That'll give us plenty of time to shower and get there well before eleven."

As they walked out the front door, they froze in confusion and horror as if slamming into a brick wall. Immediately across the street from their apartment building, smack in the middle of 82nd Street, stood the Apollo Diner. Dimitri, the owner, recognizable by his thick black curly hair and moustache, was turning his head side to side in bewilderment.

"Wait a minute," Shirley said. "What's the diner doing over here? Yesterday it was on Amsterdam."

"And look to your left," Melvin continued in astonishment. "There's Ivan's newsstand down the block near Amsterdam. Yesterday it was on Columbus. What the hell is going on?"

"Could this be the result of last night's earthquake?" Shirley said.

They stared at each other, disoriented and confused at the mysterious reconfiguration of the city streets around them. All of their neighbors were just as puzzled. Shirley and Melvin walked over to Dimitri, who was still standing in front of the diner.

"I don't know what happened," he exclaimed. "I closed the diner last night just before midnight and went directly upstairs to my apartment." He pointed toward his window on the second floor above the diner. "When I came down this morning, it was like this. I think I felt an earthquake last night. Could an earthquake do something like this, without destroying anything else?"

The newlyweds stared at each other, speechless. "Let's go see what else changed overnight," Melvin said, as he took Shirley by the hand and began to walk toward the end of the street. Turning the corner, they saw confused store owners and residents, wandering aimlessly and staring at their dislocated neighborhood. Several police cars lined the street. The officers, pad and pen in hand, were interviewing neighborhood residents.

Melvin and Shirley walked farther uptown until they came to 86th Street and Columbus Avenue. Shopkeepers were tending their stores and people were walking around as if nothing strange had occurred. Shirley approached a bakery owner who was in the front of her shop, arranging some window signs. "Has your shop always been here?" Shirley asked.

"Yes, why do you ask?"

"Has it always been in the same place?" Melvin asked.

"Of course," she replied.

"Did you feel the earthquake last night?" Shirley asked.

"What earthquake? I didn't feel any earthquake,"

"Well, I'm glad that you're all right," Melvin said. "Apparently the earthquake last night was unusually localized. C'mon, Shirley, let's go home."

"Wait a second," the baker said, "I did hear a little rumbling sound last night, but I thought it might just have been a truck or something. I didn't feel any earthquake, if that's what you're talking about. Hey, are you two all right?" she called to them as they turned abruptly and walked away.

They returned to 82nd Street where they saw four local news vans on their street. Reporters were interviewing several of the residents and shop owners. They went into their apartment and turned on the TV. It was early afternoon and news of the neighborhood re-arrangement was being broadcast on radio and television. No one could explain what had happened.

"Last night an earthquake occurred in two small areas of New York City," Bill Ritter, the Channel 7 Eyewitness News anchor began. "It appeared to have reconfigured parts of a four-block section in each locale – one on the Upper West Side of Manhattan, the other in the Sunset Park section of Brooklyn. Scientists and geologists are baffled by what appears to be the first time in history that an earthquake caused this strange phenomenon, that is, streets being rearranged without any damage to the surrounding buildings. David Novarro joins us live from Sunset Park, Brooklyn. What do you see, David?"

"Bill, people here are in shock that portions of a four-block section between 43rd and 47th Streets, and between Fifth and Sixth Avenues, were somehow rearranged by last night's earthquake. As we now know, it affected only this area and the one on the Upper West Side of Manhattan."

Melvin and Shirley watched Mr. Novarro interview some of the local residents, including a young Chinese couple and their four-year old son, who spoke about their plans to visit the woman's mother for a birthday brunch. The mother's immediate neighborhood, a few blocks away, was surprisingly unaffected by the earthquake.

"Thanks, David," said Bill Ritter. "We switch now to Tony Llamas with Doctor Penelope Aidala, Professor of Geology at New York University. Tony, what have you got?"

"That's right, Bill, I'm here with Dr. Penelope Aidala at NYU in the West Village. Dr. Aidala, what do you think caused this unusual phenomenon which affected only two four-block areas of New York City in such a strange and manner? Is it plausible that an earthquake can cause this kind of dramatic street reconfiguration without causing damage to any structures? None of the buildings in the areas hit by the earthquake appear to have sustained any damage."

Dr. Penelope Aidala, an eminent scholar and professor of geology, as well as a highly acclaimed author on tectonic plate shifts, appeared very confident as she prepared to respond. At fifty-two years of age, Dr. Aidala stood at 5'-11" tall and wore fashionable tortoise-shell horn-rimmed eyeglasses. She replied succinctly and confidently.

"Mr. Llamas, there are fault lines in New York and New Jersey that we know have caused minor tremors during the past ten years. But it's unusual to experience this kind of strong seismic occurrence affecting such small areas. For centuries, tectonic plates have been shifting in ways that we have been able to detect, even predict. However, there have been times when they have shifted in unforeseen and unpredictable ways that could affect small, local geographical areas. Micro-plate shifts, you might say. That could have been the cause of last night's occurrence."

"Dr. Aidala," Llamas continued, "Could it happen again?"

"Not likely," Aidala responded confidently. "But there could be an aftershock within a day or so. I don't think it will have much of an effect, however."

"Thank you, Dr. Aidala. Back to you, Bill," said Llamas.

"What do you make of it?" Shirley asked her husband as he clicked the remote and turned off the TV.

"I have no idea," he responded.

"Did you feel that earthquake last night?" Alice Yang said to her husband. "You barely moved in bed when it happened."

"What earthquake?" Michael asked. "I was sound asleep all night."

"You honestly didn't feel it? The bed shook. The whole apartment shook."

"Nope," Michael said. "Didn't feel it. Are you sure you weren't dreaming? I don't think we have earthquakes here in Brooklyn."

"Well, nothing seems out of order, nothing's broken, so I suppose it was a very small one," Alice said. "I better go wake up Luke."

Alice got out of bed, put on her pink terrycloth robe with the Chinese symbol for Love on the pocket, and went into Luke's room. "C'mon, sleepy head. Rise and shine," Alice said as she shook Luke's shoulder. Luke was always a good sleeper, even when he was an infant. Alice opened the curtains and said to Luke, "We're having breakfast at Nei Nei's this morning. And it's such a beautiful day. Your cousins will be coming in from Flushing to help celebrate Yeh Yeh's birthday."

Luke and his cousin Louie were the same age and enjoyed playing together. Louie's mother, Margaret, was Alice's younger sister by one year. As are many Chinese families, this family was extremely close knit. They enjoyed getting together at Nei Nei and Yeh Yeh's house as often as possible. Today would be special because of the family patriarch's 80th birthday. Luke always looked forward to Nei Nei's jiaozi and baozi, her special stuffed dumplings, as well as her youtiao, the most delicious breakfast crullers you could imagine.

Luke hopped out of bed and quickly began to get dressed, proud that he could put on his shirt and trousers by himself. Tying his shoelaces, however, was still a problem. He was happy that Alice had bought him a pair of sneakers that closed with Velcro.

"Are you ready yet?" Alice called to Michael, who had just finished shaving in the bathroom.

"I'll be ready in five minutes," he responded. "What time is it?"

"It's nine-thirty already," Alice called back. "They're expecting us by ten."

"It'll take only a few minutes to walk the two blocks to your mother's," Michael said. "We have plenty of time."

The Yang family walked hand in hand out of the elevator but stopped when they went through the front door of their apartment building onto Fifth Avenue. As they turned to their left, toward what they expected to be 47th Street, they were astounded at what they saw. Confused, Luke looked up at his mother's perplexed expression and asked, "What's wrong, Mommy?"

"What the hell?" Michael exclaimed.

"Oh, my god," said Alice. "It was the earthquake!"

"What are you talking about?" Michael said, his face twisted in bewilderment.

Nothing was where it was the day before. The Key Food supermarket on 44th Street was now on the corner of 47th Street. Sue Lee's Cleaners was now on the corner instead of in the middle of the block.

"The earthquake I told you about earlier," Alice exclaimed. "You didn't believe me. You slept through the whole damn thing. Look what it did to the streets!" Alice and Michael walked through their surrounding neighborhood with the same sense of astonishment and consternation that gripped Melvin and Shirley when they noticed the rearrangement of their own Upper West Side neighborhood.

"This makes no sense," Michael replied. "Let's go back inside and call your mother to see if she's all right."

"What do you mean, earthquake?" Nei Nei remarked. "I didn't feel an earthquake. I'll ask your father," her mother said. Alice heard her mother speak in Chinese to her husband, then heard her say, "No, your father didn't feel any earthquake either. Are you still coming to breakfast?"

"We'll be there soon, Mom, soon," Alice responded as she hung up the phone and turned to Michael saying, "They're fine. They're not even aware that anything happened!"

Upon learning that her mother's street was normal and unchanged, Alice and Michael could not understand what caused the rearrangement of their neighborhood. As they looked in amazement at the other overnight changes to their immediate vicinity, they were approached by a man holding a microphone with the number 7 in a circle on it. Another man wearing a baseball cap turned backwards followed close behind, carrying a huge video camera on his shoulder.

"Good morning. I'm David Novarro with Channel 7 Eyewitness News. What do you make of what happened here?"

"I can't say," Michael replied.

"I can," said Alice. "We had an earthquake last night. My husband, Michael and our son Luke apparently slept through the whole thing. I just don't understand how the streets could have been rearranged without any of the buildings collapsing." Their immediate neighborhood was soon inundated with police cars and news reporters.

Tumultuous scenes on both the Upper West Side of Manhattan and the Sunset Park section of Brooklyn continued throughout the afternoon of Sunday, June 18th. By evening, the streets of both neighborhoods were swarming with newspaper and television reporters. Curiosity seekers flocked to both areas, which had been cordoned off with yellow 'DO NOT CROSS' tape put up by the police. By 11:30 pm, things began to quiet down. The onlookers and curiosity seekers left, and the local residents had retired for the night. Both affected neighborhoods, however, were still brimming with police in anticipation of crowds the following morning.

At the stroke of midnight, Monday June 19th, New York City experienced mild aftershocks, just as Dr. Aidala had predicted. The aftershocks affected only the same two four-block areas of New York; the Upper West Side and the Sunset Park section of Brooklyn, restructuring them back to their original configurations. Dimitri's Apollo Diner returned to its location on Amsterdam Avenue. Key Food was back on 44th Street. Sue's Cleaners was again situated in the middle of the block. The Addlers, Yangs, and all their neighbors awoke that morning to find things as they had been on the morning of June 17th. All that remained was a bad memory of an earthquake that seemed to have never happened.

Zoey and Gunner Wiley were disappointed to discover that their cityscape slide puzzles no longer worked. "My puzzle pieces won't slide anymore," Zoey cried. "Mine, too," shouted Gunner. "They're fused in place, back in their original formats," their father replied. "Well, they were probably cheap puzzles anyway. You might as well throw them away, kids. You have all your other presents to play with. We can always buy more puzzles."

Corey Meyers, a precocious and inquisitive child in Denver, Colorado celebrated his eleventh birthday at the Mountain Lanes Bowling Alley on Saturday, June 17, where his parents hosted a party for several of his close friends. Upon returning home, Corey opened his presents and was excited to find an unusual slide puzzle that was wrapped in gold and silver foil. Curiously, there was no birthday card that indicated who sent it. Each of the puzzle pieces had pictures of houses, trees, stores and buildings. Corey could design any scene he desired by sliding the sliding puzzle pieces. He played with his new puzzle that evening before going to bed. The following morning, the people living within a four-block radius in downtown Seattle, Washington which included the Pike Place Public Market, were stunned and perplexed when they went outside their homes.

Some kind of mysterious force, possibly a localized earthquake, had rearranged their neighborhood.

In Marseilles, France, Antoine Bonhomme received an unusual slide puzzle for his eleventh birthday. The residents of a four-block section of Montmartre, Paris awoke the following morning to find their neighborhood reconfigured after experiencing a small earthquake overnight. No one could explain the phenomenon.

Note:

The mathematical puzzles that Carol Wiley gave her students included the following fallacies: In the 2=1 algebra puzzle, division by zero yields a meaningless answer. In the right triangle, the angle bisector and the opposite side bisector always intersect outside the triangle.

Eduardo's Death

MY HUSBAND, EDUARDO ACOSTA, died as a result of medical malpractice in what was supposed to be a routine operation to improve his hearing loss. I'm telling you this, baring my heart and my emotions, in the hope that you will never have to experience the anguish and sorrow that I have had to endure, both from the medical profession and even from my family. Specifically, Eduardo's family.

Eduardo suffered from complications during a mastoidectomy in which infections remaining in his middle ear affected his brain, causing his death. The doctors were negligent in his post-operative treatment. It was as simple as that. The hospital attempted to cover it up, but it was only through the courage and ethics of one of the nurses that we learned how he died.

Before I go any further, let me give you some background. Eduardo and I met as teenagers in San Juan, Puerto Rico. We dated for a while and I became pregnant. Eduardo said he loved me and wanted to do the right thing. I was in love with him, so when he proposed, I immediately said yes. His older brother, Miguel, never liked me, claiming the only reason that Eduardo married me was because I was pregnant. His family attempted to convince Eduardo that he was not the father of my child, but I knew with absolute certainty that Eduardo was the father.

Eduardo's family did not attend our wedding and I was considered an outcast. Six months after our son, Luis, was born we moved to New York, where we shared an apartment with my older sister, Francesca and her husband. They allowed us to stay in the extra bedroom and we contributed to the rent.

Francesca, the oldest of my five siblings and fifteen years older than I, was like a second mother to me. Most of the time she was bossy, but as the eldest, it was to be expected. She was a very independent woman who seemed to know what she wanted. I was not surprised when, right after she married Oscar Melo, they moved to New York to start a new life. Francesca was a marvelous seamstress who could make a decent income with her talents. Oscar was an accountant. Between the two of them, they lived comfortably in the Bronx.

Eduardo loved cars and working on automobile engines. It did not take him long to be hired as a mechanic in the Shell gasoline station only two blocks from the apartment. I helped Francesca clean the apartment and share in the cooking. It seemed to be working out well for all of us. Then tragedy struck our family. When Luis was nine months old, he died suddenly in his crib. SIDS, Sudden Infant Death Syndrome, the doctor said. It was very hard for us to understand, let alone accept. Thank God Francesca was with me. I don't know what I would have done.

Two months later, Oscar suffered a massive heart attack while at work. He collapsed at his desk and died at the age of thirty-eight.

Apparently, the doctor said, he had had a weak heart from the time he was a young boy. Suffering these two untimely deaths was agonizing for us all. Again, thank God, we were there for Francesca, as she had been for us. We were a family.

In the years that followed, Eduardo assumed the role as head of household. I got a job as a sales clerk in Millie's Dress Shop on the Grand Concourse. Francesca continued as a dressmaker working at home, and Eduardo was fortunate to get the position of lead mechanic at the Chevrolet Dealer on Fordham Road. We were making ends meet.

During that period, Miguel and his wife Isabel and their five-year old daughter, Juliana, moved to Brooklyn so that Juliana could begin her schooling in the New York City school system. The brothers stayed in touch with each other, but Miguel would not allow me to be present when they got together. Blaming me for roping Eduardo into marriage, Miguel never got over his hatred for me.

As time went on, tension began to mount between Francesca and Eduardo. Both were stubborn and headstrong. They argued about the most mundane and unimportant things. "My beer isn't cold enough in the fridge," he'd complain. Or "Why did you hang up my jacket? I left it on the couch for a reason," he'd yell.

Francesca yelled at Eduardo for leaving the toilet seat up or for not putting his supper dishes in the sink. They'd scream at each other day after day, until Eduardo left one evening and didn't return for two days. When he returned the yelling continued. Eventually, Eduardo would stay away for a week, sometimes longer.

Valentina, my younger sister, telephoned from Puerto Rico to tell me that Adriana Dias had arrived in New York a week earlier. Adriana had been Eduardo's girlfriend for two years just before he met me. Eduardo's family were fond of her and there had been talk of their getting married. Miguel had given Adriana Eduardo's work number. I now understood why Eduardo had not been coming home for all those nights. Shortly afterwards, Eduardo announced that he would be moving in with Adriana because he could not stand living in the same apartment with Francesca. I was hurt, but I still loved Eduardo very much and felt certain that he would eventually leave Adriana and come back to me.

After more than a year, Eduardo had not returned. I found out too late that he was dead.

My brother-in-law was quick to petition the court to appoint him administrator of Eduardo's estate. He claimed that Eduardo and I were no longer married. He produced a Divorce Decree from the court in San Juan, Puerto Rico, alleging that we divorced a year after Eduardo moved out of the apartment. Miguel then filed the medical malpractice lawsuit in the amount of $5 million against the surgeon and the hospital where Eduardo had been treated. The trial lasted three grueling and anxious weeks. The jury took into account Eduardo's employment record and estimate of his future earnings potential, reducing the award to $400,000. I was completely left out of the picture.

Miguel filed the lawsuit as the administrator, demanding the full amount of $400,000 for himself and Juliana, whom he claimed was really Eduardo's daughter. Juliana, he asserted, chose to live with her Uncle Miguel and her Aunt Isabel in order to grow up in a more normal family. Upon learning this, I collapsed into hysteria, requiring several weeks of medical attention.

Returning to my senses, I felt I had to fight back against the lies and arrogance of Miguel. I was especially upset at Isabel, who knew the truth and chose to remain silent. I decided to telephone Isabel when I knew Miguel was not at home. "How can you stand by while Miguel does this to me?" I asked.

"Ana, you and I were never really close as sisters-in-law, but I've always liked you."

"I know, Isabel," I replied, "But Eduardo's family never did."

"Miguel and his family were unreasonable. I went along with him in order to save my marriage. You know that I wouldn't do anything intentionally to harm you," Isabel replied. "Miguel threatened me if I said anything to you. I just hope he doesn't walk in while we're on the phone. All I can say to you is that you should hire a lawyer. I wish you good luck."

I sat in silence for some time after she hung up the phone. That's when I began to think of a strategy. I remembered that I had met an attorney named Paul Miles who worked for the New York Puerto Rican Family Association when I was on the committee for the Puerto Rican Day Parade last year. The secretary at PRFA gave me his contact information. We met the very next day at his office in The Bronx. I related the entire story to him – how my brother-in-law had cheated me out of Eduardo's estate and my rightful part in the medical malpractice settlement.

"Eduardo and I had problems during the past couple of years," I explained, "but we were still legally married. Juliana is my niece, the daughter of Isabel and Miguel, not Eduardo's.

"I can check the validity of her birth certificate," Miles said. "Were you and Eduardo legally separated?"

"No. We had no such agreement," I replied.

"Then why wasn't he living with you?"

"Sir," I responded a bit ashamed, "Eduardo and my sister, Francesca, did not get along at all. They fought constantly. It is true that Eduardo stayed away most of the time, but he often came back to the apartment to give me money for my support. All those days and nights that Eduardo did not come home he was with his mistress, Adriana Dias. They were lovers in Puerto Rico before Eduardo and I got married and moved to New York."

"And you did nothing about it?" the lawyer asked.

"I turned my eyes away from his affair because I believed in my heart that Eduardo still loved me. Miguel believed Eduardo married me only because I became pregnant with his child. But I knew that wasn't true. Eduardo truly loved me," I explained.

"I see," said Miles. "Where is your child now?

"It was a tragedy. Our son died from SIDS less than a year after he was born."

"I am so sorry to hear that, Mrs. Acosta. Please accept my condolences. Is that when your husband's affair began?"

"No, that started later – after Adriana moved here from Puerto Rico."

"Did you and your husband ever discuss divorce?" he asked.

"Of course not," I answered. "The church would never allow it."

"But Miguel showed the court a Divorce Decree from Puerto Rico."

"I don't know how he could have gotten such a document. My husband and I were never divorced!" I insisted. "Can you help me, Mr. Miles?"

"I'll open an investigation and get back to you as soon as I have information," Miles replied.

"What do I have to pay you?" I asked, nervously. "I have very little money."

"There is no upfront cost to you," said Miles. "It sounds like you have a good case. If what you told me is true, your brother-in-law may have paid someone to forge the Divorce Decree, which would nullify his claim as administrator. In that case, you would become the sole legal survivor, entitled to the entire judgment."

"I swear – everything I told you is true, Mr. Miles," I said tearfully.

"I believe you said the amount of the judgment was $400,000. Is that correct?"

"Yes, sir."

"Please don't worry, Mrs. Acosta," Paul Miles said encouragingly. "If you win the case, my fee is one-third of the judgment plus out-of-pocket expenses. Does that sound reasonable to you?"

"Yes, Mr. Miles. Thank you very much."

"The next step is our contract. I'll have my secretary draw it up for you to sign, and we can begin. What I need from you are the details about the initial filing of Miguel's lawsuit plus your marriage documents. I'll take it from there and get back to you within two to three weeks."

I returned home feeling confident that I hired the right attorney and that the case would be adjudicated in my favor. Later that evening, Francesca opened a bottle of wine to share at dinner, a treat that I rarely had occasion to enjoy. Two weeks later, I received a telephone call from Mr. Miles' secretary. "Mr. Miles would like to meet with you in his office. Are you available tomorrow at 2 pm?" she asked.

I arrived at Mr. Miles' office at 1:45, eager to hear what he had to tell me. "I have proof that the Divorce Decree is phony," Mr. Miles said, as I sat, eyes wide open and waiting to hear his next words. "I contacted the court clerk who gave me a copy of the document filed by Miguel Acosta, your brother-in-law. In the first place, the document numbers make no sense at all. The alleged Divorce Certificate he submitted were investigated by the court clerk in Puerto Rico, who testified via affidavit that no such Certificate of Divorce was ever issued, nor did the registration numbers contained on the alleged Certificate ever exist. In addition, the clerk in Puerto Rico was able to verify the registration of your Marriage Certificate, proving the legal status of your marriage to Eduardo Acosta. What's more, I have obtained the legal Birth Certificate of one Juliana Acosta, signed by her parents, Isabel and Miguel Acosta." Quite proud of his investigation, he continued, "You, Ana Acosta, appear to be the sole survivor of Eduardo Acosta, and legally the sole beneficiary of the final medical malpractice settlement."

It took two years to finalize the case, but the court awarded me the full amount of $400,000, less $5,000 which they gave to Miguel to cover the amount he laid out for Eduardo's funeral. After I paid Mr. Miles his fee and expenses, I was left with a bit more than 250,000. This was more money than I had ever seen in my life, or even expected to have. With the help of Mr. Fornasieri, my new financial advisor, I will be able to live comfortably for some time. America...what a country!

I still cannot believe my good fortune. Not only for the monetary award, but also to have found the most amazing lawyer in The Bronx! Yet I would rather have had Eduardo with me, alone.

Epilogue

What Mr. Miles did not discover was that Juliana was, in fact the daughter of Eduardo. Several years later, Isabel told me that on one of his brief homecoming visits to his family in Puerto Rico, they had become inebriated and disappeared into Isabel's bedroom. That's when Juliana was conceived. It appears to be a well-kept family secret.

Love in the Time of Invasion

"IT'S FOR YOU," Susan said, nudging her boyfriend out of a deep sleep and handing him the phone.

"Why in God's name would anyone be calling you at 3 am?"

"I have no idea," Billy grumbled. "Who is this?" he blurted into the phone. "Do you realize what time it is?"

"It has been more than two months, Beely," the strange voice intoned. "Why haven't we heard from you?"

"What?" Billy bellowed. "You got the wrong number, dammit," Billy answered. He handed the receiver back to her. "Crazy bastard," he continued.

As she hung up the phone, Susan leaned over and turned on the lamp on her night table. "What was that about?" She asked. She was now sitting up, wide awake.

"Please, honey, turn off that light and go back to sleep. It was a wrong number," Billy said as he rolled onto his side. "let's get some rest. We have another full day on the lake tomorrow." He punched his pillow twice and went back to sleep. Susan turned off the lamp but lay awake wondering why someone who dialed a wrong number would ask for Billy, by name.

Gjonxga, aka Billy Sauria, and Cjxlas, aka Charlie Walla, arrived on Earth one year earlier from Gjorvan, a planet in the Bellatrix star system located in the Orion Constellation, some 245 light-years from Earth. The Gjorvans, a reptilian society with a history of more than two million years, are warlike in nature and devoid of emotions other than the basest forms of territorial domination, aggression, anger, and survival instinct. They have a herd mentality and separate themselves into tribes ruled by alpha males. They procreate in a lustful animal fashion, initiated at the desire of the males, who lack any feelings or emotions associated with the act. Female Gjorvans are equally aggressive, but are relegated to a lower-class status than males. Only when a female cares for her young do Gjorvans display anything similar to a tender emotion.

In spite of their primal nature, the Gjorvans developed a sophisticated technological system of physics, chemistry and astronomy including a highly advanced and complex system of space travel. Gjorvanian scientists had long been warning Gjordjrix, the leader of the Council of Elders, that one of their neighboring stars, Betelgeuse, would soon go nova and cause a major calamity to the planet Gjorvan. The Council of Elders commissioned Gjordjrix to determine how and where to relocate the Gjorvan population to another planet. If the host planet were populated, the Gjorvans would move in slowly and quietly. When a sufficient number of them established their presence, they would conquer and, subsequently, annihilate the population.

Gjorvan astronomers had become aware of a small spacecraft traveling through interstellar space that was approaching their planet's proximity. To ascertain its origin and purpose, they captured it and discovered that it had been sent by the planet Earth and its inhabitants in an attempt to contact extra-terrestrial civilizations.

Gjorvan scientists studied the spacecraft's strange and unfamiliar markings: the word VOYAGER engraved on one of its sides. They translated its messages and became sufficiently proficient in the languages to determine that Earth was the planet to conquer.

When they were satisfied with the knowledge they had gleaned, they devised a plan to learn more about the Earth humans. They would send a small party of two Gjorvans to Earth for a period of one year during which they would accumulate detailed information about the Earth humans' defenses and weaknesses. This would be followed by the arrival of more Gjorvans over the course of the next year, after which they would overtake the Earth by force.

Pictures of Earth humans that were included in the VOYAGER spacecraft enabled the Gjorvan scientists to create and perfect a human skin-type outer layer that could completely envelope the Gjorvan's scaly epidermis. They were so proficient in the production of this skin that one could not detect that the entity wearing it was anything other than human. They even perfected a human-type tongue that covered their own forked tongue.

Once the Council of Elders selected the two members of the advance reconnaissance party, the plan would be ready to implement. Earth's 245 light-year distance from Gjorvan would not be a problem for the journey, as the scientists and astrophysicists had already developed a method of creating worm-holes in space that would enable them to reach Earth in only one month. Gjordjrix selected two of his most trusted troops to make the journey: Gjonxga and Cjxlas. Each was fitted with the new skin and were given rudimentary Earth-like clothing to wear upon arrival.

The monthlong journey to Earth went smoothly for Gjonxga and Cjxlas. They spent much of their time improving their proficiency in Earth language, predominantly English, although they continued to struggle with its nuances and idioms. Contractions were especially difficult for them to master. They also had to become more comfortable in their new outer flesh covering. Getting used to the prosthetic tongue was more of a challenge but the highly adaptable Gjorvans were able to overcome this hurdle without much difficulty.

Gjonxga navigated the spacecraft to land unnoticed at the edge of an isolated field in Wharton State Forest, not far from Atlantic City, New Jersey. Gjonxga and Cjxlas had been commanded to destroy the spacecraft immediately after landing, leaving no evidence of their arrival on Earth. This meant that it would be a one-way trip. The Gjorvan strategy was that subsequent arrivals would ensue and that conquering the Earth would be inevitable. The two now Earthbound Gjorvans covered what remained of their destroyed spacecraft with downed tree and branches in the woods, where they waited until nightfall.

The next step in their plan was to obtain Earth identities. When darkness fell, they used their sophisticated GPS instruments to lead them to the nearest highway, County Road 563. Their immediate strategy was to commandeer a vehicle. They had been hiking northward for fifteen minutes when a car approached from behind, heading in the same direction. Seeing the two men walking alone, the driver stopped, opened his window, and called out to them.

"You guys want a lift?"

"Yes," responded Gjonxga, "that would be most nice." He and Cjxlas got into the back seat of the black Jeep, alongside one other man as the Jeep headed north. A third man occupied the front passenger seat. Gjonxga turned to his companion and uttered several sounds that were undistinguishable to the three men.

"You guys aren't from here, are you?" said the driver.

"No," Cjxlas responded. "We are not from this place."

"You guys sound Russian, is that it?" said the man in the front passenger seat.

"You are correct," Gjonxga responded. "Yes, that is where we are from."

"Where are you guys headed?" the driver asked.

The two aliens uttered some additional sounds, followed by Cjxlas's response. "We like going to big city, please. You take us there?"

Amused by the awkward phrases, the three men had difficulty stifling their laughter as the driver pulled the Jeep off to the shoulder and shut the motor. His companions removed pistols from their shoulder holsters and pointed them at Gjonxga and Cjxlas. "Get out of the car," the man in the front passenger seat demanded. The Gjorvans, looked at each other in bewilderment. "I said, get out!" he repeated. Gjonxga and Cjxlas did as they were told and stood on the side of the road at gunpoint.

Billy Sauria, Charlie Walla and Ralph (Rocky) Jones were goons on the bottom of the mob's ladder that covered the South Jersey circuit. They were headed to meet some of their colleagues in New York City after having spent a few hours at The Golden Nugget Casino with their winnings of over $60,000 stuffed in a small duffle bag. In the presence of their superiors, those who were "made men," they were totally subservient and obedient. But their inflated egos took over when they were by themselves. When they encountered the two men walking along the highway, they decided to flex their muscles and have some fun victimizing them. They had no idea with whom they were dealing.

"Okay now, where the hell are you clowns really from?" the driver said, waving his gun in their faces.

"They talk awfully funny, Rocky," Billy said. "I don't think they're from Russia."

Gjonxga whispered a few more indistinguishable phrases to Cjxlas.

"Quit that jabbering and just shaddup," Charlie ordered. "What'll we do with these jamooks?" he continued.

"I don't know. What do you think, Billy?" Rocky replied.

"Let's just take what they have, rough 'em up a bit and dump 'em in the ditch," Billy said, while Charlie and Rocky continued to waive their guns at the aliens.

Facing what they recognized as primitive weapons and aware that they were in danger, the two aliens exchanged glances. In the next instant the three mob wannabes didn't see what was coming. Faster than one could say *Gxldon Clxmdf* (Jack Robinson in Gjorvanian), and with lightning speed, Gjonxga and Cjxlas swung their arms and lunged forward, disarming all three, breaking their necks in a single motion.

"I am pleased that we encountered these Earth men," Cjxlas, said.

"Yes. We have experienced this good fortune so early in our journey. We shall acquire their identities and proceed to the big city in their vehicle," said Gjonxga.

Cjxlas rifled through the dead men's pockets, retrieving their wallets and some small amounts of cash. When they opened the duffle bag, they were surprised to discover more money than they imagined. "This will do very nicely," said Gjonxga. They proceeded to remove the clothing from the bodies and bury them in the roadside ditch, covering them so they wouldn't be found.

"How fortuitous was this event that solved our need to establish Earth identities," said Gjonxga.

"And," Cjxlas added, "we have acquired extra clothing, and so much Earth currency. We should each take some of this Earth currency – I think they call it money – and keep it with us to spend."

"That is a very good idea. I will take the identity of this one," Gjonxga said. "I will be William Sauria."

"And I will be known as Charles Walla," said Cjxlas.

"Did you notice," Gjonxga remarked, "that the one named William was also called 'Billy' by the others?"

"Yes. And Charles was also called 'Charlie,'" Cjxlas responded.

"I am supposing that they are using a familiar form of the name," Gjonxga said. "There is much more we have to learn about this Earth language. This English language. From now on, you shall only call me Billy, and I shall call you Charlie," Gjonxga said.

"Agreed," said Cjxlas.

The pair of space travelers got into the Jeep and quickly figured out how it operated. They drove north towards New York City delighted with their first Earth conquest. During the three-hour drive on back roads, they listened to news stations on the car radio and began to hone their speech pattern and English vocabulary. They were intrigued by the pop music stations, never having heard anything like it. Gjorvanian music was quite different – simplistic, with only three notes. They swayed to the some of the rhythms, even enjoying the melodies. "I believe I will find our visit to this planet most interesting," said Billy.

"Indeed," Charlie responded, "but let us not forget our mission. We must learn about these Earth people and advise Gjordjrix of their weaknesses prior to the invasion and conquest of the planet."

"You are correct," Billy added. "We have already witnessed that they have a violent nature and are hostile to strangers."

Billy drove while Charlie navigated. Driving to the "big city" was no easy task. The darkness and their unfamiliarity with New Jersey's backroads presented a challenge. Their GPS relieved the problem, but only somewhat.

"Look, Billy," he said, "There is a sign with an arrow that says New York City. That must be the name of the big city we are looking for."

The sign led Billy onto the New Jersey Turnpike. He continued following signs that led him to the Lincoln Tunnel. The toll booths were a bit of a mystery to Billy. He stopped the car in front of the gate. "I am from out of town," he said to the woman in the booth. When she held out her hand, Billy gave her a $10 bill. She beckoned for more, and a slightly confused Billy gave her another $10. When the gate remained closed, Billy realized that the woman was waiting for Billy to take the change from her hand. When he took it, the gate swung open and Billy proceeded to drive into Manhattan.

"You are successful dealing with Earth people," Charlie said.

"You are correct," Billy responded. "They do not suspect anything."

After leaving the Lincoln Tunnel, Billy noticed a sign that read, PARK HERE. "It is as if they have been waiting for us to arrive," he remarked as he drove the car into the parking lot.

"How long?" asked the parking attendant.

"I am sorry," Billy said. "What do you mean?"

"How long you gonna park here," the attendant responded, impatiently.

"I do not know for how long. Perhaps a week or longer," Billy said. "We are from out of town."

"Okay, just pull over there," he said, pointing to his right, "and see the cashier."

"How long?" the cashier asked. This time Billy knew how to respond.

"About one or two weeks," he said.

"That'll be two hundred," the cashier said. "Just leave me the keys."

Billy handed the money to the cashier, along with the keys to the Jeep. The cashier handed Billy a receipt, saying "Show me this receipt when you want your car."

"Thank you," Billy said. "Can you also tell me where we can stay for our visit to this city?"

Unfazed by Billy's awkward phrasing – New York City is no stranger to newcomers – the cashier said, "There's a hotel right around the corner."

Billy and Charlie walked around the corner to discover a building with an awning that read *The Galaxy Hotel*. "How appropriate this name is for our stay on this planet," Billy commented.

The hotel foyer was dimly lit. A small chandelier hanging in the lobby emitted the only light. Two of the eight bulbs were burnt out. The clerk, a tall, thin man with a two-day growth of white stubble, was seated behind the front desk in an alcove, reading a newspaper.

As the two men entered the lobby, the clerk looked up and removed his reading glasses that were hanging from a braided eyeglass holder. "Can I help you?" he said, glaring at the two strangers who stood quietly in the lobby.

"We just arrived here," Charlie said. "We would like to stay in a room."

"For how long?" the clerk asked.

"For two weeks," Billy replied.

"That'll be five hundred bucks, in advance," the clerk said. He put his glasses back on and handed Billy a pen. "Sign the book here."

Billy unrolled five one-hundred-dollar bills from the wad they took from the dead goons and handed the money to the clerk. He didn't seem to care who they were and gave them no trouble when they registered, paying $500 in cash. He was also oblivious to the fact that they had no luggage. Billy managed to copy the name, William Sauria, from the driver's license that was now in his possession.

The two Gjorvans were now officially William Sauria and Charles Walla, men whose real bodies lay buried in a ditch, along with their fellow goon, Rocky Jones, somewhere in New Jersey near Wharton State Forest.

More tired than hungry – it was 3 am – the two Gjorvans climbed the stairs to the second floor, followed the dusty and somewhat tattered carpet runner to Room 7 at the end of the narrow hallway. Struggling with the key, they opened the door to reveal a dingy, but clean, 15 'x 20'room. The meager furnishings included two single beds, a vinyl upholstered chair, and a four-drawer dresser on top of which sat a small television set. The beds were separated by a small nightstand with a lamp, telephone and wind-up alarm clock that ticked loudly enough to keep a light sleeper awake. Oblivious to the condition of the room, and tired from their day's ordeal, the two newcomers to New York City tumbled onto the beds and immediately fell asleep.

Billy and Charlie awoke hungry at noon the following day. "We should acquire some provisions to sustain us," Billy said.

"Agreed," Charlie replied. "I am also experiencing hunger."

"Where can we eat, please," Charlie asked the desk clerk.

"Try Benny's at the end of the block."

After enjoying a breakfast of sardines mixed with soft-boiled eggs at Benny's Coffee Shop, Billy and Charlie decided to walk through the neighborhood and study some of the local customs. They window-shopped, sat on a bench outside a clothing store and observed the people walking by, took notice of the variety of vehicles and traffic patterns, and sampled foods from street vendors. That evening, they ate dinner at a local Italian restaurant and were surprised to experience the pleasure of being served by a waiter. Afterwards, the two retreated to their hotel room where they turned on the TV and learned more about life on Earth.

They watched the local, national and international news programs. Channel 13 aired "The Blue Planet" where they absorbed more information about Earth and its inhabitants. They continued to watch PBS each evening to learn even more about the different cultures on Earth. They found it interesting to learn about the variety of crimes being committed and wars being fought on this planet. "In some ways, the people here are a lot like we are," Billy commented.

"Yes," Charlie responded, "but more primitive."

"It will not be difficult to conquer the inhabitants here," Billy stated confidently.

Charlie changed the channel and stopped at what was a totally unfamiliar concept to them. A man wearing some sort of uniform returned home from work, put his lunch pail on the table, and greeted his wife with a kiss as she prepared dinner. *What a strange greeting,* they both thought. A neighbor, wearing a vest over a white tee shirt and a funny hat, entered their apartment and greeted the man and his wife. *Interesting,* Billy thought, *he did not touch the woman's mouth with his.* The two men began to argue with each other over several things that Billy and Charlie could not understand, such as sewers, something called bowling, and going on vacations. As they continued to watch *The Honeymooners,* starring Jackie Gleason and Art Carney, Billy and Charlie felt a strange sensation, one that neither of them had ever experienced – amusement. For the first time in their lives, they laughed. Especially when the husband said he would send his wife to the moon. They experienced a sense of humor. Coming from a planet that studied only war and cruelty and focused on conquest, humor, for its own sake, was totally foreign to them. The more they watched, the more they wanted to watch. And laugh. Humor was unknown on Gjorvan.

"Our strange response to those people on the television set is not

Gjorvanian. It is weakness that the Earth people have." said Billy.

"You are right," Charlie remarked. "It makes them vulnerable. We must avoid falling into this trap or else we will become weak, like the Earth people. We must capitalize on their weaknesses in order to facilitate our conquest." Charlie quickly arose from his chair and turned off the television. "We must watch more programs that present news and other problems that we can use to our advantage," he continued.

"You are correct," Billy said. "Let us now take some time to figure out our next strategy to observe the people. But first, we must take stock of our assets."

"And," Charlie added, "we must improve our ability to speak this Earth language."

Charlie opened the bag of money they took from the goons they killed and counted what was left. They still had most of it. He made a budget that helped them determine how much longer their money would last – at least nine months before they would have to get more. But they decided that it was not an immediate concern. They examined the contents of the wallets. In addition to driver's licenses, each wallet contained a card bearing a series of numbers and the heading, Bank of America VISA. "I don't know what these cards are for," said Billy, "But we should hold onto them. One for you, with the name 'Charles,' and one for me that says, 'William.' The numbers are probably for identification."

"It has the word BANK on it, so it may be a means of acquiring money," Billy surmised.

"We will also have to keep a low profile," Charlie added. "We were fortunate to find those men with the car who had all this money.

But it may not be so easy to kill others, take their money, and not get caught."

"We must observe and learn more before we act. As you said, we cannot allow anyone to suspect the nature of our mission," Billy responded. "Remember, we will have to report our progress to leader Gjordjrix tomorrow. You have the communicators, right?" Charlie reached into his jacket pocket and produced two gadgets, similar in size to a flip-phone. He handed one to Billy.

"I shall contact Gjordjrix in the morning," Billy said.

On their third day on Earth and enjoying another breakfast of sardines and soft-boiled eggs at Benny's, the pair returned to their hotel room and contacted their home planet. "We landed safely and all is going according to schedule," Billy reported. "We have successfully assumed Earthman identities and are residing in a big city called New York. I am now called Billy Sauria and Cjxlas is called Charlie Walla. We are observing the population and learning their strengths and weaknesses. We shall report again at intervals of one Earth week."

"Where can I find an instruction guide to improve my English speaking?" Billy asked the Galaxy Hotel desk clerk.

"Well," the clerk responded, "you can head to the library over on Fifth Avenue. They have books on just about everything."

Billy and Charlie walked from their hotel along 42nd Street, where they continued to observe more of the sights, sounds and the people, until they reached the New York Public Library. "Look at these huge statues on the sides of the steps," Charlie commented.

"They must represent a different kind of Earth creature," Billy said. "It may be a symbol of one of their gods."

"We shall try to be aware of them while we are here," Charlie warned, "and inform Gjordjrix of what they look like. Certainly, they are different from the humans."

The two marveled at the height of the huge front doors. "It may be that this planet also has inhabitants that are much larger than the humans we have seen. We must report this to Gjordjrix also," Billy said.

Returning their focus to their immediate goal, they approached the front desk, still gaping at the immense size of the room.

"Do you have a book of instructions that will help me improve my English speaking?" Billy asked the woman at the huge desk.

"Why, yes," the librarian responded. "It's called the 'Handbook of Current English.' You can find it on the computer."

"Thank you. I am a new arrival in New York, and would appreciate your help."

"No problem. Janet," she called to her assistant, "would you please help these gentlemen find what they're looking for." Janet escorted the two foreigners to the language section and helped them locate the book.

"This is a good instruction guide for us," said Charlie.

They sat at a huge table and began to leaf through the book. "We must study it in more detail, and practice to improve our speaking," Billy said. He approached the librarian and said, "We would like to take this book back to our hotel and study from it."

"Do you have a library card?" she asked.

"I do not," Billy replied.

"Well," she said, "if you want to borrow the book, you'll need one. Here." She handed an application to Billy. "Fill this out and bring it back to me."

Returning to the reading table, Billy said, "We cannot comply with all the information they are asking. We will have to find a better way to have this book."

"I know a way," said Charlie. He looked around and, when no one was watching, he carefully tore out the pages they wanted. Without drawing attention, he stuffed them inside his shirt. A cart with a sign that read: RETURN BOOKS HERE sat at the end of the table. They placed the book in the cart, quietly left the library and returned to their hotel room.

They studied English for the next several days and became comfortable with idioms, phrases, and especially, contractions. Within a few days, they began to feel more comfortable blending in with the population.

Billy and Charlie continued their observations diligently for the next several weeks. They pretended to be tourists, went sight-seeing and sampled the sounds and tastes of New York City. During Billy's next contact with his home planet, Gjordjrix ordered his two emissaries to venture outside the big city to learn about the rural population.

One observation they found useful was that Earth people used VISA cards to pay for clothing, food, entertainment, and taxicab fare. It enabled them to frequent restaurants, theaters and nightclubs, enjoying themselves on Earth in spite of their mission.

They also became aware of how many Earth people were cordial and friendly toward one another. People were often nice and polite without necessarily having any ulterior motives. People often seemed to care about each other. What they failed to recognize, however, was that the longer they remained on Earth, the more they experienced the sensations that were unfamiliar to Gjorvans, such as empathy, pleasure, and amusement. They even began to use 'please' and 'thank you' more frequently.

"I do not understand it, but I am beginning to like this planet," Billy confided to Charlie.

"To be honest with you," Charlie responded, "I could get used to living like this, also. But let us not forget our primary mission. We cannot allow ourselves to become weak, like the Earth people."

"I understand what you are saying, Charlie," Billy responded. "But we can still try to enjoy these new sensations that we are experiencing. Is that so bad?"

"I will agree with you for now, but we must not let our guard down. What if Gjordjrix were to find out?"

"Do not worry. I will report that everything is going according to plan. Relax and enjoy yourself."

"If you say so, Billy."

For the next few months, Billy and Charlie continued to report their activities to Gjordjrix while, at the same time, requesting extensions for their observations. Gjordjrix instructed that in order for them to produce a final report prior to an invasion, they would need to become more intimate with the Earth people on a one-to-one basis. A personal relationship would reinforce their initial understanding of the Earth peoples' weaknesses. They would have to initiate and develop friendships. It was soon afterwards that Billy met Susan Janus, and Charlie met Millie Foxx. The two aliens were soon to discover yet another entirely strange sensation: falling in love.

During the first six months after Gjonxga and Cjxlas arrived on Earth, they had learned a great deal about how the people live and interacted with each other. They read newspapers, watched news programs, movies, sitcoms, nature documentaries, late-night talk and entertainment shows on the outdated television set in their hotel room. They remained aware that their mission to scout the planet in preparation for a Gjorvan invasion was paramount but the longer they remained on Earth, their focus gradually eroded, receding into the back of their minds. They were, unconsciously, becoming more and more like the people whom their own people planned to conquer and annihilate. Although they knew they were given an important mission, the planet Earth was having a major impact on their attitudes and behavior. They were undeniably and irreversibly morphing into their avatars, Billy Sauria and Charlie Walla.

As part of Gjordjrix's instructions to learn more about Earth human relationships, Billy met Susan Janus at *The Ives Have It,* a popular singles bar in Manhattan, and was instantly drawn to her. Susan had the face and form of a Glamour Magazine model. Her peach-colored skin was highlighted by her greenish-blue eyes, pageboy styled blonde hair, and full red lips. Billy was intrigued by the fact that she openly welcomed his introduction and advances toward her. In no time they were drinking and laughing together.

Charlie wasn't doing too bad for himself either. He was cozying up to another knockout, Millie Foxx, at the other end of the bar. Millie, it so happened, was Susan's best friend. She had sky-blue eyes that hypnotized Charlie, and waist-length black hair that ran down the middle of her back. Millie was equally attracted to Charlie. His boyish charm and self-assurance, plus his piercing green eyes, drew her to him. "Another round here, Steve," he called out to the bartender. And please send my friend over there and the girl he's with two more of whatever they're drinking."

Both Billy and Charlie would be considered exceptionally attractive by most women. Their choice of attire – perfectly fitted jeans and black tee shirts under sportscoats – showed off their muscular physiques. Billy exuded animal magnetism. Charlie's charisma was irresistible.

Tonight marked their first adventure into a bar, let alone a singles bar. And though neither intended to get involved with Earth women, they were fascinated by them. There was something about the place that generated sensations they had never experienced. The ambiance, music, and the actions of humans who were genuinely enjoying themselves pervaded the room and drew them into it. Their intention had been to observe humans in a social setting and to educate themselves about their habits and weaknesses. Billy and Charlie were not aware of it yet, but they were succumbing to their own weaknesses.

In their zeal to conquer and dominate, the Gjorvans relied heavily on brute force and numbers, more than developing extensive knowledge of their enemies and victims. Their dependence on fleeting political alliances was no match for the values of long-standing and lasting personal relationships. Once Billy and Charlie began to experience more of the feelings and sensations that came naturally to humans, especially their attraction to Earth women, their own weaknesses became apparent.

During the ensuing two months, both men had fallen under the spell of the two most beautiful women they had ever seen – to the detriment of their entire mission. Unbeknownst to both men, the strong feelings they developed on Earth had erased the memories of who they were, where they came from, and why they were there. Billy and Charlie actually believed that they were Earthmen. They spent most of their time together with the women, sharing their lust for life on Earth, making love whenever and as often as they could.

Susan had arranged for the two couples to spend a summer weekend together at her cabin on the New York end of Greenwood Lake, half of which also straddled New Jersey. The weather forecast was delightful – two warm, balmy, sunny days. They grilled steaks for dinner on Friday night, went swimming after hiking on Saturday, and had a lobster fest on Saturday night, complete with corn-on-the-cob and steamers. Charlie brought two bottles of Pinot Grigio to accompany the meal, which they downed completely.

The mysterious phone call for Billy at 3 am interrupted what had been a wonderful weekend. After she hung up the phone, Susan stayed awake when Billy fell back into a deep sleep. She remained troubled about the "wrong number" in which the caller, with a strange accent, asked for Billy by name. Convinced that it was not a wrong number and fearing that Billy and Charlie were possibly involved in some kind of scheme, Susan nudged Billy. When he didn't wake up immediately, she shook him again, inadvertently scratching his neck. To her horror, a small amount of Billy's skin flaked off, revealing an underlayer of reptilian scales. Before he awoke, she scraped off more skin from Billy's neck, exposing a false epidermis that covered a full layer of scales.

Finally aroused out of his deep slumber brought on by all the outdoor activity earlier in the day, and an evening of exhaustive love-making, Billy sat up in bed clutching his neck. Seeing that Susan had scratched off part of his false outer skin layer, a host of suppressed memories raced to the forefront of his mind. Billy suddenly remembered that he was a Gjorvan.

"What have you done to me, Susan?" he shouted.

"Who the hell are you, Billy? What the hell are you?" she yelled.

In an attempt to overcome his own uneasiness, Billy responded, "Calm down, Susan. Let me explain."

"Explain what?" Susan yelled back at him. "What was that wrong number about? You knew who that was. And what's the matter with your skin?"

"Let me get my thoughts together," Billy said, trying to regain his composure. "Please."

Billy sat in bed, struggling to figure out what he should say to the woman with whom he had fallen in love. The excitement and horror of the moment were beginning to shake Billy's memory back to who he really was and why he was here. In the next moment Susan reached out towards the wound on Billy's neck, tearing away more of the false skin that covered Billy's scaly hide. Billy's hand responded in an immediate reflex grabbing Susan's wrist, restraining her from damaging his façade any further. "Stop it!" he yelled. "I can explain it now," he continued.

"Please do," Susan implored, while she stared at him angrily.

Alarmed by the commotion coming from Susan and Billy's room, Millie and Charlie knocked on the door and entered, uninvited.

"What's going on in here?" Millie asked.

"What happened to your neck, Billy?" Charlie asked, the look of horror overtaking his entire demeanor.

"Okay, everyone, I can explain," Billy began. "Please bear with me and understand where I'm coming from."

Charlie and Millie stood side by side at the foot of the bed. Susan sat upright alongside Billy while he explained where they were actually from, and that their mission was to scout the Earth in advance of an invasion. Then he explained how he and Charlie had been transformed into their new avatars, influenced by how the Earth had affected them. He claimed that he no longer wanted to complete his mission and that he planned to contact the leaders of Gjorvan and convince them to abort the invasion. He was convinced, without a doubt, that all the new sensations and emotions he experienced during his short visit to Earth, especially love, were able to cause a mutation in his genes that ameliorated all the aggressive, anti-social, warring and conquest traits of the Gjorvans. He wanted to remain here on Earth and live in peace and in love.

Turning to Susan, then to Millie, he said, "I'm sure that Charlie feels the same way as I do, don't you Charlie?" Charlie put his arm around Millie's shoulders and said, "Millie, I love you. I feel exactly the same way as Billy."

Susan stared at Billy, then at Charlie, and finally at Millie. She caressed the gash on his neck tenderly, her long red fingernails glistening in the lamplight. "What do you think, Millie?"

Millie nodded her head, as if to agree with Susan. Susan looked at Billy again while Millie looked into Charlie's sad eyes. As if on cue, both Susan and Millie opened their mouths wide, their jaws unhinging like a snake's, displaying their huge, sharp pearly whites as if to devour an animal larger than itself. Those were the last two images that Bill and Charlie saw. With lightning speed, both women simultaneously snapped their hyper-extended jaws over Billy's and Charlie's heads, severing them completely, killing both men instantly. Blood spattered in every direction as the two women spat the two heads onto the floor, watching them roll in two different directions, the eyes still opened in horror. The headless bodies trembled, their limbs flailed, as their reptilian nerves took a few more moments to die. Then, slowly, they ceased all movement.

At 4 am the telephone rang again. "I want to speak to Beely" the voice demanded.

"Don't bother, Gjordjrix, if that's who you are," Susan said. "Gjonxga and Cjxlas are dead. You'll have to find a different planet for your invasion. The Kalians have been here for more than ten Earth years, and our conquest is nearly complete. No hard feelings. Good-bye."

Susan (nee Kali-alfa) and Millie (nee Kali-beta) were shape-shifters from the planet Kali in the Saiph star system in the constellation of Orion. The Kalians had also been aware of the impending demise of Betelgeuse and beat the Gjorvans to the invasion of the Earth.

After hanging up the phone, Susan turned and spoke to Millie.

"We must prepare ourselves and our minions for an attack by the Gjorvans. They may want to avenge the deaths of Gjonxga and Cjxlas. Or, they might invade a different planet. We can't be certain. Meanwhile, our plans to completely dominate the Earth must continue uninterrupted."

The invasion of planet Earth by the Kalians continued for another hundred years. It was never fully successful. Or was it?

Stellar Rendezvous

"HAVE YOU DOUBLE CHECKED your figures, and are you sure you're not mistaken?" asked Dr. Ginsberg. "That would be a pretty catastrophic discovery," he added, scratching his head, with deep concern. "Mauricio, I think it would be a good idea to verify this with Dr. Gruber's staff."

Dr. David Ginsberg was in charge of a prestigious group of astronomers, cosmologists, astrophysicists, and planetary scientists at the Krinsky Center for Interplanetary Research and Discovery (CIRD) near the peak of Mauna Kea on the Big Island of Hawaii. Ginsberg idolized Carl Sagan. Now in his early fifties, his hair style emulated Sagan's shag cut but with a noticeable bald patch in back. His beard and round wire-rimmed glasses added to the image of the stereotypical mad scientist. Mad he wasn't; genius he was.

"Dr. Ginsberg, I've been watching this anomaly for a couple of hours and I'm fairly certain about my calculations," answered Mauricio Alvarez, Dr. Ginsberg's assistant. "But I'll get right over to Dr. Gruber's office immediately and check with her."

Alvarez, who grew up in Chile, was interning under Dr. Ginsberg's wing in preparation for his Ph.D. He was a straight A student at Cal Tech's graduate astrophysics program. When Mauricio was a child, his father introduced him to astronomy, taking him to the La Silla Observatory, just north of where they lived in Santiago de Chile. Mauricio knew then, even at the age of ten, that he wanted to study the planets.

Mauricio's only other passion was soccer – he was the star goalie on his high school soccer team, as well as a brilliant academic student. He earned a scholarship to Amherst in Massachusetts as a scholar-athlete. He was graduated Cum Laude, majoring in engineering science, and received his Master of Science degree in physics from Cal Tech.

Tall, dark and handsome, Mauricio drew the attention of several young women on his way to becoming a top student. The only one who gained Mauricio's interest, however, was Stella Garcia, with whom he fell madly in love. A senior at Cal Tech's chemical engineering program, Stella wrote love letters to Mauricio three times a week while he was interning with Dr. Ginsberg in Hawaii. They missed each other terribly and planned to become engaged as soon as possible after Mauricio completed his Ph.D. dissertation.

Dr. Ginsberg recruited Julia Gruber, his second in command at CIRD, three years ago directly from Princeton University where she earned her MS in astronomy and Ph.D. in astrophysics. With her BS in biology from the University of Virginia, Dr. Gruber had hoped to pursue the study of interplanetary life forms, whatever forms they might be, if at all. Her focus on the universe left her no time to develop a social life.

Dr. Gruber's staff routinely and meticulously monitored the myriad comets and asteroids hurtling through the Milky Way Galaxy in order to detect whether any object could be on a potentially hazardous collision path with Earth. Many meteorites often hit the Earth but were too small to have a major impact. However, a larger asteroid colliding into the Earth would be devastating.

Mauricio walked past the row of desks at which the skywatchers, as they called themselves, would normally be tracking and charting a host of astronomical bodies on their computers and radar screens. But today he noticed that most of them were huddled around Leslie Garson's desk.

"Come see Leslie's engagement ring, Mauricio," one of them beckoned.

"Sure," he said. "I'll be there right after I speak with Dr. Gruber."

"Dr. Gruber, Dr. Ginsberg asked me to check something important with you. Have you got a few moments? It's rather urgent," Mauricio asked as he approached her desk on the far side of the room.

"What's up, Mauricio?" she replied, lifting her head from the stack of graphs and charts she was studying.

"I noticed an anomaly from Hubble that I've been watching for a few hours. I hope I'm wrong, but have any of the skywatchers observed anything unusual lately? If I'm not wrong, I may have discovered an object heading towards our solar system, something traveling at an extremely high rate of speed. I don't think we've ever encountered anything moving that fast," Mauricio explained.

"None of the skywatchers mentioned anything to me yet," Dr. Gruber replied. "Tell me what you saw."

"Well," Mauricio continued, "The object is just beyond Pluto's orbit, somewhere in the heliosphere, placing it some nine billion miles from Earth. After watching it for a while I made some initial estimates. It's traveling at about 27 million miles per hour. That's an incredible rate of speed. Other than gamma rays, that travel at the speed of light itself, I don't know of any other object that travels at anywhere near that velocity. It's mind-blowing. On its present path, it could reach the Earth in about two weeks. Voyager took over forty years to travel that distance. Nine billion miles in only 14 days! That's terrifying, don't you think?"

"My God!" Gruber exclaimed. She stood and stared directly into Mauricio's eyes. "You better not be shitting me! This better not be a damn joke!"

"I wish," Mauricio responded.

Dr. Gruber grabbed Mauricio by the sleeve. "Let's go," she said. As they passed the crowd at Leslie's desk, Gruber grabbed Steve Chuebon, Leslie's new fiancé. "Steve, drop everything and come with us."

Gruber didn't bother to knock on Ginsberg's office door as the three of them burst in. "David, what's all this about Mauricio's observations?"

"Close the door, Julia," Ginsberg said.

"What's going on?" Steve asked.

Mauricio reiterated what he had explained to both Dr. Ginsberg and Dr. Gruber.

"Come on," Steve began, "we don't know of anything traveling at that speed except energy rays or gamma rays. And those travel at nearly the speed of light itself."

"It's not that I could identify any one thing in particular," Mauricio said. "It's the effect the object was having on the space around it – the way the light appeared. I'm thinking that it could be a black hole, but I'm not exactly sure. It's not the distance I'm concerned about. It's the speed."

"If Mauricio is correct," Dr. Ginsberg said somberly, "we'd be in for a worldwide calamity."

"Of course, it would depend on whether the object maintains its present trajectory and speed, and whether Earth is in the just the right place in its own orbit," Dr. Gruber said in her inimitable style of problem analysis. "But first, let's not panic until we can substantiate Mauricio's findings. Steve, why don't you select one of the other experienced skywatchers and work quietly – very quietly – with Mauricio on this. I don't want to cause any unnecessary uproar. Meanwhile, I'll get everyone else back to their stations; see if they can pick up anything out there." Turning to Dr. Ginsberg, she said, "David, let's you and I talk in private."

"Mauricio, bring your calculations into the conference room," Steve said. I'll ask Harvey Eisenberg to join us. He's been watching the galaxy for a while. Maybe he can shed some light on this."

Raised in an Orthodox Jewish family, Harvey Eisenberg never, in his wildest dreams, would have considered a profession in astronomy. Anything outside of the creation story in the Torah, especially that the scientific age of the universe was 13.8 billion years, was anathema to his family. As a headstrong teenager Harvey began to question his father's dogmatic and simplistic approach to religious life, and the world in general. He became frustrated with religion's inability to satisfy his curiosity about the universe. He would sneak off to the public library and ask the head librarian for recommendations. Carl Sagan's book *Cosmos* emboldened Harvey. He followed up with Christopher Hitchens' *God is Not Great* and then *The God Delusion* by Richard Dawkins. Ultimately becoming an atheist, he was shunned by his former religious community. Once a month, however, he would telephone his mother, the only family member with whom he maintained a secret and loving relationship.

While Steve, Mauricio and Harvey sat at the conference table evaluating Mauricio's initial findings, Mauricio pondered one of his greatest goals: to make a significant discovery in the field of astronomy. *How ironic,* he thought. *If I'm correct, my discovery could mean the end of the world.*

"David," Julia began, "What's your opinion about this?"

"I haven't formed one yet, Julia," he replied. "Mauricio just came to me with this and I asked him to check with you and your staff. Let's not jump to conclusions, though. You should have them check their own computers and charts to see if they can verify Mauricio's initial calculations."

"Sure," Dr. Gruber said, "but if his estimate of 14 days is anywhere in the ballpark, we need to consider a worst-case scenario."

"You mean the end of the world, don't you?" said Dr. Ginsberg.

"Sounds improbable," she replied, "but we need a plan. Do we alert the government? Should we confirm it with other observatories? What if they've picked this up already?"

"Let's wait and see what the boys come up with," Dr. Ginsberg said. "Then, if Mauricio's initial estimates have any merit at all, I'll have him follow the movement of the object for the next couple of days to see whether its path changes. Or even if there is actually something headed our way."

"Agreed," Dr. Gruber said. "I'll check with the team in the conference room in a little while."

When Dr. Ginsberg, Dr. Gruber, Mauricio, Steve, and Harvey met in the conference room at 5:30, the rest of the skywatchers began to suspect that something was up.

"We've gone over the numbers and it appears that Mauricio's initial calculations are in the ballpark," Steve stated. "Something is on the way towards the inner solar system. We can't actually see it, but it seems to be affecting the space around its path. If it is a black hole, as Mauricio believes, it's a relatively small one and definitely not supermassive. We're not aware of any collapsed star in that region of the galaxy."

"We need to keep this under wraps for the next few days," Dr. Ginsberg said. "Not a word to anyone, even to the other skywatchers. The three of you will take turns monitoring it for the next 48 hours, working in four-hour shifts. If word of this leaks out, it could set off worldwide panic. Steve, you take the lead. Start immediately. Keep me and Dr. Gruber apprised at the end of each shift. We'll be on call 24/7."

Mauricio was assigned to the first shift from 6 to 10 pm. Harvey took the second shift. Steve was on from 2 to 6 am. They nicknamed the project, "MA-1." Anyone who asked why the three men were working these special hours was told that it was a special project of Dr. Ginsberg's for the next two days, and that they would all be informed of the details afterward. It sounded perfectly normal that from time to time Dr. Ginsberg or Dr. Gruber would require assistance from the skywatchers for special governmental or NASA projects. Leslie Garson was a bit disappointed, however, that she and Steve had to postpone their engagement party. But she knew that was the life of dedicated scientists in the field of astronomy.

For the next two days and nights, the MA-1 team diligently observed the mysterious object and its path into the solar system. At the end of the initial two-day observation period, Steve reported that the object had traveled another 1.3 billion miles. To Leslie Garson's dismay, Dr. Ginsberg extended the survey period for another 48 hours. Steve reported that the object was more than 2½ billion miles closer than when Mauricio first detected it. If it remained on its current path, it would reach Earth's orbit in about ten days.

Dr. Gruber could no longer hide her concern from Dr. Ginsberg and the project team. "It's worse than I imagined," she said.

"We should enlist the assistance of the James Webb Space Telescope as a backup to Hubble," Dr. Ginsberg advised. "With its longer wavelength and greater sensitivity, it should identify what we're looking at much more clearly."

"This is nothing like the Oumuamua comet of 2017," Dr. Ginsberg said. "That was close but not like this. Even if it comes anywhere near Earth's orbit, it'll destroy us. It's possible it could even wipe out our entire solar system. Call your entire staff into the conference room," he instructed Dr. Gruber.

Dr. Ginsberg stood at the head of the conference table and addressed the entire scientific team at CIRD. "As you all are aware, we've been conducting a highly secret and confidential project here at CIRD for the past 4 days. The reason for its secrecy is to avoid creating a panic. As you are also aware, Voyager 2 Space Probe has stopped communicating with NASA. We now believe that it has been destroyed by a black hole that appears to be on its way toward our solar system. Unlike the supermassive black holes that we've been able to detect with reasonable certainty, this black hole has a much smaller mass which made it more difficult to detect at first. Thanks to Mauricio Alverez's astute observations, we have identified it. That's the good news. The bad news is that it's traveling at an unheard-of velocity, roughly 27 million miles per hour. At that rate and on its present path, it could now reach Earth's orbit in about ten days."

Disbelief and horror echoed in the conference room. "Wait a minute," said one of the skywatchers. "Are you saying that Earth will be destroyed in less than two weeks?"

"That can't be possible," exclaimed another skywatcher.

"Please, everyone, try to remain calm," Dr. Gruber insisted. "Let Dr. Ginsberg finish."

"Yes. Please Dr. Ginsberg, tell us what the hell is going on," another skywatcher demanded.

"All right," Dr. Ginsberg continued, "here's what we know."

One by one, skywatchers began to express their doubt, shock, frustration, anger and desperation as Dr. Ginsberg enlightened his staff of stunned scientists about the possible end of the world.

"What do we do now?" Leslie Garson asked. "Do we, what I mean is...how do we..." She dropped her head onto her arms on the conference table and began to cry. Steve ran immediately to her to try to console his fiancée. Leslie lifted her head and placed it against Steve's chest, threw her arms around him and wept uncontrollably. Several of the other skywatchers were overcome with grief as well.

"Please, everyone," implored Dr. Ginsberg. "Please let's try to control ourselves. I just need your attention for a few more minutes," he urged, trying to cover his own desperation. "What we have to figure out now," he said calmly, "is how to convey this information to the rest of the world. Granted, it will be only ten days before the black hole reaches us, but there's always a chance that it could change course and avoid us altogether."

"I've thought of that," Mauricio added. "As you all know, a black hole thrives on devouring whatever it comes near or in contact with. As it travels through the Kuiper Belt, it will consume many of the comets and other icy bodies out there. That could change both its path and its speed, possibly slowing it down somewhat as it grows larger. Then, of course, if it nears any of the outer planets, such as Neptune, Uranus or Jupiter its course and speed could change yet again. Slow down, I mean."

"Do we know whether any other observatories around the globe have identified the object?" asked Dr. Gruber.

"I haven't heard from any of them yet," said Dr. Ginsberg. "Until we have more information, I've decided to keep it to ourselves for the time being."

"But don't we have a responsibility to warn everyone?" asked Harvey Eisenberg. "I mean, just in case..."

"Yes," Dr. Ginsberg replied. "But I want to wait another day or so before we inform the world – just to see where it goes. Everyone agree?"

After a brief silence, Dr. Gruber responded, "I agree. How about the rest of you?" One by one, each skywatcher promised to go along with Dr. Ginsberg and wait before sounding the alarm bell.

By noon the next day, the object, designated MSH-1 by the project team, was well on its way through Kuiper Belt. If it remained on the same path, the team's calculations indicated that it would intersect the orbit of the dwarf planet, Pluto in another four days, placing it just over three billion miles and then only five days from reaching Earth's orbit.

At 5 pm on the fifth day following Mauricio's discovery, Dr. Ginsberg received a telephone call from Dr. Joaquin Soto, Director of the La Silla Observatory. "Hi Jack," said Dr. Ginsberg. "It's been a while. How've you been?"

"I'm fine," said Dr. Soto. "And I'm sure you are, too, David. Let's not waste any time. I'm sure you do know why I'm calling."

"The black hole, isn't it," said Dr. Ginsberg.

"That's what we think it is. What's your take?" Soto asked.

"My intern, Mauricio Alverez, first identified it five days ago. We've been maintaining silence on it until we could determine where it's headed. And we now think it's highly likely that it's headed our way. We also think that we should inform the world governments."

Dr. Ginsberg and Dr. Soto continued to compare notes on MSH-1 and share their ideas about notifying the public. Their initial conversation developed into a conference call that included the MSH project team and their counterparts in Chile. Within an hour, the lights on Dr. Ginsberg's phone were flashing with incoming calls from several other observatories around the world. They had also become aware of the black hole that was entering our solar system. It was time to inform world leaders.

Dr. Ginsberg was put through to the President at 8 pm. "How soon can you get your team here to Washington?" the President asked.

"Sir," said Dr. Ginsberg, "May I respectfully request that you come here to the observatory instead? I'm certain it will be a lot easier for you to understand once you see it all first hand. It may give you a greater basis for developing any strategy that will be necessary under the circumstances."

"All right," President Ellison said. "We'll be at your office at ten o'clock tomorrow morning. Please make sure you have all the facts we need as soon as I arrive."

"Yes, Mr. President, we'll have it all ready for you," Dr. Ginsberg said.

"I love you so much," Leslie sobbed.

"And I love you, too," Steve replied, attempting to hold back his own tears as they hugged each other. "I have an idea," he continued. "Let's get married right away. Immediately after President Ellison leaves, we can take the car into Waimea and get married by the Justice of the Peace. I know you would have preferred a big wedding with all the trimmings, and with our families, but that doesn't seem to be in the cards."

"Let's do it sooner, before the President comes," Leslie implored. "If the Justice of the Peace can come up here, we can get married with all our friends as witnesses. They're our family now."

"That's even better," said Steve. "I'll call right him now."

At 7:30 the next morning, Drs. Gruber and Ginsberg and all the skywatchers assembled in the observatory hall at the base of the giant telescope to witness the marriage of Leslie Garson and Steve Chuebon.

"I now pronounce you husband and wife," declared Judge Mahi'ai.

Steve stomped on the glass that Leslie insisted be included in the ceremony, and embraced as if they never would let go of each other.

"Mazel Tov," called Harvey Eisenberg.

"Thank you, Judge, for coming up here so early," said Steve as he handed him a personal check for $500. A thousand Mahalos."

"It was my pleasure," said the Judge. "And this is more than enough. Aloha."

Steve turned to Leslie. "We may have to delay our honeymoon until we get things set up for the President."

Leslie laughed and sobbed simultaneously.

Dr. Gruber handed out paper cups from the water cooler while Dr. Ginsberg retrieved a bottle of Champagne from his office refrigerator. He then poured out just enough to give everyone a sip.

"Congratulations to Leslie and Steve," he toasted, raising his paper cup. "May you have a long and..." but before he could utter another word, his voice cracked as he, along with everyone else, began to tear up. Finally, regaining his composure, Ginsberg continued, "I'm so happy that you found each other. God bless you both."

Air Force One landed on the Big Island of Hawaii at 8:30 am. President Ellison and his Chief of Staff, Michael Corkery, were greeted by Dr. Ginsberg at the Mauna Kea Observatory at 10 AM. Although several other staff members accompanied the President on this trip, no one was permitted to attend the highly classified and top secret meeting they were about to hold, with only one exception, Army General Todd Bennett. The initial presidential briefing concluded, President Ellison sat at the conference table distraught, his hand holding his forehead. After a few moments of silence, the President lifted his head and said, "You say that that thing will hit the Earth in what, a week?"

"Sir," Dr. Ginsberg replied, "at its present speed and path, it would only be in the vicinity of Earth's orbit. That doesn't mean it would actually strike the Earth."

"What's the goddamn difference if it strikes us or not?" the president snapped. "Could we survive if it just passed by?"

"We don't know exactly, Mr. President," Dr. Gruber said. "The fact that its trajectory could be affected by the gravity of Jupiter might possibly alter it so that nothing at all happens."

"So, we just wait and see?" the president said. "How long would we have?"

"If I may, sir," Mauricio added, "we expect it to pass by Pluto in about three days, Neptune three days after that, then Jupiter the following day. Once it nears Jupiter, it would take only one day to arrive here. If we're lucky, Uranus might be able to alter its path."

"Worst case scenario, the Earth is destroyed, right?" President Ellison said, mournfully. Everyone remained silent and motionless.

"I really hate to say this, Mr. President," said Dr. Ginsberg in a most soulful manner, "but the end won't be pretty. A black hole, with its immense gravitational pull, would suck out our atmosphere, evaporate the oceans and, ultimately, disintegrate the planet, along with every living thing on it."

"There's no way out, is there? I'll have to go on the air and inform the country," the President said. "Although I don't know what good that will do. Except maybe give the people a chance to say goodbye to their loved ones. How do you tell everyone that they have only one more week to live?"

"We've spoken with our counterparts at other observatories and some of my colleagues at NASA. Sadly, everyone comes to the same conclusion. We always knew that one day our solar system would come to an end – several million years or even a billion years from now. No one ever thought it would be next week," Dr. Gruber added.

"Thanks for those words of encouragement," Ellison remarked. "God, give me the strength to do this," he continued as he and his staff prepared to leave. "You are sure of this, right?" Ginsberg uttered only one word to the president as they shook hands: "Godspeed."

The entire observatory team watched with trepidation as the President walked toward the limousine that would return him to the airport. Once aboard Air Force One, President Ellison downed a glass of Chivas Regal and began to prepare his speech to the nation.

At noon the following day, seated behind his desk in the Oval Office, President Ellison addressed the nation with his "Farewell Speech."

Immediately following President Ellison's speech to the nation, the country erupted in panic. The science-denying right-wing conservative media responded immediately to his message by imploring their viewers to ignore the obvious left-wing, liberal plot to bring down the economy. They also told their listeners to hold tight to their guns and rifles in order to ward off the liberal enemy who would be coming to destroy them.

Within two days supermarket and grocery store shelves were bare. The first items to go were toilet paper, ice cream, candy, cookies and cakes. What use would dieting do anymore? All deliveries ceased. Gasoline stations closed. Most people stopped working and stayed close to home with their families. There was barely enough time for people to telephone their loved ones to say goodbye. Mass transportation came to a halt. Highways were filled with cars carrying those who were trying to join their families. Religious people prayed. Some agnostic and atheists suddenly became believers. Churches, synagogues and mosques were packed morning through evening. On the fourth day, telephone lines became inoperable. Utility company generators ultimately stopped producing electricity. Law and order ceased. The world was in chaos.

Hospitals remained open. Doctors and nurses continued to honor their oaths to help the sick, handle emergencies and deliver babies. Mothers who had just given birth clutched their newborns to their bosoms and wept. Joy and sorrow became one.

At 10 am on the fourth day, Dr. Ginsberg held what would be his final CIRD staff meeting.

"You've all been amazing during this crisis," he began. "I'm sure all of you have been able to reach your families by now. From what we've been observing for the past week, it's become obvious what's in store for us and the world in the next three days. That said, I see no reason for any of you to remain here at the observatory. I'd suggest that you go home, make any final plans you want to make, watch the sun, listen to the birds chirp, pray, do whatever you feel is necessary. It has been an honor to have worked with all of you here at CIRD."

"I echo the sentiments of Dr. Ginsberg," Dr. Gruber said. "I love you all," she added, after which she sat down and wiped the tears from her cheeks. The skywatchers clasped hands and circled the conference table. They all began to weep with her.

Mauricio broke the silence. "There's no need to shut down completely. I'd like to stay here and keep an eye on the black hole, since I was the one who first identified it. Don't worry about me," he said, forcing a smile.

"You don't have to do that, Mauricio," Dr. Ginsberg said.

"I know, I just want to. I called Stella to say goodbye and tell her that I loved her. I've said my goodbyes to my family in Chile. I've done all I can do. I'll be okay now."

"I'll stay here with you," said Dr. Gruber. "I have nowhere else to go, and no one in particular to see. I've said my goodbyes as well. And while we're still here, Mauricio," she said, "call me Julia."

The skywatchers had a difficult time saying goodbye to Leslie and Steve. All they could do was to hug and kiss.

"No problem," Steve said. "We got married, and that's what's important right now. At least we'll be together...forever."

On the fifth day, countries around the globe were shutting down. Panic began to subside. Many wandered aimlessly in the streets. Some committed suicide. Many who finally accepted what they perceived as fate sought a quiet refuge where they could remain peaceful until the ultimate end. Mountain lakesides experienced an influx of people trying to enjoy the beauty of nature while they awaited their final days.

On the sixth day following President Ellison's broadcast, the black hole forced the planet Uranus to spin out of its orbit. As it continued on its way toward Jupiter, the planet's immense gravity affected its path. Instead of it merely approaching Earth's orbit and continuing unhindered towards the sun, the black hole made a beeline for Earth itself.

At 3 o'clock that afternoon, Julia and Mauricio walked out of the Mauna Kea Observatory, never to return. "Come home with me," Julia said, looking into Mauricio's emerald green eyes. She took him by the hand as they walked towards her car. "No one should be alone tonight."

On the seventh day, the day that God rested, the black hole collided directly into the Earth, causing its immediate disintegration and destruction. It happened so quickly that the people hardly knew what hit them. Everyone on Earth died almost instantaneously. The planet Earth no longer existed. The black hole absorbed Venus and Mercury on its way towards the sun, which itself was consumed. Mars, Jupiter and Neptune were flung out of their orbits to roam as vagabond planets in outer space. The Milky Way didn't even notice their absence. God's work was finished. It took only seven days.

ACKNOWLEDGMENTS

MANY THANKS TO MY WIFE, Maxine, for her editing, proof-reading, story ideas and especially, her patience and support. Thank you to my writing coach, June August (yes, that's her name), for additional editing, proofreading, and ideas that helped improve the manuscript.

I appreciate the suggestions of my friends and family who shared their thoughts and encouraged me during the writing of this book. I'm grateful to my granddaughter, Julia, for proposing the title for *Money Hungry*. I appreciate the long-distance assistance from my cousin, Jackie Patchick in England, who helped identify key locations in Manchester for *Visions of Lorelei*.

A shout goes out to my friends at The Players Guild of Leonia for suggesting that I write my first one-act play, *They Answer Our Prayers* which, along with two other one-act plays I wrote, developed into short stories. I appreciate the help and advice of my publisher, Bobbi Benson, for her guidance and marketing advice.

Made in the USA
Middletown, DE
23 March 2021